YOUNG AMERICANS

Josh Stallings

HEIST
PUBLISHING

Dedicated to Tad, a fiercely loyal friend and a brilliant sweetheart of a man. We stomped the wild glittery terra of the '70s, recreating ourselves into something that could last.

"I am the King of Glitter Rock. It's true–I am a bisexual. But I can't deny that I've used that fact very well. I suppose it's the best thing that ever happened to me. Fun, too."
—*David Bowie, 1976*

CHAPTER 1

"It's a handicap isn't it? Being so obviously American?"
—Man from U.N.C.L.E.

1976, WINTER BREAK.

Jacob lay down on his waterbed, staring at the poster on the ceiling—Iggy and the Stooges. He was wondrously stoned. High enough to feel nostalgia and whimsy, straight enough not to be consumed by the need to power eat a sack of Jack in the Box tacos.

He was eighteen and slight. Hair, a long rock shag. Jeans, Sticky Fingers. Skintight, of course. T-shirt, Gumby. Two sizes too small, thank you. Yellow scarf, to his knees. Boots, platforms with a three-inch heel. Pot, Panama Red. Music filling the apartment—Bowie, always.

Earlier he'd smoked a pinner, wanting to get a little buzz on before he and his best friend, Terry, went to the midnight movies. It was John Boorman night and they were playing *Deliverance* and *Zardoz*.

Jacob thought about the silver-framed family photos sitting on his mother's nightstand, where they'd always been. His family moved often. Neighborhoods and houses changed, but the pictures by her bed remained—his parents' and grandparents' wedding photos, and a black-and-white shot of his five-year-old sister, Sam, standing near a spring driven hobbyhorse. In the plastic saddle sits a three-year-old Jacob. Their heads lean into one another, co-conspirators. Jacob is laughing. Sam has a sly grin. He wonders how he and his sister drifted so far apart. Wonders why she left the Bay Area. After high school she split, headed north. For the last two years he only saw her on holidays.

Jacob worshipped his older sister, though he'd known his young age bugged her since she became a teenager and he was still a kid. A kid who wanted nothing more than to hang with his big sister. Their mother always demanded Sam include him, which made Sam resent him all the more.

Like many siblings, they were connected by blood, torn apart by too close proximity. And yet, all she would have to do is ask and Jacob would crawl across broken glass for her.

Three hundred miles between them made it easier to idolize her.

Closing his eyes, he drifted back to 1966. A suburban street, pleasant homes nestled amongst an orange grove. An eight-year-old Jacob backpedaled hard on his Stingray, locking the rear wheel. Skidding on the pavement, he kicked out the rear, stopping inches from the garage door. He let out a long-held breath. Looking down, there was a four-inch patch of black rubber he'd laid down. *Bitchin.* He headed into his home. He didn't even try the garage door, he knew better.

Esther, his mother, sat in the breakfast nook, smoking a cigarette and perusing the want ads.

"We moving?" Jacob asked.

"I didn't hear you come in."

"Are we moving?"

"Can't hide anything from you, smart guy."

"Because Sam got in a fight at school?"

"They called. She shouldn't have done that."

"Skinny Johnny asked for it. Everyone knows he's an asshole."

Esther took her son's face in her hands, meeting his eyes. "What is rule number one?"

He looked down. "Don't draw attention."

"Right."

Pulling away, Jacob dug into his backpack and pulled out a dog-eared copy of *James and the Giant Peach*. "Mrs. Sharpe got it for me. It's for fourth graders. Really cool."

"You have always been the smart one. The rest of us are clever, but you're smart. Smart will take you farther than clever any day."

"I know." He rolled his eyes. It wasn't the first time he'd heard this rap.

"OK, time for your home—"

"Work? Finished it on the bus." What he didn't tell her was he had also done his big sister's math homework in trade for her doing his chores. "Can I go play spy?"

"Just remember to break your cover for dinner."

He gave her a smart salute and was gone to his room to supply up.

Inside the garage, ten-year-old Sam was working on a secret project. But nothing could remain unseen by the all-seeing eye of Jake Stern, international spy. He had a periscope built from a cardboard packing tube, an X-ACTO knife, black electrician's tape, three mirrors and two lenses he'd salvaged from a broken stargazer. He also had an old stethoscope Doc Willard had given him for his birthday. Jacob took a Mason jar and very slowly drilled a hole just the size of the chest piece. The jar helped amplify the sound. Jacob liked to overcomplicate a task to the point where it sometimes became unmanageable.

He circled the garage twice and was about to go a third. While he walked he was trying to figure out how to build a harness rig to lift him up to the window. If only he had a grappling hook gun like Napoleon Solo. Pulling out an empty trash can, he stood on the lid. He was able to reach the dust-covered window; it wasn't locked. He pried it open far enough to slip in his Mason jar rig. Putting on the earpieces, he heard his grandfather's voice. "Shhh, Samula, gentle. Stroke it like it's a long-lost lover."

"Gross a go-go."

"No, hush. Now start again."

Jacob wiped away a patch of dust and grime from the periscope. He watched his big sister and grandfather. Sam was hunched over something hidden from view. She raised her hands, shaking the tension out of them.

"Time is not on your side. Any moment someone could come through that door and our secret will end. Then you will never know what is in the safe."

"Fine," she said, with just enough edge to let him know she was pissed, but not enough to get a cuffing.

Sam was sweating. The garage was hot and smelled of old oil, paint and solvents. She had trained with picks; grandpa taught her to unlock any deadbolt in less than two minutes. Blindfolded. But between her legs was an AMSEC safe—four tumblers, double cams. Two inches of hardened steel, so drilling was out of the question. Small shape charge? Grandpa said they were amazing, but noisy. No, unless they had unlimited time at a remote location, she would have to finesse it open. Her grandpa had all his attention on the stopwatch in his hand. From when you broke in until you were out needed to be less than six minutes.

Sam closed her eyes. For a moment she just took deep breaths, then let her mind wander to San Gregorio beach. She was holding hands with her best friend, Candy. They walked into the waves.

Back in the garage, Sam's hand started to rotate the dial, one tick at a time until she felt the first sear drop the first bar. Three more of the same fell.

At the beach, Sam and Candy were shrieking and laughing silently. The waves crashed with perfect silence.

The fourth and final rod fell into place and she opened her eyes.

"Amazing. Never have I seen anything like it. Two minutes, forty seconds. Even I, in my prime, couldn't have beat that." He gave her a kiss on the forehead. "Now, open it. The contents are yours."

Pulling down the large handle, the safe's door swung open. Inside was a little blue box. "Tiffany? No, too much," she said, while she was already tearing off the ribbon. In it was a simple gold heart with the words *Best Friends* on it. It was broken, so she could give half of it away. She couldn't wait to show Candy.

"Friends, true friends, are the best tools a thief has. Don't you ever forget this. Look at the people in your life and ask who would take a slug or do a stretch for you. The ones that won't, cut them out like cancer."

CHAPTER 2

"Like old momma said, next best thing to playing and winning is playing and losing."

—*Hard Times*

1976, WINTER,
HUMBOLDT COUNTY, CALIFORNIA.

Rain sluiced off the small cabin. The wind snapped at the blue plastic tarp used to patch leaks in the roof. Inside its one room, a rusted potbellied stove gave the only warmth. Sam sat in a camp chair wrapped in her sleeping bag. She was a big girl, with the kind of curves that started wars. Zaftig. Out of fashion. The Thin White Duke, David Bowie, made looking underfed fashionable. You could count every one of supermodel Margaux Hemingway's ribs. Sam's body was luxurious. It said screw you, have a burger and relax awhile. Her glitter platforms jutted out of black satin jeans. Her hair was cut in a spiky shag, just like Suzi Quatro. It was a blonde-red. Shiny. Her body, her stature, demanded a wider view of what a glitter rocker could look like. Not that anyone wanted an ass kicking enough to screw with her about her size.

Smitty, Sam's skinny shaggy-haired boyfriend, was putting freshly cut wood into the stove.

"It's too green."

"You speaking to me?"

"Won't burn, just smoke." She watched, waited. When the smoke started to invade their cabin, she hopped over and cranked the tin chimney's flue to wide open.

"Fine, fine, so no merit badge for me."

"You should have listened."

"Yes, ma'am, boss lady."

"Smitty?"

"Yeah, Sam?"

"What do you like about me? And if you say my tits or other bull, I will clock you. That's what the guys at the club like about me. But you?"

He looked at her searching for the answer. He fixated on her damn-near perfect tits. *Not melons, not half peaches. Navel oranges, that was it. Really large, soft, overripe oranges.*

"Your hair is really pretty."

"Bzzzzzzzz! Wrong answer." True to her word, she feigned a haymaker with her left arm, and while he was defending against the blow she used her right to jab his nose two solid hits.

"Ow, that fucking hurt. Get me some ice." Blood was running through his fingers.

"Have your shit gone by the time I get off tonight."

"But Sam . . . no. I make you laugh."

"Not often enough,"

"I make you come like a freight train."

"Ooooowwwwwaaaaaaa, yes." She faked a climax, her eyes dead cold on him. "Be out by two-thirty."

Turning away, she fired up the Coleman and started to heat some water. She needed a quick whore's bath. She could take a real shower at the club, where they had actual running hot water. Why had she left the Bay Area? Not for this. Did she really think she was going to make her fame and fortune stripping in the hick-filled forests of the North? It hadn't been the plan, it just happened. She'd been headed for Seattle, but ran out of cash in Humboldt. Her plan had been to dance at a club here for a couple of weeks, get up a stake to keep moving up North. That was a long time ago.

"Hey, Smitty, you know how to boil a frog?"

"No, Sam, I don't think I do know how."

"Put it in a pot of cold water and slowly, slowly, bit by bit add more heat until it's boiled."

"You're talking to me, that mean you want me to stick around?"

"Oh, hell no."

Rapunzel's was just another sad strip club trying to scrape by. It had rough redwood planks covering the walls and sawdust on the floor. The bar top was a finely carved and polished piece of driftwood. The room smelled of wood sap, sweat, sex, disappointment and disinfectant.

"Rocker like you, I bet you know some kinky moves, stuff make even a worldly guy like me blush." Sheriff Winslow was pushing fifty, had a sunken chest, sloped shoulders and a weak chin.

"It is never going to happen. Never." Sam spoke, but his eyes stayed glued to her cleavage.

"Oh, a day will come you'll need something from me, then girl, it's off to the races." He made a neighing sound, slapped her ass and walked out. Sam had to remember he was the law to keep from tearing after him.

Sam stomped up to the bar and stood looking at Breeze. He was the club owner and local small-town kingpin. He was a tall, thin man, bejeweled with multiple earrings, bracelets and rings on every finger. He didn't do subtle. He had long hair and a General Custer beard.

"Our sheriff is a dick," Sam said.

"No shit, but he's my dick. Not like that. Stop laughing."

"It's OK if you like cop dick, Breeze, really it is."

"One hundred percent pussy hound, got it?"

"No one is a hundred percent anything, boss. But I get your point."

"Good." Breeze leaned over the bar and took a bottle of Jack Daniels. He poured them each a shot. "Other than pissed off at the sheriff, how you doing, darlin?"

"Tips are tight. Mouth to God, one squid was tossing coins. But I'm getting by."

"Put that useless boyfriend to work. He could make a bundle trimming for me. He has a skill few do. I think it's those tiny little girl hands of his."

"He's paranoid about getting busted. Thinks he's too pretty to survive in the joint."

"Probably right. Fuck President Ford and his bullshit war on drugs. It's got everyone freaked."

"Doesn't look like you're sweating it."

"I hide my assets. Plus, I'm a visionary. The pH of a redwood forest and our climate are perfect for the weed craft. One day this whole forest will be full of pot farmers."

"Bullshit. Feds get wind of your grows they will drop a net on your ass."

"Have to find the dope first. Not so easy in all this wilderness. Yep, in a blind world I got 20/20 eyesight."

Sam let out a deep laugh. "Yes, you do."

"And in case of a downturn in the pot market, I diversified my portfolio with this joint and the working girls."

"We can't all be captains of industry, some of us are worker bees."

"Times get hard enough, you know I always got a crib for you up at the motel."

"I'm not a whore, Breeze."

"Oh hell, we're all whores. We just have different thoughts on how deep we'll let them stick it in."

"OK, then maybe I'm just not that desperate yet."

"Could make a bundle—truckers love big girls."

"You are so sweet."

"Just like molasses," he said to her back as she headed for the dressing room.

By ten o'clock the joint was a bit livelier. When Sam took the stage, six frat boys sat at the rail. She moved slowly to David Bowie's *Fame*. Closing her eyes, she let the man's shirt she wore slide off her shoulder. She stripped slowly, teasing it out. The frat boys were hooting, loving it. From the bar a tall man in a black leather blazer was watching her every move. His Burt Reynolds mustache only slightly hid a smirk. The frat boys dared each other to slip dollars in her G-string. The man from the bar moved up. He put a twenty into her hand, tipped his leather porkpie hat, moved back to watch. Sam snapped the twenty for the frats to see how it was done. She watched the new guy head toward the bar. Not her type. Not glitter skinny. He was the polar opposite of Bowie or Smitty. His muscular body was built either at the gym or in the joint—you don't get that taut an ass sitting in an office. OK, there were some parts of his macho-man body that called to her estrogen.

After the song ended she collected her cash and clothes and went into the dressing room. The Doobie Brothers' "Taking It To The Streets" heralded on Angie, Humboldt County's girl next door.

"You liked what you saw?" Sam sat down on the stool next to the big spending mustache.

"Girl, do we have to play this game?" His tightly curled blond hair was pulled back into a ponytail.

"Game?"

"Whatever, um, what's your name?" He motioned to the bartender, pointing at Sam.

"Cassidy."

"Whatever Cassidy is having and a Johnny Black with a Michelob back."

Sam noticed Breeze kept glancing at the new stud from the other end of the bar. She knew that he knew everyone in the Humboldt area, and he didn't like strangers. This cat was fit. Feds and cops were fit. But he didn't vibe cop to her.

His 501s were loose fitting, tucked into a pair of Red Wing Engineer boots—expensive foot leather meant for years in the field, not a night on stakeout.

The next time Sam went on stage she played "Little Bitch Blue" by Suzi Quatro. The 151 rum she had been blasting in the dressing room helped get her into the music. She whipped around the small stage like a demon, spitting as she screamed along to Suzi. She kicked a beer bottle, which exploded over the bartender's head. He just laughed. She watched mustachio man watching her. His undisguised desire turned her on. Glitter rock boys were fine, some were fantastic, but many of them thought androgyny meant they should act like pussies.

Dancing, Sam was an amazing combination of Kali the destroyer and Marilyn Monroe, cooing one moment and lashing out the next. Whipping her belt off, she cracked it like a whip. The leather tip hit the dollars stacked in front of the frat boys. One fast flick and their bills were raining down around her.

"Thank you, boys." She leaned down and kissed the first one on the cheek. He flinched. She laughed.

Sam stepped off the stage onto a chair, tipped it over, riding it to the sawdust. She stalked up to mustachio man, wrapped her belt around his neck, and pulled him close enough for their lips to touch. They didn't. She pulled back. His eyes said the battle was over, and she was the victor. All that was left to be settled were the terms of his surrender.

Sam's shift was done a 2:45 a.m. At 2:48 she was in the front seat of the stranger's 1967 sky blue Firebird, tongue deep in his throat. She didn't remember her shirt or bra coming off. Her nipple plumped in his mouth. Then she was on him. He fit just perfect.

MYTH: Bigger is always better.

FACT: It is all about the fit.

At least that was Sam's view, and man did he fit. There was nothing faked in her orgasm. After, she collapsed onto his thick chest hair.

"That was . . . was . . . unexpected." She was panting.

"No it wasn't." He barely broke a sweat.

"Oh, I knew the minute I saw you we'd be bumping uglies."

"Very full of yourself, girl."

"Woman. Girls don't do what we just did."

"So what was the 'unexpected'?"

"That it would feel so fucking good."

"Did feel great," he puffed up his chest, "didn't it."

"Lucky I'm not ovulating. We would have made a man-child. Science says male sperm swim slower, so deep thrusts give you a better than average chance for a boy. We can call him Bill, after the money you gave me."

Mustachio slumped against his Firebird.

Sam moved very close to his ear, filling it with warm air and words. "I'm on the pill. You get extra points for not bolting."

"Any chance the rest of the test is written? I'm hell on wheels with multiple choice."

"I'll keep that in mind." She was really starting to like this stud-muffin. "My car is the piece of shit Valiant across the lot."

"You in a hurry to get down the road?"

"Nope. I'm hoping you aren't either. Damn, that sounds pitiful. Trust me, I'm not usually this pliable."

"I don't intend on going anywhere. My name is Callum."

"I'm Sam."

"What happened to Cassidy?"

"She dances in the club. Sam inhabits the rest of my life. Boundaries."

"Nice to meet you, Sam."

The handshake felt a bit formal and silly, so he kissed her out-stretched hand. Then he ran his tongue across her knuckles. The second time they took their time, enjoying every movement. He came rocking slowly deep inside her.

Smitty looked comical flying out of the shack. A mostly strap-ping-tape suitcase came flying after him. He tried to speak but the door slammed shut.

Callum took in the one-room cabin. "You live in this rathole?"

"Yeah."

"With that punk?"

"Not anymore."

"We are going to have to make some adjustments if this is going to work."

"Um, like what?"

"Tomorrow we're moving you into my apartment in Arcata. Two bedroom, view of the water."

"No. I pull my own weight. You wanna be with me, this is where I live."

"OK, so you keep your things here and we make love in my place, where the roof doesn't leak."

"We'll see." They didn't leave the cabin that night. Instead, they made love twice more. Both were raw and slick when they fell asleep.

By noon, the rain let up. Birds were chirping. T-Rex was on the turntable. Sam was cooking—Sam never cooked. She set a steaming plate of eggs, potato hash and a mug of coffee in front of Callum. "Now that we are done screwing my cooch raw, how's about some talk?"

"Talk?"

"Yeah, like I was born and raised in Redwood City, down in the Bay Area." It was a lie, but only by fifteen miles. She was raised in Mountain View. Just because her hormones called his name didn't mean she had to be stupid.

He gave her a blank stare.

"Your turn."

More blank stare.

"Boy, you sure were talkative when you wanted to get into these fine, fine, fine panties. Asking me to move in with you and all. If that was just pillow talk and now you want to split? Cools-ville. I had fun. You had fun. Adios." She picked up the plate he wasn't done eating and shattered it in the sink. "Oops."

"Flagstaff. I was raised in Flagstaff."

"That's a start. You splitting or staying."

"I'd like to stick around, if you'll have me."

"We'll see. Take it casual. One day—"

"At a time?"

"You been in the program?" she asked him.

"No. I did go to AA meetings, but just as a way to get out of my cell. Some words must have sunk in."

"My pop was twenty years clean and sober when a semi crushed him." She poured him another cup. "How long were you down?"

"Four years. San Quentin."

"Am I your first since raising?"

"Yes."

"Was I worth the wait?"

"Hell yes."

"Right answer." She let out a laugh that swept the tension from the room.

Walking through the redwood forest, jays were cawing and the leftover raindrops dripped from the redwoods' branches, feeding the lush ferns and lupine. This trail, this view, made it almost worth the stripping for cheap hicks and college boys. They were following a thin game trail deeper into the woods. It wasn't long before the road noise from the highway was muffled into silence. Nature abhors a vacuum; the silence was filled by beetles clacking, birds calling, unseen critters flapping their wings.

"I love how small my life feels in the face of this forest."

Callum said, "I know just what you mean," but his eyes told a different story.

"Always a city boy?"

"How could you tell?"

"Fear in your eyes."

"That's not fear—dust, got some dust in them." He smiled at her. "On the upside, we get attacked by rats, roaches or sewer gators, I have your ass covered."

1968, ATHERTON, CALIFORNIA

Most Jewish girls get a bat mitzvah at twelve. Sam got to go on her first heist.

Her father and grandfather argued back and forth. Sam feigned disinterest.

"She isn't ready," her father said.

"She was ready a year ago. Neither of us can fit through that window. And with my arthritis, I don't know if I can finesse the safe."

Her father was as angry as she had seen him. It took her grandfather an hour to convince the younger thief they had no choice. A gem merchant had a bag of uncut diamonds locked in a safe at his friend's house while he was in town. "It is now, or say goodbye to my retirement."

The guilt worked.

On the job, Sam was brilliant. Her father boosted her through a small window. The house was quiet. She moved to the back door and let the men in. In the master bedroom there was a wall safe hidden behind a Remington painting of cowboys racing across the plains. They owed the maid a small cut of the action for tipping them to where the safe was and what was in it. That was one of their chief sources of information—a network of gardeners and domestics who were all looking to get ahead. The way Grandpa explained it to Sam, if rich folk didn't want to get robbed they should treat their people better.

Sam cracked the safe in three minutes—not a record, but good enough.

After, dividing up the haul, Sam could tell her pops was proud of her.

Jake, on the other hand, would never join the crew. The school ran a buttload of tests on him that year, and it turned out he was some kind of genius; the kind who forgot to tie his laces unless she told him to. But also the kind who went to Ivy League schools and got rich without risking spending time in lockdown. He was their golden child.

But not this night.

This night Sam was special.

She was an earner.

"What are you thinking about, babe?" Callum said. They were walking through a wildflower-strewn meadow. A red-tailed hawk's shadow slid past them. Sixty feet above it circled in the wind.

"Nothing. Choices. What did you go down for?"

"You pull no punches."

"I have to know." The red-tail folded its wings in and plummeted to the earth. Opening its wings at the last moment, it swooped up, a fat field mouse in its talons.

"Drugs. An eight-ball and a bad lawyer."

"You on parole?"

"No. I did the whole jolt, why?"

"I don't care what's coming as long as I know in advance. I have only two rules. One, never lie to me. Never. Two, no other women. Can you live with that?"

"Sam, you know we just met, right?"

"We did, and I offered you the getaway clean card. You stayed, so as long as it lasts those are the rules."

"Cool. What time is lights out, Cap?"

"Screw you." She was smiling. She was happy. Callum draped his arm over her shoulder, letting his hand slip down onto her breast. His thumb slowly stroked her nipple. She didn't mind one bit.

"What do you know about him?" Breeze was sitting in the booth he conducted business from, drinking a mug of coffee. By day, Rapunzel's was a bar and Breeze's office. By night, it was a strip joint and Breeze's office.

"He's just raised and could use a break," Sam said.

"Good in the sack?"

"None of your damn business."

"OK, you and me go way back, so I'll look into him. His tale holds agua I'll find him some farmer johns." Sam kissed Breeze, making him uncomfortable. "If, Sam, a big, huge stinking pile of *if* he checks out."

"He will."

"Now I need a favor from you, little miss slick fingers."

"You lock your keys in your car again?"

"No, bigger."

One lonely, drunken night Sam made the mistake of bragging to Breeze about her criminal past. Later, sober, she'd told him it was bullshit. He hadn't believed her. In the back room sitting on the desk was a Denver 923, one of the sweetest safes made in the last fifty years.

"You know I gave this up," Sam said, playing it casual.

"I know that's what you said."

"What's in the box?"

"Mine, that's all you need to know."

"Ten percent, and you hire Callum."

He nodded. "Done."

Fact was, the safe was calling her name. Two years. Maybe she'd lost it. She was pure old school. It was all touch and feel. The Denver 923 had four tumblers in a standard pattern of four clockwise, three counter, two clockwise, one counter to zero and bingo. Slowly she moved the dial, getting the feel for the mechanism. She kissed her fingers for luck. She closed her eyes and saw an open field. She and Callum were walking, a flock of multicolored finches flitted playfully around them. Her fingers felt the lock's cogs and wheels moving as she slowly stroked the dial. It barely moved, but to her it was like climbing a mountain. Every click rocked her. Time disappeared. It was just her in the field, her with the lock. She always felt she went away so that the images would distract the logical part of her brain. Finessing a lock was intuition. It was an art.

When the safe snapped open, Sam was surprised to find herself standing in the back room.

Breeze looked at his Rolex. "Two minutes, ten seconds. That has to be a record."

"I don't think it's an Olympic event."

"It should be." He was grinning as he pulled out a small pile of bills. $750 was the total. Sam got a massive $75 bucks. "Callum gets the gig, right?"

"I said it. So be it."

Callum was hired to work the graveyard shift guarding one of the grows deep in the forest. After the first night in his leak-free apartment, Sam moved in. She kept her cabin, to make a point, but only returned there to pick up her mail. For two wonderful weeks, they made love and ate and laughed. When her Valiant threw a rod he started driving her to and from the club. She bought him a lunch pail, and in a nod to a domesticity she never really would capture, she started making him meals, mostly PB&J sandwiches, and sending him off to work with them. In their own strange way, Sam and Callum played house. Even stranger, she didn't entirely hate it.

Everything was copasetic. Until it wasn't.

At midnight the only light in Breeze's office was on his desk. He leaned back and looked at Sam and Callum. She was dressed in a gauzy gown and G-string. Callum wore hunting camouflage and a shoulder holster filled with a Colt Python.

"Glad to see you both. Drinks?" Breeze asked.

"What the fuck, fellas," Sam said. "I got a wealthy bigmouth on the hook out there. Can we cut the foreplay before Angie snags him?"

Breeze let out a laugh. "Love the mouth on this girl. The intercourse of the matter is, your man here wants to step out big. He wants me to front him a sweet pile of our best bud. Says he has a pal in Texarkana will pay double. I want to know if it's bullshit."

"Callum told me about his friend, but shit, Breeze, I'm just a dancer with a bone for the guy, what do I know."

"Come on baby, it's more than—" Callum started.

"Shut up, I'm talking to the lady," Breeze said. "Gut up time, girl. You give him the nod and you two could be sitting high on that hog. He burns me . . . you owe me, large."

Sam gave Callum one long look. She always wanted a rich outlaw for an old man. She nodded at Breeze. "I'd trust him. I'd also send one or two of your boys along."

"He said he was leaving you and his Firebird as collateral."

"Ain't that romantic. Send the boys."

"My buyers see strangers, they could freak," Callum said.

"Then they freak. I got to get back to work."

The bigmouth was an English professor from Humboldt State University who had just sold a book and was tossing his advance around. He offered Sam three hundred to come home with him. She declined, but didn't slap his face. What would be the point? Angie disappeared with him, so that was that. On stage Sam could hardly keep it together long enough to finish her shift.

That night after she and Callum made love, they lay in the moonlight panting, catching their breath. She lay on his chest, content. "Sam, if something goes wrong . . ."

"Like what?"

"Like I don't know, but if it does."

"How will I know?"

"I'll call everyday at two a.m. I don't call, something has gone wrong."

"And what do I do?"

"Split."

Sam wrapped herself in a quilt. He took her to the carport, to the Firebird. He showed her where the nitrous switch was under the dash. He showed her a hidden kill switch under the driver's seat. No one could hot-wire the car if that switch was on. In the trunk, he showed her a hidden false floor. He kept a twelve-gauge pump and a gym bag in there. With the trunk floor locked in place the hold became invisible. Cops had even searched it once and came up empty-handed.

"Why are you telling me all this? You getting froggy?"

"No, but you never know on a run like this. Anything goes hinky, you get in the Firebird and take off. This bitch will outrun the CHP if needs be."

"If."

"Yeah. It won't happen, but if... How do I find you once I straighten it out?"

"Find me, or your car?"

"I don't give two shakes of a rat's tit about the car. I love you." He had never said those words. They struck Sam hard. She rewarded him with a deep kiss.

"Where do I find you?" Callum said, stroking her face gently.

"No one up here knows about my family. It has to stay that way, OK?"

"Cross my heart." Callum traced a cross over his heart.

"Mountain View." She wrote out her mother's number in a matchbook and pressed it into his hand. "Breeze and them, no one can find this."

Callum looked at the number, saying it under his breath several times, then lit the book on fire. It flared as all the match heads went up. He dropped it into a large glass ashtray. After the number had turned to ash he smiled at Sam. "Feel better?"

"Better. If your deal blows up, that is where I'll be."

"You'll wait for me?"

"At least for a couple of days."

Back in Callum's bed, they made love again, hungry to stave off the fear.

When Sam woke, Callum was gone on his run.

Night one, he called like clockwork. He joked about what hicks Breeze had sent along to cover him.

Night two, called again. This time he whispered sweet endearments. Told her when this was over he was taking her to Mexico for a fun and sun vacation.

Night three, she waited all night. No call.

She phoned in sick the next day, sitting by the phone waiting for Callum to call. By the afternoon of day four she knew she was screwed.

Sam called down South. Her brother answered. She said she was coming home for a bit. She played it off as just needing a break from Hicksville. He said he was glad regardless of the reason.

Everything Sam owned fit into the Firebird, with room to spare. One of two things had happened: either Callum got jammed up by his buyer, or he had stolen the load and left Sam holding the bag. If Callum had screwed her it was maybe to be expected. Hurt, but what was a cat like that going to see in a big girl like her? Hell, he could be boning any Twiggy he chose.

Regardless of why, she was screwed. Breeze would be hunting her, that was a fact. He might care about her, but cash was the temple at which he worshipped. It was time to run, hard and fast. South.

She almost made it, too.

CHAPTER 3

"You wouldn't shoot an 18-year-old girl. Would you?"
"You bet I would. You bet I would."

—Killer Elite

"Breeze's money or his weed. You got to give us one or t'other." A bicycle chain pinned Sam to the barn's center joist. Shadows leapt and fell with the gas bursts of the cutting torch. Sam had been filling the Firebird's tank when they nailed her. A cut-down twelve-gauge in a shaking hand had convinced her to drive to their farm. She knew these guys. Not bad men. Not real bright, but she doubted they were killers. It wasn't until they chained her to the beam and lit the torch that she started to worry.

"Don't make Cracker get down to scorching that pretty flesh of yours." Sardine was a grimy pig of a man. Sweat and grease stuck his sparse hair to his skull. "Nothing? OK, Cracker, time to put in some work."

"Wait." Sam scrambled to make her brain fire quick enough to save herself. "Breeze, you dumb hick. He hired you to get his money back."

"Of course Breeze hired us. So, you gonna give it up, or does Cracker get on with this here BBQ?"

"I cleared it up. Ask Breeze. He'n me, love will keep us together." She was tap dancing so fast she was starting to quote Captain and goddamn Tennille. She didn't have time to think. "I was you, I'd get my ass on the phone with Breeze. We're together now, Breeze and me. He tell you that?"

"No, you're with that Callum fella. He's who ripped Breeze off."

"Was with. Now it's Breeze and me all the way."

"Oh hell, every bitch he bones thinks they is together."

"See this ring?" She was twisting to show her finger.

"Get the ring."

Cracker did as told. He pulled at the ring, but it wouldn't budge, so he pulled harder. It felt like he was going to tear her finger off. Sam tried not to cry out. "It's not coming," Cracker said.

"Then get a hacksaw."

"Wait!" Sam said. "Think Breeze will want you cutting up his ring?"

"Not gonna cut the ring."

Cracker spit on her finger. He realized what he'd done, gave Sam an apologetic smile. The ring slid off. Sam mouthed 'thank you' to Cracker as he passed Sardine the ring. It was 18k gold. Victorian. It had belonged to Sam's grandmother. "Careful, been in Breeze's family forever. And he gave it to me. That sound like he's mad at me?"

"A ring, hmmmm? Now that's a bitch of another color. How do I know? I mean, well, you could be laying down a bullshit trail."

"Ask him. But first tell him what you did to me."

Sardine furrowed his brow, struggling to think. "I didn't do shit."

"You didn't rape me?"

"Wait a minute, slow up."

"Because that's how I'll tell it. Breeze hates rapists. The pigs will eat your balls for breakfast."

"Bullshit. Breeze ain't gonna believe some Bay City bitch over kin."

"Let me talk to Breeze, get this straight. Or call him yourself. Don't forget to mention I'm chained to a goddamn barn post and getting splinters up my cooch."

"You still want I should light her up?" Fire danced on Cracker's childlike face.

"No. Not yet. No. What I want from you, what I need, is ten seconds of silence. Think! Think!" Sardine started pounding his own forehead with the palm of his hand.

"You want help?" Sam said. "Give me a shovel and I'll see what I can do."

"Damn, damn . . . win, lose, damn. OK burn her. No, stop. I'm calling Breeze."

"Wha, what about the rape thing? You didn't rape her did you, Sardine?"

"What? You haven't left my side. Been like a third tit since we snatched her, right?"

"Sure."

"Then when exactly would I have raped this bitch?"

Cracker was trying to puzzle this out.

Sam worked her arms straining against the chain. It cut into her wrists. She knew sooner or later these boys would melt down.

"Keep an eye on her. But don't speak to her."

"Where you goin'?"

"The house, make a call. You, bitch?" Sardine gave Sam his full tough guy stare. "Don't try nothin'."

Blood was running down Sam's wrists, but one hand was free. The chain hung loose, still attached to her left hand. She looped it once over her knuckles and watched Sardine walk out. Cracker turned around, looking her over. "Never did get to see you dance up to Rapunzel's."

"Didn't miss much."

"I bet you was good. Kinda hope I don't have to fire you up." He was moving in on her, the torch in his hand hissing. "Don't be afraid. Like you said, Breeze will straighten this out." He looked from the torch, up to her. "You ain't gonna' tell them lies about rape and all."

She mumbled a response. He leaned in. The chain took him in the temple and almost popped his eye out of its socket. She stepped into the second blow, this time using her chain-knuckled fist to break his nose. He was howling, blood smearing his face. His upper lip quivered as he swung the torch at her. Flame singed her spikes as she leapt back. Working the wound, she swung the chain again, hitting the growing hematoma over his temple. His eyebrow burst. The blood blinded him. Reaching to clear the blood, he took off his eyebrows with the torch. He squealed and dropped it. The dry hay around him exploded to life.

Sam was out and gone before Sardine cleared the farmhouse's front porch. The Firebird spat up a rooster tail of gravel and dust as she bounced away. In the rearview mirror she saw Sardine grabbing a garden hose and spraying his brother's burning shirt. Hitting asphalt, she slid sideways until the T/A radials hooked up and she was gone into the night.

One hundred feet past the Humboldt County line was a liquor store/gas station. She did not buy skunk weed from the kid selling it out of his wizard-painted van. She did make a phone call.

"Breeze?"

"Where you calling from? I don't hear flames and moaning, so it looks like I'm going to have to send you to hell myself."

"Hey, I know it means shit and all, but I had no idea that dick was planning to take you down."

"Your vouch, your debt. Don't play dumb. Cash, grass or ass, and as fine as your big ass is, it ain't worth no twenty grand." Twenty grand. He could have said a million, wouldn't be any easier to get.

"What happened to the boys you sent with him, why aren't they on the hook?"

"James bros. Dead."

"Damn, I liked them. Breeze?"

"Yeah, Sam?"

"You see any plan where I don't end up dead?"

"Not yet. But I'm ruminating my ass off. I like you girl, fact. But I let this pass, every hick with a gun and some balls will think he can take me down. They will come at me hard if I don't make an example out of you."

"Breeze, we are both fucked here."

"You, little girl, you are fucked."

"I'll get you your money, you know I will."

"Twenty large, plus five for the barn. Due, um let's see, hmmm, how about we say . . . now."

"It's going to take time, but I'll get it, promise I will."

"Or die trying. Look, call me in two days, I may have a gig that could square us."

"Breeze?"

"Yeah, kid?"

"We had some fun didn't we?"

"Sure did. Gonna' miss you down at the club."

Sam hung up. Breeze was the swinging dick in Humboldt County. Owned cops. Any pussy or pot got sold he was sure to get his taste. Did his power extend down the coast? She didn't think so. She hoped she was right.

Sam shoved Ziggy into the 8-track. Cranked up "Rock 'n' Roll Suicide." She sparked a Marlboro and mashed down the gas pedal.

Owing Breeze big money had never been Sam's plan. Hell, stripping hadn't been in the cards either, but life did what life did, she was just along for the ride. Pulling alongside a VW bug, she saw it was driven by a handsome young man. His girlfriend leaned into him, twirling his long hair in her fingers. An "HSU Rocks!" bumper sticker pegged them as students. This happy little picture pissed Sam off. Fuck did they know about real life, living on daddy's dole. They were blissfully stupid sheep to be sheared.

At heart, Sam was a thief.

Fact.

By fifteen she had formed her own crew. Candy, her best friend, was her partner in crime. Bobby Willis, sixteen, was a druggy and a bit of an idiot, but he had a car and driver's license so they used him. In trade for head, Bobby taught Candy how to boost cars. As it turned out, she was a natural. When Bobby fell in love with Candy they cut him loose. But with her looks they never had trouble finding meatheads for grunt work.

The baby bandits, as Sam's grandfather called them, pulled small-time scores, mostly creeping houses while the owners were away on vacation. Sam would scan the want ads for folks wanting pet sitters, or even better, plant tenders. No one needed their plants tended if they were going to be in town. They were never even close to being caught. Sam had two skills. Yes, she could finesse a lock, be it a dead bolt, safe or padlock, but she also was a hell of a heist scriptwriter.

By seventeen, they started to feel invincible. Creeping houses started to lose its thrill, was becoming a job. So they upped the ante. Took more risks. They traveled down to San Jose to pull their first armed robbery. A liquor store. Sam had cased it. It went down slick, but they only cleared a couple hundred bucks apiece. The risk to reward ratio was out of whack. They decided it had been a thrill, but going in armed made no real sense.

It was time to return to what they knew. Fate sent Valentina their way. Sam and Candy met her at Taxi Dancer, a gay disco in the city. They were seventeen, flying on fake IDs and grown-up attitudes. Valentina knew lots of rich men with lots of pretty things she didn't mind helping Sam steal. "Girl, they have massive in-sure-ance. 'Sides, they will never miss what crumbs we take. Them that's got shall get, them that's not shall steal."

The added danger of alarm systems and guard dogs perked Sam and Candy up. They'd still be at it, but two weeks before Sam's eighteenth birthday her father was arrested. The cops found him with sixty thousand dollars in gems from a jewelry store heist. His inside man sold him out. "You think you're bulletproof. You're not," he'd told Sam. He was out on bail awaiting trial. If convicted it would be his third fall and they would treat him as a habitual offender. He was looking at a long, long sentence. "You're almost an adult, kiddo, no more juvie or community service. Time you hang up the picks and become a citizen."

"Someone has to earn," she said.

"True, but you're no good to your mom or brother if you're locked down. You're a clever girl. Find another way." It took some work, but he ultimately made Sam promise to go straight. She was stoned at the time and never meant to keep her word. Then a week later he was killed by a drunk truck driver and she figured she had to do right by his memory.

Admittedly, stripping was a fucked up way to do it.

She spent her high school years high, drunk or on a heist. It hadn't prepared her for a lot of straight gigs.

The sun was coming up when the Firebird crossed the Golden Gate Bridge. Fog-shrouded girders disappeared above. The city was mysterious and magical, always had been for Sam. For this moment, her spirit rose. She would find a way to get straight with Breeze. Or she would leave him hanging. She would find a better way to knock out the bills, a way that didn't involve letting hillbillies ogle and touch her. In this city, at this moment, everything was possible.

CHAPTER 4

"Caught in a landslide, no escape from reality."
—*Queen*

MOUNTAIN VIEW.

Sam was exhausted when she pulled the Firebird into the Creekside Apartments visitors' parking. The long, two-story, L-shaped stucco building sat across a drainage ditch from the 280 freeway in Mountain View, California. Nestled amongst high-power lines and other equally shabby apartment buildings, it lacked both a mountain view and a creek. What it did have was apartment 3B, Sam's family home. Or the home they'd lived in for the longest stretch—two and a half years and counting. When your dad is a thief and a gambler, the family income fluctuates with his luck. When he was up, they rented nice houses in Palo Alto. Other times they rented a double-wide in Watsonville. Now that he was dead, it was Creekside. Sam lived in the crap shed in Humboldt while most of her cash flew south to help her mother cover the bills. She didn't begrudge the money sent. Sam understood there was us and them; she took care of us, and clipped them whenever she got a shot.

At the front door, Sam took out a leather case, in which was a set of lock picks she made with her grandfather when she was eleven. They took apart a bicycle wheel and flattened several spokes with a hammer and anvil. With a file and needle-nose pliers they shaped the picks. It wasn't long before she could open any keyed lock faster than it took most people to find their keys.

The apartment was silent. The living room was trashed. On a wall hung a torn sign that said WELCOME HOME SAM! Empty beer and whiskey bottles littered the countertops. Ashtrays overflowed. The rhythmic clicking of a record needle playing the empty final groove over and over droned on infinitely.

Sam crept into her little brother Jacob's room and flipped open the curtain.

Sunlight exploded through the window, popping Jacob's eyes open. He leapt up, striking a cheesy kung fu pose. The room spun and he fell back on the bed, fighting down the bile.

"I'm gonna puke." Jacob grabbed for a trash can, leaned over and after a moment sat up. "False alarm. Pukeus interruptus." He let out a loud laugh.

"Shut the fuck up, you little freak, you'll wake Moms."

"She's in Mexico with Karl."

"Oh, yeah. With Karl? As in dating?"

"Are you asking is she boning the honorable Karl Fuckwad? Just thinking about it makes me want to pull an Oedipus Rex and stick a needle in my eye."

"Me too, kid." Karl was a lawyer. A shady lawyer. He'd been on retainer for the family as long as Sam could remember. Looked like he'd swooped in and started dating their mom. "She left you alone?"

"No big. Terry's been here, a lot."

"I feel so much better then. Two teenage boys with no supervision, what could go wrong? You keeping up with school?"

"Winter break. And I'm eighteen. Can legally buy smokes or enlist and go kill me some nice little brown people."

"Right, point made. I don't have to worry about you, do I?"

"No."

"Couldn't she do better than Karl?" Sam chewed on her inner lip.

"Guess not." Jake thought for a moment. "Is switching out a thief for a lawyer trading up or down?"

"Pop for Karl is a definite down turn."

"Yeah . . . Sam?"

"What?"

"We had a party for you."

"Did I enjoy it?"

"You weren't here. Were you?"

"That fucked up, huh? No, just got in. Bet it was a blast. Valentina hit on Terry?"

"Of course."

"He's passed out in the living room and Val's in Mom's bed with Candy, so I guess she failed."

"Doomed. He's straight."

"So you keep telling me."

"He is. You OK?"

"Just rode hard and put up wet. Be fine with some sleep."

"Are you lying?"

"Probably."

"Sam?"

"Yeah, Jake?"

"I missed you."

She gave her brother a smile and a tired headshake. Sam was home, Jacob was massively hung over and all was right with the world.

By one that afternoon, Sam was rested and hungry. It was time for breakfast and a massive injection of coffee. Of course the only thing in the fridge was either booze or mixer. Stepping into the harsh daylight, Jacob saw the Firebird and let out a low whistle. "Tight short. The Valiant?"

"Died an ignoble death." Sam unlocked the driver's door.

"Where did this beast come from?"

"It was payback from a douche I'd rather not talk about."

"A douche you were banging, yes?"

"This is me not talking about it." Sam slid into the Firebird. Jacob got in beside her. Terry and Candy got into Valentina's two-tone 1963 Ford Galaxie, bronze over green metal flake. Regardless of Sam's reason for returning, she was glad to be back in the bosom of her people. Surrounded by them she safe and protected, almost.

The crew was:

TERRY. Jacob's best friend. Cute. Glasses. Long hair. A Todd Rundgren tee worn loose to hide the fact he was ripped. Sports had given him muscles, love of pale, skinny rock stars made him hide them. Seventeen and hairy. Five o'clock shadow. He could score chicks and booze.

CANDY. Model looks. Lithe, pale almost translucent skin. Straight, jet-black hair framing her perfect face. She was the quintessential glitter rock girl. Every glitter boy's wet dream. Toujour Moi was her signature perfume. Her lips always tasted of cherries, courtesy of Bonne Bell flavored lip gloss. Around her neck, half a best friend's heart. The other half was where it had been since the fifth grade—around Sam's throat. She was the sweet Candy that men dreamt of tasting while Sam robbed them blind.

VALENTINA. She spun though life trailing glitter and feathers molting from her thrift store boa. Smoking hot, low-cut gown, nice tits, fine ass. Six foot two inches of drool inducing chocolate wonderfulness. If it weren't for her dick, Terry—hell, anyone—would have done her in a second.

When Sam got out of the life, so did her crew. All except Billy Quinn, a muscular punk and their last driver. He kept going. He was now serving ten years at San Quentin for trying to stick up a Stop-n-Shop with a pellet gun.

Lions on the El Camino was a pure old-school, working-class coffee shop. All the waitresses had beehives and cat glasses, not one of them was under sixty. Sam and the others sat in a booth laughing and finishing their greasy feast. Jacob slumped over his mostly untouched food, smearing the yoke around with a piece of toast.

"You gonna' eat that bacon?" Terry snatched it off the plate without waiting for an answer.

"No, go right ahead, pal."

"Hash browns?"

"Knock yourself out." Jacob slid the plate to his friend. His stomach did a slow tumble when Terry dug in with sloppy gusto.

"You feeling OK, little brother?" Sam moved her sunglasses down her nose and looked him over. "You pickle any important organs while I was gone?"

Aware the others were checking him out, Jacob sat up. "Nope, organs are in fine working order."

"Handsome and a working organ? Ladies, be still your hearts." Valentina fanned herself with a pie menu. Jacob looked from her to Candy, who shot him a playful wink. He struggled for a smartass quip but his hungover brain left him stranded by the side of the conversational road.

Sam was about to add to Jacob's misery when she caught the eerie feeling that someone was watching her. Spinning around she saw a middle-aged man in a wrinkled suit staring at her from the counter. From his thick-soled black shoes to the tip of his buzz cut flattop he vibed cop. Midnight dark Ray-Ban Aviators hiding his eyes.

Sam froze. The others followed her gaze then went silent. Seeing the cop, they all looked with intense interest at their dirty breakfast dishes. "Think he saw us?" Sam whispered to Valentina.

"Pray to the blessed virgin or whoever for a no."

Jacob flicked nervous eyes at Terry, who shrugged, unconcerned. Cops didn't freak him one bit. He wasn't by nature a lawbreaker.

The cop dropped a couple of bills on the counter and drifted quietly up to their booth. He stood behind Sam, who was starting to sweat. "Boo," he said, without humor.

Valentina was the first to look up, all smiles and twinkle. "Why, if it isn't the Korean Burt Reynolds. Detective Pahk, what a pleasure. You look manly as ever."

"Aren't you about forty miles south of Sodom by the bay, Henry?"

"Valentina." She slid a steel edge into her voice, then a quick reverse back to coquette. "Bad boy, you missed me. Those shades don't hide the way you're eye-fucking my titties." She pressed her breasts together, mounding them into an impressive display of cleavage. "You're like a hungry bear looking at a pick-a-nick basket."

"What, um, ever you say, Henry." A bit flustered, Detective Pahk turned to Sam. "Heard you were living up north. Doing the naked hoochie coochie for loggers, burnouts and drooling frat boys, right?"

"Mostly loggers. Burnouts and drooling frat boys would have been a welcome change." Sam kept her face flat, giving him nothing while remaining conversational. "Why haven't they put you out to pasture?"

"Either it's my solid arrest record or a picture I have stashed of the mayor banging a lady-boy, you choose."

"I'll take the union is protecting your ass for five hundred dollars."

"Funny. This permanent, or just a visit?"

"You know, Detective, I'm not sure. But you will be my first call once I decide."

"Crime rate dropped when you left town. You planning on raising it again?"

"I have no idea what you're talking about."

"I see you and these two," he motioned to Valentina and Candy, "I have to think you're getting the old crew together."

"Again, you lost me. Old friends sharing a cup a joe. Not breaking any laws."

"Unless there's a law against hotness." Valentina bit her lower lip and struck a sultry pose.

"If there is, we are guilty as charged." Candy licked her finger, touched Valentina's cheek and made a sizzling sound. Staring into the detective's eyes, she sang, "I say, hey, babe, take a walk on the wild side. And the colored girls say . . ." She winked at Valentina.

"Doo do doo do doo do do doo," Valentina sang, eyes closed, head tilted back.

"You, you and you—you three are a mug shot away from the pen. You're the brother, Jacob?"

"That's my name." It wasn't a clever quip, but at least Jacob purged the quiver from his voice.

"Heard you were some kind of Einstein, omitting the kooky hair; I don't see it." Pahk turned his attention to Terry, who just grinned at him. "Who are you, pretty boy?"

"Terry." He put a hand out to shake, but seeing Sam's eyes he wilted and let it drop.

"You play for the Spartans, wide receiver, right?"

"Yes, sir."

"Are you wearing women's eye shadow?"

"Yes, sir." Terry's smile didn't falter.

"Why in the name of Jesus H. Christ would you do that?"

"Brings out the green in my eyes."

Pahk looked sad and disgusted. "What's your last name, son?"

"None of your business," Sam said, flat. "Unless you want to arrest us, we're done here."

"Not near done, little girl. You are going down, you can take that to the bank."

"Bank? That's from Baretta, right? Corny."

"I don't know, Princess Samula, that Rooster was steamy, in a skinny hot chocolate fur collar pimpy way."

"I am going to relish slapping the cuffs on you two."

Sam affected a Texas drawl. "Your cart is way out in front of the horse. You have even one, no matter how shaky, piece of evidence against us?"

"I will. Then you, this gargantuan chicken-hawk tranny and the rest of you limp-wristed girls will be pulling a train up in the big Q."

Terry's grin fell and he stared at his glitter polished pinky finger anxiously. Jacob looked to his sister for support, but she wouldn't take her cold eyes off Pahk. Even the ever-cool Candy looked unsettled. Valentina stood, towering over Pahk. All the flirt was gone. Her jaw muscles popped. Her hands balled into fists.

"Sit down, Henry, before I call the fruit squad." Pahk looked at Valentina's fists and forced a laugh. "Watch it, Henry, don't want to break a nail." He reached into his jacket pocket, feeling for his sap.

"Do it, I'll go beaucoup dinky dau on your ass. Then the ACLU will destroy what's left." Tension was rippling off Valentina in waves.

"ACLU? They might protect your Afro-American half, but the dick-licking dress-wearing side? I don't think so."

Valentina was about to lose control when Sam got between

them. She put a hand gently on Valentina's shoulder. "This is what he wants. Hit him, and you go down. Fuck him."

"Not even on a dare. I only go down for charmers in too-tight jeans." She let out a breath. Curled her lips into an approximation of a smile and sat down.

"Call the family shyster." Sam flipped Jacob a dime that, amazingly, he snatched out of the air. "Time to decide, detective, bust us or politely fuck off."

"Politely fuck off, huh? Nice." He gave the crew one last hard look, then relaxed. "See you geeks around the playground." They were silent until Pahk walked out, got in his unmarked cop car and drove down the El Camino.

"Nice guy, very personable," Jacob said.

"A charmer, and so good looking," Candy said. "Amazing he has no wedding ring on."

"I guess a Casanova of his caliber doesn't want to be tied down," Jake said.

"Unless he does. That man is a poster child for a closet sub," Valentina said. "Yes, mistress, may I lick the dog brown off your boots?"

"Shiny, shiny, shiny boots of leather. Whiplash girlchild in the dark," Terry sang the opening to a Velvet Underground song. Even Sam laughed at that. The last of the residual tension left the booth.

"What we need, my fab compatriots, is this." Valentina opened a pill bottle with nails that were smoky dark purple, to match her lips. She plucked out a large white pill. "Vitamin Q time." She took a glass of orange juice out of Jacob's hand and chased the lude down. She let her tongue circle the glass. "One of these boozy days, young Jacob, we are going to have to see just how straight you are."

"My man Jake is straighter than a . . . well, something that's really straight," Terry said.

"Mmmmmm, you just keep decorating that closet, Terr-Terr, it will look dazzling when you come out." She ran a finger over Terry's cheek, down to cross his lips. He started to blush.

Sam watched the scene and smiled. "Candy, during my banishment to the cold north, did you relent and give my little bro the wool he so wants?"

"I wouldn't risk losing my surrogate little brother for a tumble in the hay. Regardless of how good it might be." Candy gave Jacob a consolation kiss on the cheek, leaving a classic red lip print.

"That, and face it," Valentina said, "she's Rolls Royce and he's VW bug. Sorry, Jake."

"No, please, a fact's a fact." Jacob nodded agreement.

Back at Creekside Apartments, the crew was fed and loose on Quaaludes. Terry and Jacob sat on stools by the bar top that separated the kitchen from the living room. "That cop has a real boner for your sister." Terry's neck was a limp noodle, leaving his hands to hold up his face.

"It's a family thing. He's the idiot donkey dick who busted Dad."

"He's not an idiot, Jake." Sam was sprawled out on the living room floor, dark glasses covering her closed eyes. "Don't believe the dumb cop crap, it's a smoke screen. Pahk was slick enough to take down Pops."

"OK, not an idiot, but definitely a donkey dick." Jacob jumped when the phone started ringing. "Casa de loony tunes, how can we help you?" He listened for a moment, then passed the receiver to Sam. "It's for you."

"Callum?" Sam asked.

"Not even close." Breeze crackled across the line. "This is your past racing to catch up to you."

"How did you get this number?"

"You can't hide from me. Shall I have Sardine and Cracker go to work on that cute little brother to prove it?"

"No. Breeze, I said I'd handle it and I will."

"People say all kinds of bullshit when they think a blowtorch is in their future. Now here is what will go down. I will get my cash. You know how I know that?"

"Because you trust me?"

"No. Because I know how you're going to get it for me."

"How?"

"Steal it. New Year's Eve Sylvester and the Hot Band are playing at Taxi Dancer, along with The Tubes and a third, opening act. It's going to be a massive party kissing 1976 goodbye. There will be twenty-plus grand in the till by the time the ball drops. That's not counting the bar and popper sales."

"I'm a creeper, Breeze, a sneak thief. Brazen stick-up gigs are a good way to end up on a slab."

"True, there is a chance of bodily harm, but . . ." Breeze paused for effect. "You don't do it and I can guarantee you will need a toe tag."

Sam wound the phone cord around her index finger. "If I did this, what would I pay my crew with?"

"The plus goes to them. Anything over your debt you keep. I'm dropping Sardine's barn, so you owe me a clean twenty. Thank you, Breeze. You are ever so welcome."

"Up fronts? I'm broke."

"All this you should have thunk over before vouching for your scheming boyfriend."

She was going to tell him to fuck off, she wasn't a thief anymore. Tell him she'd find another way. Then she looked at her goofy brother flirting with Candy and she knew she would do whatever it took to keep him safe.

Breeze gave Sam the number of his inside man, a bartender named Bruce. It was December fourteenth—she had slightly more than two weeks to set up the heist. It wasn't enough time. Robbing the joint might be easy, getting away with it was the trick.

CHAPTER 5

*"Give yourself over to absolute pleasure. Swim the warm
waters of sins of the flesh—erotic nightmares beyond any
measure, and sensual daydreams to treasure forever."*
—*Rocky Horror Picture Show*

The Bay City Rollers commanded that Saturday night was for
dancing to rock and roll. But judging from Taxi Dancer's dance
floor, Saturday night was also and mainly for getting laid. Men
of all shapes and sizes were doing that wonderful mating ritual
known as disco dancing. The bump, the hustle, the cha-cha, the
robot, the boogaloo—they all had distinct moves and styles, and
all were danced to turn on your partner. When Diana Ross sang
"Love Hangover" the dancers all sang along. Ohio Players' "Love
Rollercoaster" had them rising onto their toes then dropping down
and yelling as if they were all riding that rollercoaster.

Valentina used several Quaaludes to bribe a bouncer, who let
Sam and Candy in the back door. Their fake IDs weren't good
enough to get past the new man watching the front door. Taxi
Dancer had been taken over by new management since Sam left
town. They were hell on females now, demanded triple picture IDs,
crap like that.

"This used to be our fucking club. What the hell, Val?" Sam
said.

"Times change, princess, pendulum swings. Watch, in another

year it will be a straight club and they'll be keeping the leather boys out and playing Rush albums."

Jacob and Terry cruised through the front door. They had really lousy fake IDs but they were cute boys. The hairy doorman in a leather vest and not much else didn't even look at the Xeroxed Stanford student ID cards.

Once inside, Sam and crew headed for the couch room—the crotch room they called it, because it was where guys went to play open the package. Tonight Sam and her friends had taken it over. Valentina scared off anyone who wasn't a friend. That wasn't many. Most loved Sam. Most were glad to come and give her a hug and kiss, take a toke off a joint or a sniff off a popper. The welcome home party had been delayed but not forgotten. Candy took Jacob onto the dance floor. She was dressed in tight snakeskin print pants. Her scoop-necked tee shirt was studded with rhinestones spelling out *Rebel Rebel*. The mirror ball sparkled over Jacob and Candy as they danced. He wore bright yellow platforms, making him a few inches taller than her in her stilettos. Glitter and confetti swirled in the air. A man in chaps and no underwear handed Jacob a popper. A deep sniff and the amyl nitrate hit his heart like an alligator. The dance floor smelled of sweat and amyl and sex and Candy's Toujour Moi. She glowed. She leaned in whispering something he couldn't hear and he felt her warm breath across his ear.

Terry was suddenly between them, yelling over Donna Summer. "An Indian chief just grabbed my dick in the men's room."

Candy laughed. She looked even more beautiful when she laughed.

"What the fuck you go in the men's for?" Jacob asked.

"Woman's was full."

"Dude. You went in the men's. No bitching now."

"He. Grabbed. My. Dick."

"Was he good-looking?" Candy asked.

"Fuck both of you."

"Three way? You up for it, Jake?"

"Not with this hairy beast-boy," Jake yelled. "Sorry man, didn't mean that. I'd so bone you." The last part was said just as the DJ dropped the music out. The whole dance floor heard, "I'd so bone you." They erupted with blasts from their whistles. Even Jacob had to grin at his own mistake.

"Twenty large, girl? Damn, when you screw up, you go big," Valentina said to Sam. They were drinking sloe gin fizzes.

"This man I was hanging with, he had a plan."

"Oh, baby, man gets a plan it's time to duck and motherfucking cover."

"I know that now."

"This man who planned it, was he cute, filled out his Levis? We girls get wet and stop thinking."

"Wasn't like that. OK it was like that, but . . . damn, Val, I thought he was real. Thought I meant something to the creepoid. Maybe I was just tired of shaking my titties and cooch for five bucks a grope, thought maybe he was my ticket off the stage."

"Heard that, girl."

"Heard what?" Jacob, Terry and Candy came in off the dance floor.

"Nothing, little bro."

"An Indian chief tried to grab my dick."

"I'll let the society editor at the *Chronicle* know, Terr-Terr."

Sam looked from Jacob to Candy then back to Jacob. "Candy?"

"Yes, my dear?" Candy fell into the couch, leaning her head on Sam's shoulder.

"Are you planning on balling my little bro?"

Candy put her hand on her chin and made a damn fine pantomime of someone thinking. "'Cause if you ain't, you gotta stop giving him those eyes. Kid looked like he was going to bust a nut on the dance floor."

"Fuck I was. We were just having . . . I don't, um . . ."

"Little bro, you don't want us to know who you're planning on boning, don't wear such tight jeans." She arched an eyebrow and looked down. "Hell, the whole room can see you want her, and that you're Jewish."

"Fuck you. No really, fuck you." They were all laughing at Jacob. "Come on, Terry, I need a drink."

"Come back, Jake, we're kidding," Candy said between giggles.

When Jacob was clear, Sam told Candy and Valentina all of the ugly truth. Told them about Breeze and his inside man, why she had chosen Taxi Dancer tonight—she was casing the club. As they talked, danced and drank, Sam watched the money. Every twenty minutes a big guy in a leather jumpsuit and dog collar went around the different bars and the door collecting cash in canvas envelopes. He then would disappear into the back.

"So are we crewing up?" Candy asked. "One big score to get clear of this Humboldt bastard?"

"Yes. Something like that."

"Girl, I'm in. If you two white bitches going on a job, so am I. We're the three musketeers. I'm Darktanya. Ha, that's funny. Smile, Sam."

"I will once I figure this gig out."

At the bar, a drag queen in a Marilyn wig and massive gold platforms poured Jacob and Terry rum and Cokes. Over the speakers, Sylvester and the Hot Band were kicking out their version of "Southern Man." Terry sparked his Bic and fired up a Marlboro. "Jake, A, you're cute when you blush."

"You too?"

"And B, Candy wants to fuck you. So, um, fuck you."

"No, what Candy wants is to drive me crazy and then laugh about it with Sam."

"What you need, what you really need, what you really, really need is . . ."

"Yes, oh wise Terry?"

"What you really, really, really need is some trim."

"Yes I do. What are the odds of finding a willing and cute and dickless girl in here, who isn't my sister or Candy?"

"Zero to, um, zero. Vitamin Q time?" Terry held a lude between his finger and thumb.

"Oh, hell yes."

Sam sashayed around the room, swinging her full hips to Gloria Gaynor's "Never Can Say Goodbye." She was memorizing the room. Upstairs was the dance floor. The room was thirty-two feet by forty feet. Downstairs was the front door and the cabaret where the live acts played.

At three a.m., while the friends scarfed down Chinese food in the Golden Pot, Sam worked on a sketchpad, drawing Taxi Dancer's floor plan. She took notes. She didn't look up or notice Jacob standing behind her.

"You planning to take down Taxi Dancer?"

"No, just an old habit. It calms me down."

"Bullshit. I'm in."

"No. You graduate high school. You go to college. Then, you support my tired ass. That is the plan."

"Plan? Your plan? Mom's plan? My plan is I go with you. I cover your ass for a change. You let grungy hillbillies maul you so Mom and me could eat. My turn is now."

"Me, too," Terry said. He was shitfaced, and very serious. "Jake is in, I'm in."

"No, and no," Sam said. "I mean it Jake, no shit."

"So do I."

"Ooh la la, look who just grew a set," Valentina said.

"Stay out of this Val, really. Subject is lock-boxed." Sam stood, closed her sketchbook and walked out.

Jacob watched his sister through the front window as she walked down the neon-lit sidewalk of Chinatown. "This is bogus. I'm in. Whatever the hell it is, I'm in."

"Jake," Candy said, "Sam's full of shit sometimes, but she's right this time."

"Valentina?"

"Yes, Jacob, sweetheart, love of my dreams, Sam is correct."

"Why? I'm not man enough, not tough enough? Think I'll crumble when it gets hot?"

Valentine shook her head, running out of steam. "No, precious. No. You're too good."

"Jake, let it rest and trust Sam. Please." Candy flashed her hottest smile.

Jacob melted. "OK, for now."

On the sidewalk, Sam smoked and thought. She had no operating capital, no plan, no chance in hell of pulling it off. Yet, she had happy butterflies. Back up on the reef and ready to rip and scam. She was feeling more alive than she had in two years.

CHAPTER 6

"I'm always prone to do things very quickly, which has distinct advantages—you leave all the mistakes in, and the mistakes always become interesting."
—*Brian Eno*

It was early afternoon and the fog draped over the city when Sam parked in the alley behind Taxi Dancer. Bruce, the inside man, met Sam at the service entrance. He was five feet nothing and skinny. He was in his mid-twenties, cute in a Lucky Charms kinda way. In the daylight his ruffle-fronted tux shirt and black velvet sport coat seemed a bit extravagant, but this was San Francisco, The City.

"I can get fired just for opening this door."

"Is there an alarm?" Sam asked.

"Off. Cleaning crew is in there."

"Then what's the sweat?"

"Jo Jo or Maurizio. If either one of them are here I'll lose my job. I love Breeze, much as anyone, but I need the work."

"First, nobody loves Breeze, you owe him. Second, slow it down. I know Jo Jo. Big guy, likes to wear a leather jumpsuit, he's the manager, right?"

Bruce nodded, then looked around nervously.

"Who is Maurizio?"

"He took over a year ago. One day Freddy Quinn is running the club, next he's gone and Maurizio is in charge. He's the GM, or maybe the owner. They say he's . . ." Bruce tapped his finger to his nose.

"A coke hound?"

"That too, but no." He tapped his finger to his nose again. Sam shook her head. Bruce let out an overly theatrical sigh. "Mob."

"Bullshit. Mob owning a gay disco? Bullshit."

"It's a rumor."

"So is Elvis being dead, don't make it true."

"Have you seen him?"

"Maurizio?"

"No, Elvis. Might as well be dead. I had a mad crush on skinny Elvis."

"OK. Wanna open this door?"

"Yes, no."

"Let's go with yes, OK? Standing out here we look like two mooks casing the joint." After a painful fumbling of keys, two drops, Sam wanted to bitch slap Bruce, but little as he was it might break his neck, and then who would be her tour guide? Finally, on the third try, he got the door open.

The first room was filled floor to ceiling with cases of booze and kegs of beer. Next was a hall that led to a freight elevator. Past that was the band dressing room and a room for their sound equipment. A hall led to backstage of the cabaret. The front door and main staircase were beyond that.

"Let's take the elevator," Sam said.

"It's noisy. Can't hear it at night, but it really is . . ."

"Noisy?"

"Yeah."

"So let's live a little." Sam pushed him into the elevator, pulling the accordion gate closed behind them. Flipping the lever up was, in fact, noisy. Gears gnashed and metal on metal screeched.

The elevator was just a platform; they could watch the brick walls moving past them. Nearing the second floor, Sam saw a pair of tasseled Italian loafers facing the lift. Moving up it revealed expensive-looking wool slacks. A Pierre Cardin belt buckle. White linen shirt coving a tight gut and chest, top two buttons undone exposing a rug of black chest hair and a thick gold chain. Then the face—aquiline nose, thin lips pursed unpleasantly, black hair swept back and lacquered in place. He was handsome in an Al Pacino/Michael Corleone sort of way.

It took Bruce three tries before he could line up the elevator's platform with the floor. Throughout, the man stared at Sam, and she stared right back at him. Nothing to hide here.

"Hey, Maurizio," Bruce said as he pulled open the door.

"You're sweating."

"Am I?"

"Yes. We working you too hard?"

"No, sir."

"So, here's a question: what is my head bartender doing here—" he checked his gold Omega "—six hours before his shift?"

"I was just, see, um—"

"He was showing me the club," Sam said, flashing Maurizio her best innocent but I might fuck you smile. "It's impressive." She let her eyes wander down Maurizio, checking him out.

"Who the fuck is the skirt?"

"She's, um—"

"Bruce's sister from Phoenix, nice to meet you." She extended a hand. Maurizio looked at it and then at Bruce.

"You don't look like his sister. Not one tiny bit."

"Different fathers. Mom was a bit of a whore."

"Whoa, that's no way to talk about your mother."

"Sporting lady? Lady of pleasure? Those sound better?"

"You mean she really was a . . . ?"

"Afraid so."

"That's rough."

"Wasn't easy. Nice club you got here. Bro was just giving me the dime tour."

"We like it, the fags seem to have fun, no offense, Bruce."

"None taken, sir."

"I got to get back to work. Have a fun tour, Miss."

"Cassidy. Call me Cassidy." She leaned even harder on him with her smile, this one with slightly parted full lips, saying you can have me if you ask. He didn't ask. He turned and walked down a short hall and into an office. As the door swung closed, she caught a glimpse of a safe. Wells Fargo M7721. It was a beauty, with gold inlaid letters and a large elegant dial. She couldn't wait to stroke it.

The M7721 could be broke, but it had three false tumblers to feel for. She would need to take her time. Sam's grandfather had a notebook with the specs on every safe he could find out about. Sam stayed up late nights memorizing the details. The M7721 was a lady; she needed a tender hand, but she would give up the goods. A Safeco 6620 was a slut, opened its box at the merest of touches. The Diamond 2301 was an ice queen; take her to dinner, stroke her soft and long, and she still might not open.

After Bruce's pulse stabilized, Sam convinced him to continue their sweep of the joint. Most of it Sam knew well, but she had never been in the DJ's booth. "That switch is for fog, that for glitter," Bruce pointed at the switch labeled FOG and one labeled GLITTER. "The lights are controlled on this console." Sam took snaps of it all with her Polaroid.

He showed her where the bouncers' stations were—four per room, two on the door and two floaters. She had never noticed them because they just looked like more leather boys cruising. They could be a real problem. Trick would be to get them as far away from the back of the club and keep them there. After walking down the stairs and checking the cabaret, pacing the hallway and sizing up the three dressing rooms, she finally let Bruce lead her out the back door.

"You tell Breeze we're even now, OK? Tell him that."

"I guess your love for him was a bit coerced."

"Just pass the message. You get caught, don't look at me for anything."

"Understood."

Candy and Valentina were waiting in Chinatown at the Golden Pot. "Val, what have you heard about Maurizio?"

"Mobster Maurizio? They say he's related to James 'Jimmy the Hat' Binasco. Love that name."

"Binasco is a no shit, real deal, put a horse head in your bed gangster," Sam said. "What is the macho mob doing in a gay disco?"

"Got me, little sister. Lord knows there are plenty of straight joints out there."

"I think Maurizio is gay," Sam said.

"Nope, way off."

"I think so."

"Based on?"

"He didn't make a move on me. I left the door wide open, he walked on by."

"Maybe he likes his girls skinny and tight like Miss Candy."

"Leave me out of this," Candy said, without looking up from the latest issue of CREEM Magazine. It had Mott The Hoople on the cover.

"Men are dogs, correct?" Sam said.

"Yes, baby, I give you that."

"You offer a dog a free bone, even if it ain't his favorite flavor, he's still gonna chew it."

"So if he don't rush after your big ass, he's gay? Vanity, sister, goeth before that fall."

"OK, so maybe he's straight," Sam said. "And speaking of straight, Jacob isn't backing off."

"Princess, I've been thinking . . . Jacob and Terry, they're full-grown men. Time we recognize what's standing in front of us and start treating them like adults."

Candy looked over her heart-shaped glasses and shook her head slowly.

"We are gonna need some eye candy," Valentina said, "and in Taxi Dancer our Candy is the wrong flavor."

"You're not wrong," Sam said. "Any way you turn it we are going to need help turning heads."

"You're going to pimp your brother?" Candy asked.

"No, but I might use him to bait a trap or two," Sam said.

"Your moral compass is bent, you know that don't you?"

"No, I promise I'll set it so he's safe."

"Sam, there is no safe place on a heist. You, me, Val we all know that."

"Glitter girl's right," Valentina said. "Don't mean they don't have the right to step up, danger or no. It's on them."

"Candy, leave it to me. I'll keep them clean." Sam made it clear the discussion was over. Jacob was her brother, her responsibility.

CHAPTER 7

"Watch yourself, sister! Everything in these woods'll either bite ya, stab ya or stick ya!"
—*Rooster Cogburn*

"All right, princess, if we gonna do this, we gonna do it right." Valentina passed Sam a handwritten note:

10 smoke grenades, 2 M16s with folding stocks, 1 cut-down pump twelve-gauge, 3 revolvers, clean plates for a 1967 Firebird, 5 sets of handcuffs, 5 large bandanas.

"A lot of firepower, Val. You know how to use an M16? Cause I sure as hell don't."

"I know a lot of things you don't know. A mountain in fact."

Wexler's sporting goods shop in San Jose sold rods, reels, camping equipment, and legal firearms. Caleb Wexler paid his taxes, filed a DROS on all gun sales, and kept open ledgers clean enough to please any audit. Next door to the sporting goods shop was what appeared to be a long-abandoned textbook company. Behind a Winchester sales poster in Cable's office was a hidden door, connecting the two buildings. He never sold to strangers and always spoke code. It was a sweet arrangement, kept Caleb out of the jug for the last thirty years. Sam stood in the office, set the list in front of Caleb, then stepped back beside Valentina and waited.

Caleb Wexler was a deeply overweight man in an oilskin Aussie hat and safari jacket. Sweat popped on his brow. He was panting from the exertion of living. "Let's say four apiece for the two water buffalo guns, a buck fifty for the goose. I have some older pocket warmers, sixty a pop. The cigars, twenty-five per. The rest you get at army surplus or a junk yard."

"Twelve forty-five? That's a lot of cabbage," Sam said. "What about I cut you in two to one after the gig. This is solid, swear on my pops."

"I'd love to Sammy, we got history. Can't. You get lost in the jungle or run over by a stampeding elephant, I'm sitting with my thumb up my ass."

"What if I can come up with some cash and some auxiliary collateral?"

"What kind of collateral?"

"Family heirlooms, some jewelry and such."

"Not my business. Hiram, you remember him? He is still handling estate sales. He does a fair deal. See him, then come back."

"You sure you don't—"

"Can't, Sammy, can't."

Sam and Valentina kept their mouths closed and eyes open until they were back on the 101 headed north. "Princess, that was one cryptic mumbo jumbo fab confabulation you had going there."

"Need me to translate?"

"Oh no, I got the gist. We are boned, and not in a good way, unless we find an investor."

"The silenter, the better."

"One big, rich, mute sugar daddy coming up."

One night later, Sam sat alone in the Firebird watching a massive fake French chateau just off of University Avenue in the heart of Palo Alto's richest neighborhood. Jacob had given her the address. The man who owned it was a brain surgeon or some shit at Stanford. When his wife and kids were out of town he liked to throw parties. All the high school rockers knew the doc had good drugs and plenty of free-flowing whiskey, even tanks of nitrous oxide. He was forty-five. He liked to fuck teenage girls, younger the better. If in fact it was their first time, or they convinced him it was, he always gave them a treat—jewelry, money, coke. Something to make them feel special.

Tonight the good doctor was taking a limo-load of teens to Half Moon Bay, where he owned a sweet beach house.

"I gave you the house. Terry told us about the beach party. I say we go in with you," Jacob had reasoned earlier in the night.

"No. Any other questions?" Sam said.

"All my life I've been excluded. At school? Terry is my only friend. I'm not like other people because of my family. At home, you make it clear I'm different. I didn't choose to be smart. All I wanted was to be like you."

"Look, I'll let you in on the heist, but not like this. This is a bull-shit B&E, we can do it eyes closed. Not worth risking your record on."

"Not fucking fair. Not. You wanna go all John Wayne? I'm going or I'll call the doctor and tell him."

Sam moved slowly toward her brother, backing him up against the wall. She was dead serious. "You never rat. Not even as a threat. Never. If Pop taught us anything it was that. There is us or the squids. Who you gonna be?"

"Us. I ain't no squid."

"Damn straight. Val says you're ready to cut your teeth."

"I am."

"She says you're a man and I should treat you like one."

"You should."

"But you're also my little brother, see?"

"It doesn't matter how you see me. I am man, hear me roar." Jacob beat his chest and made a Tarzan call. Sam couldn't help but smile. "Besides, me and Terry are the only ones know the layout of the doc's crib."

Sam waited twenty minutes and then flashed her headlights. A white plumber's van rolled up the driveway. Candy boosted the van that afternoon. It was Saturday, so no one would notice it was missing until they opened on Monday. By then it would be back in its stall with the ignition wires taped up and out of sight.

Sam walked to the front door, had the deadbolt tripped fast. Anyone watching would assume she used a key. With a flashlight she found her way to the side door. Jacob and Terry stepped in looking nervous as hell. Candy and Valentina took up the rear. Valentina stood by the back door, looking out. In her hand was a stopwatch. "Five minutes and we are gone, my children of the revolution."

Sam motioned for the lads and Candy to take upstairs. She had given strict instructions— jewelry, watches, anything sterling silver. No other bullshit. TVs too heavy, art too hard to move. Keep it simple. Precious metals and gems always had a market.

Sam searched the downstairs, finding the doc's den exactly where Jake said it would be. He told her the doc took girls in there to get them high. A Mont Blanc pen set. That went in her pillowcase. Then, in the corner of the room, she found a fire safe. It was new. Needed a combination and a key.

"Three minutes, then we book," Valentina called.

Sam scanned the room. She sat in the doc's chair and swiveled to look down at the safe. Then back to the desk. There were grooves in the carpet like he made that trip a lot. In the distance a police siren wailed. Then it was clear. She reached under the ink blotter and found a key. Below it was a slip of paper with the combination. Sam was slightly disappointed at not getting to finesse the safe.

Upstairs, Terry heard the siren and started to panic. He came out of a little girl's room, shaking. Jacob met him, equally freaked.

"Do they really rape pretty boys in jail?" Terry asked.

"Yes, so you don't have to worry." Jacob's joke fell flat. Over his shoulder Jacob had a pillowcase filled with silver picture frames, two flintlock pistols and a jewelry box. Terry had nothing but a stuffed toy.

Candy came out of the parents' bedroom with a pillowcase that looked near full. "Terry, why are you holding a unicorn?"

Terry looked at the unicorn as if he had never seen it before. "I don't know," he said and dropped it.

"Time. We are off like a virgin's panties," Valentina called.

Candy spun and ran down the stairs. The lads rapidly followed her out of the house and into the back of the plumber's van. Sam let herself out the front door. Once in the Firebird and two blocks away, she allowed herself to smile. She turned up T. Rex's *The Slider* 8-track, let Marc Bolan woo her with "Ballrooms of Mars." It had been a good night. In the safe she found a cornucopia of uppers and downers, screamers and wailers. Plus she found the Holy Grail—two of the doctor's script pads. In the right hands those scripts were golden.

Hiram Goldstein had helped prepare Jacob for his bar mitzvah. Hiram was also the fairest fence in the South Bay. They went to a very liberal synagogue.

"How is Jacob, studying hard?"

"Straight A's. He's shooting for Stanford, or Berkeley," Sam said.

"What does he want to major in?"

"Film or theater, but I think he should be practical. He's smart enough to study earth science, rare metals and such."

"Rare metals, just like you?"

"And you."

"True. So, bad news always first. Mont Blanc, made in Japan, fake. The silver frames are cheap plate, and these?" He held up the flintlocks. "Crap replicas. Now, the good. The watch is gold, necklace is diamonds and rubies, all of fine quality."

Everything Candy pulled was valuable. The boys had brought crap. Creeping wasn't as easy as it looked.

"So, Hiram."

"Yes, my little Samula?"

"What is the family, dang we need a break, price?"

Hiram acted like he was running numbers in his head. Sam was sure he already knew what he was going to say. "I can go seven hundred and at that I'm losing money, hand to God."

"Can you get me a glass of water? I suddenly feel sick." Sam feigned a swoon.

"OK, miss dramatic, what would you say it's worth?"

"Eighteen hundred and fifty, all night long."

Hiram clutched his chest. "You are killing me."

"So you will say eight fifty, right?"

"Close enough."

"I'll say seventeen ninety, back and forth we'll go, and I bet we settle at eleven hundred even."

"How can you be sure?"

"Because it's the only price we both can live with."

"Do you know what, Samula, you're right." He stuck out his hand and they shook. "You ever want to come work for me steady, I could use you. I'm getting old. Mira says I have to slow down."

"Crazy talk, Hiram. You will be doing this when you're a hundred. Why?"

"Why?"

"Because you love it."

"True." He nodded in happy recognition.

The next deal wasn't nearly as cordial or safe. The meet was in a biker bar in Boulder Creek, nestled in the redwoods where Skyline Boulevard dumped down into Santa Cruz. Johnny Salt was the head of the local chapter of the Grim Reapers, a biker gang feared in the Midwest. In NorCal they didn't draw much water. Still, if you wanted to unload a bunch of pharmaceuticals they were the best bet.

At the door, a greasy biker patted them down. He got a bit too close to Valentina's dick. She grabbed his wrist and drove the biker to his knees.

"If he doesn't back off, Valentina may rip his arm off."

"Let him go. My apologies to both of you, but I have to be very careful. The Angels put a bounty on my head."

"Why would they do that?"

"Because they are assholes."

"So I heard."

Johnny Salt looked Sam up and down, slow. "You have filled out in all the right places. Damn, girl. Hot motherfucking damn."

"I was twelve last time you saw me. My pops and I were selling you a case of whites."

"And look at you now. Yummy, yummy, love to have you on your tummy. How is your pops?"

"Run over by a drunk truck driver."

"Shit does happen, don't it."

"Could say it that way."

Valentina was bent over the pool table completely distracting all of Johnny Salt's bodyguards.

"Show and tell time, babe," Salt said.

"Gentlemen first."

"No, I insist." His face went cold. Sam slowly lifted her purse onto the table, dumping out the contents. Then she dropped the script pads on top of the already impressive pile of narcotics.

"So how much you want for it all?"

"Three grand, just like I said on the phone. Non negotiable."

"Everything is negotiable, especially when you come onto my turf unprotected."

One of the boys started to reach into his jacket. Valentina flipped a cue, connecting the heavy end with the man's temple. It made a meaty thud and his legs went Jell-O. He was out before he hit the floor. Valentina dove and rolled across the pool table, swung the cue again, taking the man who had pat-searched her just below his chin, smacking his Adam's apple hard. He dropped down, gasping to keep air moving to his lungs.

The last bodyguard aimed an ugly little .44 bulldog at Valentina.

She grabbed the cue ball off the table and hurled it at the gun. She missed, but the man flinched as he jerked the trigger. The gun went off, filling the room with a deafening roar. The bullet passed over Valentina's head and blasted a hole in the wall over the bar. The dust was still falling when Valentina threw the eight ball. It took the man with the .44 between his eyes. He went down like a sack of rocks. She moved over, kicking the gun from his hand. She walked the room, taking the fallen's firearms.

"Hey, asshole, I'm over here," Sam said.

Johnny Salt slowly turned away from the carnage.

"My money, or I sell you to the Angels. Your choice."

"I have—"

"Time's up."

"OK, it's behind the bar."

"Val, get the cash."

Valentina moved behind the bar, dropping the handguns into the dirty water filled sink. Leaning down, she grinned. There was in fact, miracle of miracles, a paper bag filled with bundled up cash.

Sam looked at Johnny Salt, then at the bag again. With one massive roundhouse she clocked the punk. He did a clumsy pirouette then hit the floor.

In the Firebird, Sam and Valentina started to laugh.

"Vitamin Q time, Princess Samantha?"

"Yes, good plan. And never call me that."

"What, princess or Samantha?"

"I can live with princess, almost."

Valentina looked at her friend and smiled. "That hand hurt?"

"Like hell."

"Two Qs coming right up."

Day thirteen and they were funded.

Now all Sam had to do was work out how to get their arsenal into the club. And how to get out once they had the cash.

Minor details.

CHAPTER 8

"This is gun country."
—Death Wish

"Settle down you dazzling bitches, class is in session." Valentina unzipped an olive canvas duffle bag that was sitting on the coffee table in the Creekside Apartment living room. It was full of guns.

"Oh, fuck me." Terry turned a lighter shade of pale.

"You OK, Terr-Terr, this shit getting a little too real?" Valentina tossed a snub-nosed .38 to Terry. He recoiled and the revolver bounced off his chest, landing on his lap. "Pick it up, Ms. Cutie." Terry looked scared. "Pick. It. Up. Bitch."

"Leave him alone, Val," Jacob said, reaching for the gun.

"Stop. Terr-Terr either pulls his weight or he walks."

"Fine, fine, I'm cool." Terry picked up the snubnose and snapped back the hammer, waving it around the room wildly. He squeezed the trigger by accident. Flame spit from the short barrel. The crew hit the floor. All except Valentina, who stood calmly looking at Terry.

Terry looked from the gun to Valentina. "Sorry."

"Point it at the floor. Not your foot, the floor. Everyone alive?"

"I spilled my beer," Sam said.

"I swallowed my gum," Candy said.

"I shit my pants," Jacob said.

They all started to laugh, even Terry. Nervous laughter, but laughter nonetheless.

"Lesson one, my lovelies, a gun is always loaded." She took the snubnose from Terry and looked in his eyes for a long moment. "Baby, no shame in walking away. This gig here ain't for everyone."

"I'm cool. I'm cool."

"You don't look cool, baby, you look snakebit."

"You threw a loaded gun at me. Yes, I'm freaked. But next time warn me, OK? I'm not a pussy. I'm not a wimp. I just don't like having loaded guns thrown at me. OK?"

"OK. You're cute when you're all riled up." She stroked his cheek, then turned back to the room. She went through the care and feeding of all the weapons. She explained that knowing how to use them made them safer. She was fabulous in her tube top and flowing purple velvet skirt. She had on a Farrah Fawcett wig, frosted tips and all. She was the sexiest drill sergeant on Earth.

"I want the nickel-plated Smith & Wesson," Candy said. "I have a silver snakeskin belt that will go perfectly with it."

"Done, girl. Style points are always appreciated. We may be robbing this joint, but there is no excuse for looking tacky."

Terry got the snubby Valentina had tossed at him. It was missing most of its bluing and the handle was wrapped in electrician's tape. But its action was smooth and he had already proved it shot just fine.

Jacob was given a Smith & Wesson Chief's Special. Black-blue. Five shot. Light. Deadly. He didn't like to think about the last part. It was *Dog Day Afternoon* or *The Godfather*—just a movie if he didn't dwell.

"I'm not a pussy." Terry was drinking a beer, looking down into the drainage ditch. The 280 freeway droned on beyond where he and Jacob sat.

"I know that. No shame in walking away."

"You too? Nobody keeps asking you if you want to walk."

"I'm family."

"So am I."

"Fact," Jacob said.

Terry was the product of a late-in-life mistake. He didn't know his father and his mother was over sixty. She worked as an executive secretary to the History department head at De Anza College. She was a nice woman, just sort of vacant. In high school, Terry spent more nights at Jacob's than at home.

"Jake, if you're in, I'm in. I'll always have your back."

"OK, so now that we know we're going to do this, I mean no shit going to do this, are you a bit freaked?"

"Oh, hell yes, totally freaked."

"Good, me too. Don't tell Sam or Valentina, but when we were in the doctor's house I thought my heart would explode."

"At least you didn't try and steal a purple unicorn."

"What the fuck was that about?"

"I haven't a clue, Jake. I looked down and it was in my hand."

"I'm glad Candy didn't tell Sam or we would never—"

"She'd nickname me unicorn-boy or something else equally demeaning."

"Is she that hard on you?"

"No, she's that hard on the world."

"True. *The Wild Bunch* is playing at the dollar movies, wanna go tonight?"

"We're after men and I wish to God I was with them." Terry did his best Robert Ryan impression. They both loved films, and Peckinpah was the best. They also loved Sergio Leone, had seen all of his Man with No Name films from dusk till dawn at the drive-ins. And then there was Martin Scorsese. He hadn't made many films, but fuck they were fine. They hadn't seen *Boxcar Bertha* but Barbara Hershey's playboy spread convinced them it had to be a great film. *Mean Streets* nailed that baby gangster world and *Taxi Driver* completely blew Jacob and Terry away. Sitting in the Varsity Theatre, Jacob had known he wanted to make movies when he saw that film. Robert De Niro was an acting god. And Paul Schrader's script was pure crazy poetry. Oh yeah, and Terry and him were both panting after Jody Foster. Even in *Bugsy Malone* she was a stone cold fox.

In the woods high above Palo Alto, Sam and Valentina were walking on Alpine, a remote dirt road. "You tossed a loaded gun at Terry . . . what the fuck, Val?"

"It was a blank, darling. I had to see how he would react."

"You are evil, you know that?"

"You would have done the same."

"Yes, I would. Still evil. But you're right. This deal gets twisted, I couldn't stand to lose any of them." This wasn't Sam's baby crew pulling creep and sneaks. This was brazen. Taxi Dancer deposited the night's take early every morning after the count out. Armed men—armed and looking for a robbery—took it to the bank, so unless they wanted a shootout, taking them down was out. This left robbing the disco while it was open. If nothing went wrong the guns would be for show. If it went sideways, they might be the only way out.

"Shoulder that arm and put two rounds in the oak," Valentina said.

Fumbling, Sam snapped the M16's selective fire onto semi the way Valentina had shown her. She flinched when the gun went off. Valentina taught her to keep her eyes open and to gently squeeze the trigger. Sam was a natural.

"Val, we aren't going to shoot anyone."

"We aren't going to plan to shoot anyone. But you bring out a gun, you open a door that can't be closed easily. Thing about a firefight is, it starts fast, goes crazy, and when it's done there may be some dead bodies. I want to make sure none of them are ours."

"You ever kill a man?"

"Sam, I done worlds of things I ain't gonna talk about up here in these woods on this fine day. Three shot burst, pine tree, now."

Sam clicked the selective fire to burst and blasted the sapling, chopping it to pieces.

CHAPTER 9

"I don't know where I'm going from here, but I promise it won't be boring."
— David Bowie

"A band called Sound and Fury is the opening act," Candy reported. "Local, just out of high school. The lead singer works at Kenny's shoes."

"Corruptible?" Sam asked. They were in a booth at Lions, drinking coffee served by a waitress with a platinum beehive.

"They come off as smart, arty, not criminals or druggies."

"Damn. Doesn't do us much good."

"Opening act at Taxi Dancer is a huge break for them."

"Tubes, Sylvester, not a shabby rep builder."

"I was thinking, just say Sound and Fury lost a bandmate, guy took a powder, wouldn't that be terrible. Their singer is a front man, without him they might cancel."

"You think you could find a corruptible replacement?"

"I know I could. The city is full of junky glitter boys with rock star dreams. All I have to do is throw a rock and I'll hit one."

"Does seem like every boy with a spike in his arm thinks he's Iggy."

"Unless he's bi, then he thinks he's Bowie."

It was a complicated gig with too many moving parts for Sam, but she didn't have a better plan. "Scout the city. Call when you want me to have the boys pick up Sound and Fury's singer."

"Oh, I have a plan for him. Prrrrfect."

"Aren't you the bestest little minx."

Jacob pulled his ten-speed into the parking lot as Candy was getting into the Mercury Capri her parents gave her two years earlier when she graduated high school.

"Get in, little boy, I'm taking you for a ride."

"What about my bike?"

"Lock it. Don't you like candy? I thought all little boys had a sweet tooth."

Jacob saw Sam inside the coffee shop, paying the bill. He shrugged, waved goodbye to her and climbed into the Capri. "Where are we going?"

"Shopping. You are starting to look raggedy, and not in an I wanna fuck you rock star way." At the Stanford Shopping Mall she took him into I Magnin. Candy was dressed to her usual high standard and carried bags from several other high-end shops. They didn't get a second look when she had Jacob try on brown velvet bell-bottoms and skintight silk shirts, scarves and big-framed sunglasses. Even a pair of red snakeskin platform boots. In the end, nothing quite fit and they left empty handed—except for the fact that her previously empty bags were now full.

"That, my dear Jake, is how you look like a millionaire on pennies a day."

They headed her Capri up Page Mill and into the country. *Aladdin Sane* was blasting on the 8-track and they sang along to "Panic in Detroit." The curving road took them to Foothill Park.

"Cracked Actor" was on as they parked. They sang "suck, baby, suck, give me your head before you start professing that you're knocking me dead" to each other as the lyrics hit. Jacob went full blush and looked out the window. A group of high school guys were playing football. A skinny kid about Jacob's size got clotheslined, flipping into the air. Jacob would have traded places with the horizontal kid in an instant.

"Hey, Major Tom?" Candy said, touched his hand. It felt electric.

"I'm stepping through the door."

"No, wait. Something I want to tell you, it's important."

"OK." He didn't dare look at her, get lost in those eyes and start babbling.

"I didn't tell anyone. Not until I was sure."

"Tell us what, you're getting a sex change, going to be a guy and start dating Valentina?"

"Worse, I'm . . . I applied and got into Berkeley. I start in September. Art History," Candy said.

"That's fantastic, why hide it?"

"Wasn't sure I was smart enough to get in. Now with Sam back, she needs me. I . . ."

"Just tell her, Candy. She'll be proud."

"She needs me for Taxi Dancer."

"True. So it's your encore show, right?"

"Let's take a walk." She led him down a path into a secluded dell. They sat on a fallen log. She fired up a joint and they smoked in silence. Feeling embolden by the pot, Jacob imagined pulling her into his arms, pressing his lips against hers.

"You are the brother I never had, you know?"

Spell broken, Jacob took a long toke.

"I didn't want Sam getting you involved. She didn't listen."

"Fairness to her, I kinda blackmailed her, just a bit."

"Still. Jake you are the brightest of us all. You just need some time to grow up and you will be brilliant. You got into Stanford. Your mom told me you got accepted. Full ride. You just have to not fuck up your last semester of high school. Five months."

"I'm not leaving the crew hanging."

"Then think about it as 'what I did with my winter break.' Then get back to school and show all those rich bitch legacy kids how we do it."

"OK."

"I want a pinky promise." They linked little fingers. Jacob almost started blushing when he felt her heat. "Say it."

"I promise—"

"No, pinky promise."

"I pinky promise that when this job is done I will go back to school, go to Stanford and then come for you guns blazing." The pot bravado again.

Candy shook his pinky and released it. She smiled at him for the briefest of moments then looked away. "We better get going."

Jacob wanted to stay, wanted to take her in his arms, wanted to kiss her and never stop. "Yeah, I guess we better," is what he said.

CHAPTER 10

"Does your mommy know you use language like this?"
—*Starsky & Hutch*

The job was seven days out.

Sam and Jacob were searching a junkyard. A scruffy hellhound followed them, growling every once in awhile just to remind them that they could easily go from customers to dinner. "Don't worry, he won't bite," an older black man said. "Unless he thinks you're stealing. Then . . ."

"He bites?" Jacob smiled too broadly.

"Bites like a starved jackal. You ever seen a starved jackal?"

Jacob shook his head. "Nope."

"Me neither, but I bet my life it gets real nasty for its prey."

"Bet it does."

For twenty tense minutes they searched up and down the aisles of stacked wrecks. The whole time the dog paced them. On tinny-sounding loudspeakers "Rudolph the Red Nosed Reindeer" was playing, a bluesy version done by The Temptations. Then came Stevie Wonder doing "Little Drummer Boy."

"What's with the music?" Sam asked.

"You really don't know?"

"No, give."

"It's Christmas Eve."

"No shit. Hmmm. The crew?"

"All home with their people."

"We're their people."

"OK, families. They are with their families."

"Even Terry?"

"Yeah, he's with his mom."

"Do you see that?" She pointed at a totaled 1967 Firebird.

"The plates are clean. It's a Christmas miracle!"

"Yes it is, Tiny Tim."

Ten minutes, a screwdriver, some solvent and six bucks and they were on their way.

"Wanna go to midnight mass?" Jacob said. "I hear St. Thomas has a killer organ player." They were raised Jewish, but their moms loved Christmastime. They always had a tree and she would crash midnight mass. Not understanding Latin, they could imagine whatever they wanted.

"Moms blew it off. I think I'll skip it too this year."

"Sacrilege. What will the baby Jesus think when he opens his eyes and finds himself surrounded by goyim, not a Jew in sight? He'll freak out."

"The plaster baby will survive, I'm sure of it."

At a liquor store, Sam bought eggnog, a pint of Bacardi 151 and a carton of Marlboro Reds. It was time for some serious chilling out.

They sat sixty feet above the ground, hanging their legs off the edge of one of the high-power towers that flanked the Creekside Apartments. They could see across the carpet of lights to the foothills and the dark mountains above. Sam poured out a quarter of the eggnog then refilled it with 151. She took a big gulp, smiled and handed the powerful concoction to Jacob. Never one to let his sister outdo him, he took an even deeper chug.

"That, Sam, is liquid Christmas cheer."

"Yes, my brother, it is."

"I got you a present."

"What is it?"

"Open it and find out, weirdo."

"I don't like surprises, you know that."

"That's right." Every Christmas Jacob had to raid their mom's hiding place and report back to Sam. "That was odd at best, sister."

"Remember when Grandpa taught me how to finesse a safe?"

"Yeah, said you had a gift. I was just another kid to him."

"You were six when he got busted, do you remember it?"

"I don't know if I do, or I just remember hearing about it. I think Moms told me about it to keep me out of the life."

"Sounds like her. Our egghead momma's boy."

"Screw you. Do you really begrudge me my immense brain? And yes, ladies, it is massive."

"Huge. But back to Grandpa. He came home after a nice day at the track and, wham-o, he was surprised by four cops. Told me never be surprised. Know what's coming and always plan for three ways out." She dropped the spent cigarette, which bounced off the girders showering sparks as it fell. "I was eight. The case fell apart for lack, but still it broke my heart when they took him. His words stuck."

"Then I am sorry to give you this. It's Mick Ronson's *Play Don't Worry*. Cool sound." He tore away the wrapping paper and let it drift off on the wind. He handed her the 8-track. She looked at it for a long moment, then leaned over and kissed her brother's cheek.

"I didn't get you anything."

"I didn't expect you to." He took a long chug of the nog.

"If you could have anything, no holds barred?" Sam sparked a new cig.

"You'll laugh."

"Maybe, take a risk."

Standing, he leaned out over the abyss, shouting into the wind that was picking up. "Candy. I want Candy."

"Sit down. You can't have her, she's not a thing."

"You know what I mean." He plunked back down and took another chug of nog.

"No, I know what you said."

"I want her to want me. Is that plain and simple enough?"

"That's better. But she maybe already wants you. Every time I walk down the street a bunch of mooks want me. Don't mean shit. I want one of them to get me. See me. You know, see but also see what's under all these wonderful curves." She was starting to slur her words just a bit.

"So, I want her to get me."

"No, honestly, you want to bang her."

"It's not like that. OK, it is kinda like that, but more."

"Do me a solid. Wait until we drain Taxi Dancer to act on all these feelings, OK?"

"OK, you got it."

"I'm a little tipsy, brother."

"You look hammered."

"I will concede that point."

A high-intensity beam of light swept the girders. It landed on Sam and Jacob like a vaudeville spotlight.

"You on the tower. You are trespassing on private property." The voice sounded mechanical, coming from a lo-fi speaker. "Climb down now."

"Easier said than done." Sam blocked the light with her hand, trying to see who was behind the light.

"Come on, sis, we either climb down or start tap dancing."

"I don't know how to tap dance."

"We could do the hustle." Jacob moved his fists in a circle.

"I'd rather die from the fall."

"Then down we go."

Steel beam to steel beam they moved slowly down the tower. Halfway, Sam misstepped. Her arms were all that held her from the fall. Slowly she pulled herself up, and then did five more pull-ups just to show off.

"You're an idiot." Jacob smacked the back of her head.

"A strong idiot."

It took thirty minutes to make it to terra firma. Detective Pahk stood silhouetted by the spotlight on the side of his unmarked car. "I could take you both in for endangering public safety, trespassing and six other misdemeanors."

"It's Christmas Eve, Detective, what are you doing wasting tax-payer money pestering me and my brother?"

"I'm off duty."

"Pathetic." Sam stepped forward, Jacob hung back.

"I'm not the one trying to get themselves fried."

"He has a point."

"Shut up, Jake."

"Jacob, you're the smart one?"

"That is what they say."

"Then why did you follow her up there?"

"The view is amazing. Would you like a drink?" Jacob held out what was left of the 151. Pahk thought about it, then took the bottle, indulging in a long gulp. He barely coughed. Nodding a thank you, he dropped it into his coat pocket.

"Too much paperwork bullshit."

"Excuse me, Detective?" Sam asked.

"Why I'm not taking you in."

"Then you must've come to wish us a Merry Christmas. Right, Detective?"

"Someone robbed a doctor's house in Palo Alto. When going over the case an old partner of mine noticed the safe had been cracked so he called me."

"I have an alibi."

"I didn't say when it was, but you have an alibi?"

"Yep, was here playing dreidel with my little brother. You got a witness says different?"

"Look, little girl, play wiseass all you want, I'm on to you."

"You need to get a life." She walked past him. Jacob started to follow but Pahk caught his arm.

"Smart boy, it's time to act smart. Don't be around your sister when she goes down, or you're going with her."

"Solid advice, sir."

"You mocking me?"

"No, sir. Seems to me, smart one that I am, that my sister hasn't done anything and you are obsessed with her. Hassling us on Christmas Eve could look a lot like harassment to someone with more jaded eyes than mine."

"This really how you want to play it, kid?"

"Like my sister said, you need to get a life." Jacob walked away, leaving Pahk leaning against his car.

In the apartment, Jacob found the lights out. Sam was watching the detective from behind a curtain.

"Do you think he knows it was us? He couldn't, right?"

"He's trying to rattle us, that's all," Sam said.

"Um, it's kinda working. Why us?"

"I don't know." Sam kept her face turned away from her brother.

"Truth? You don't know?"

"That is what I said."

"OK. Why didn't you tell me about finessing the safe?"

"Because brother of mine, I didn't." Sam looked him straight on. "The lying doc must have forgot to mention he left the combination under his blotter. AMA frowns on doctors not keeping their scripts better protected."

"Is no one honest anymore?"

"Just you and me, pal."

"But only to each other."

"There is that."

After twenty minutes, Detective Pahk finally drove off. Sam and Jacob curled up on the couch wrapped in blankets.

"Weird not having Moms here. How you taking it, kid?"

"We're Jews, OK?"

"Nominally, but go on."

"So this whole Christmas deal was Mom's. She wants to spend the winter break in Cabo with our lawyer, power to her. Me? Other than an excuse to get you some music I can listen to in your car, it don't mean shit. Just another day."

"You sound pissed, little brother."

"I'm not. What I am is shitty faced."

Sam knew it was more. She could see how hard it had been for Jacob to be the smart one, the family's hope of going straight. "Why are you so good at school?"

"I'm a smart motherfucker." That was a part of the truth. The rest he kept to himself. Doing what is expected is all it took to get good grades, no matter what new school he was thrown into. Growing up, Jacob hadn't fit in anywhere, not really. In a family of thieves you never let your guard down in public, never shared any truth about yourself. When asked what you did with your summer vacation you made shit up. Terry was the one person who really knew Jacob. At home he was the family's great hope. He wasn't supposed to follow in his father's or grandfather's footsteps. He was on uncharted ground.

Sam didn't tell Jacob she was just as lost. Didn't tell him their father had made her promise to get out of the life. A promise she was breaking to protect the family.

"Do you miss Pops?" Jacob asked, as if he had been reading her mind.

"Yeah, all the time."

"When he wasn't on a losing streak and moody, he was a great guy."

"Yes, he was."

Christmas morning exploded in on Sam like a million shards of happy piercing her fragile, hungover head. "Zip-a-dee-doo-dah, zip-a-dee-ay, my oh my what a wonderful day." Moms was home from Mexico, and singing up a storm.

"The hell you say?" Sam grumbled.

"You didn't think I would miss Christmas."

"Mom?"

"Yes, Samantha?"

"You know we're Jewish, and I'm in deep pain."

"To point one, so what? To point two, I brought you a mimosa." Their mother, Esther, was short. She was curvy in her day, now slipping into round. More than anything she was a cheerful steam-roller. If she said they were having Christmas, they were having it. While Esther went to wake Jacob, Sam ate a couple tabs of Ritalin she'd taken from the good doctor's house. She gulped them down with the mimosa.

Ten minutes, Sam's eyes popped open. The speed and the realization she hadn't cleaned the apartment hit at the same time. Were guns sitting on the coffee table? Where was her plan book? Her mother wasn't stupid, she knew what a heist in progress looked like. Fuck.

Jacob was sitting in the living room. He had on a poncho and a sombrero with his name stitched on its crown. He smiled. "Look what Moms brought me."

"Attractive look on you." Sam scanned the room. Jacob flicked his eyes to a hall closet.

"Samantha, I didn't forget you." Esther handed Sam a white cotton dress with flowers embroidered across the yoke.

"It's amazing." It was. Sam could see it with her leather jacket and combat boots.

"I'm sorry I missed Christmas Eve. Traffic on the 101 was death. No really, death."

"You died?" Jacob smiled.

"Yes, as a matter of fact, smart boy, I was dead. Karl had to do CPR."

"Sounds dreadful. Did you see the white light?"

"I did and your Nana came to me, asked me to tell you to do your homework and be nice to me or she'd haunt you."

"Cool beans, I never had a ghost before. Bring on the haunting, Nana!"

"Your brother is a very odd child."

"Genetics are a bitch." Sam sparked a Marlboro, offering one to

Esther, who took it and greedily inhaled. After a moment she jetted the blue smoke.

"Damn that tastes good. Karl hates when I smoke."

"Welcome home, Esther."

"Thank you, Samantha. What a gift to have both my children waiting for me. You didn't lose your job did you?"

"If I did?"

"Rent is due next week."

"I quit my job. And don't worry, I have you covered."

"Good. You are welcome to be here as long as you need to be." Esther hugged her daughter tightly. Sam resisted at first, then relaxed into the embrace. Growing up, her mother was the glue that had held the family together when Dad went off the rails or was in lockdown. It was Esther they could depend on. It was in her arms Sam felt safe. For this moment she allowed herself to be.

Sam pulled away. "Karl?"

"He's nice, it was fun."

"He's kinda a tool," Jacob said.

"He is not your father. But no one is. He'll do for now, so please be nice. He's coming to dinner tonight."

"Tonight?" Sam said.

"Tonight."

"Damn, we have plans," Jacob said.

"Change them." Her smile was soft, her will iron.

"Don't fight it, bro. We'll be here with bells on."

"Good. Now I need to lie down. Saving Christmas is hard work." Sam followed Esther into her bedroom. She picked up the picture of her and Jacob on the swing sets when they were children. She stared from the photo to her mother.

"Yes, Samantha? You're angry. Karl?"

"Not really. You think it was smart leaving Jacob?"

"Oh, I get it. You can run off to whatever adventures you want. Your father, he certainly did as he pleased. But Mom wants one week for herself and the world comes crashing down. One week is too much for all I've done."

"You're a black belt."

"Excuse me? Black belt?"

"At guilt."

"That is not fair, Samantha."

"Don't mean it ain't true."

"Did something happen? Is Jacob alright?"

"He's fine."

"There you go then. He's almost an adult."

"No, he's not."

"Can we argue the semantics of your brother's age later? I'm exhausted."

"OK." Sam left Esther lying on the bed.

Sam and Jacob waited to hear Esther snoring before moving the guns, smoke grenades and other evidence of the crime to the Firebird's false trunk. "How did you get everything hidden?"

"I was sleeping on the couch, heard her come in. While she went to put her bags in her room I hustled everything into the closet."

"We are going to have to be very careful, the woman can smell a scam a mile away."

"Why not tell her?"

"No. I don't need her grief. 'Sides, it would only worry her about shit she has no control over."

Terry peddled up on his ten-speed. Sam and Jacob were sharing a warm Mickey's big mouth, leaning on the Firebird. Terry was wearing a red sweater with a Frosty the Snowman appliqué. "Don't say a word, either of you."

"It's kinda sexy in a very kinky way," Sam said.

"I think I saw Ian Hunter wearing one like it in CREEM," Jacob said.

"Fuck ya both and give me a cig and a beer."

"They're warm."

"Don't care."

"That rough?"

"She invited her friends from work. All old, all straight. 'Why do you wear eye shadow?' 'You aren't a faggot are you, son?' Like that all night." He gulped a warm beer down like he was from the UK. Took the cig offered by Jacob and sucked deep. He pulled off the sweater, revealing a black Bowie tee shirt on under it.

"Don't know what I'd do if I didn't have you two."

"Go on a Nico-style killing spree. 'Mother I want to . . . kill you,'" Jacob sang.

"It was a Doors song. She covered it on the album *June 1, 1974*, with Eno, Cale and Ayers."

"Terry, you are a god of music trivia," Jacob said.

"You're fucking with me, right?"

"I think it's sexy." Sam winked.

"And now you're fucking with me. Thanks guys."

"You know we love you. L.U.V.," Jacob said.

"We do. I might even take a run at you, but it would break Valentina's heart."

"I am straight. Tell her I like, *like*, her. More than that is never gonna happen."

"And destroy all her hope? Never," Sam said.

"You gotta admit, Valentina is smoking hot," Jacob said.

"Yes, she is. If she was a woman I would be all over her."

"You really gonna let seven inches of flesh stand between you and what could be true love?" Sam said.

"Yes!" Terry guzzled his beer.

"You staying for dinner?" Jacob asked.

"No, Mom and her pals are doing the whole turkey dealio. Got any boo?"

"Always." Jacob pulled out a Bugler tobacco tin packed with joints. He sparked one and passed it to Terry. "Panama Red, be careful."

Terry took a long hit and held it, speaking around his tight lips. "Can't be powerful enough for what I got coming." He started to pass the joint back but Jacob held his palms up.

"Keep it."

Terry rode off sitting up, hands off the handlebars, smoking the joint. He weaved a little but not badly.

"I think Terry and Val might make a hell of a couple."

"He's straight."

"So you boys keep saying. Sooner or later those lines blur."

"You been with a woman?"

"None of your business."

"Dyke. If you weren't my sister that might be hot. As it is, I want to boil my eyes to clean away the thought."

"Sorry, I won't tell you how hot she was. Long black hair, fine–"

"La la la, not listening." He put his hands over his ears and walked into the apartment, leaving Sam leaning against the Firebird.

Christmas dinner was a fucking disaster for everyone but Esther. She was happy to be left in the dark.

Karl was pushing past middle-aged into just aged. Thick gray hair permed into a white man fro. Brown corduroy leisure suit. A ruddy, moon-shaped face, red from sunburn and years of a steady diet of scotch and soda. "I want you kids to know how much I respect your mother. I would never try and take your father's place."

Jacob tuned out—this was pure bullshit. If Karl respected his pop he wouldn't be hitting on the man's widow. He was feeling very Hamlet. Just needed a sword, a skull and a tapestry to hide behind.

When Esther went to make coffee and serve the pie, Karl turned his attention to Sam. "Heard you were dancing up North. That I'd like to have seen. I'm a big tipper." Under the table, having slipped off his shoe, he stroked Sam's ankle with his toes. Her face was hardening.

"Karl, you toke?" Jacob mimed hitting a joint.

"Yeah, I'm cool."

"Then come on, dude, won't take a second." Jacob was up and at the door before Karl could resist. He did what any man who didn't want to be shown up by a younger man would. He went out back and instantly took a deep hit on the joint Jacob was sparking.

"That's good, right?"

"Fucking fantastic, kid."

"Take another hit, I have something to show you."

Karl took a long inhale. Closed his eyes. Held it. Opened his eyes. *Fuck.*

Jacob was pointing a snub-nosed .38 between Karl's eyes.

Karl let a stream of smoke escape his lips. He started to speak.

"Shhhhh. Keep your fucking mouth closed." Jacob snapped the hammer back, for effect.

Karl near shit himself. "Son, you don't—"

"Shhhhh. I will kill you and not even think twice. I'm stoned. I'm angry. You hit on my sister again, ever, you die. Clear?"

"You wouldn't."

"My pops would. I'm his son. I'm a lousy shot, so it will be close range."

"You're crazy, you need help."

"Yes I am, and no I don't." Jacob tapped the barrel on Karl's brow. "Here is how this plays out. You grow some balls and come after me, I will kill you. Or you kill me. Then Sam will kill you. You kill Sam, well then Moms is hell with a shotgun. Getting the picture?"

Jacob put the revolver in his pocket.

Karl was panicking. He moved toward the house. "My jacket."

Sam stood at the backdoor, holding Karl's jacket. She tossed it to him. It landed on his head.

He pulled it off, all dignity lost. "What about Esther?"

"We'll tell her you had to book."

Karl looked from one hard face to the other. Slowly he turned and was gone into the shadows.

"Don't fight my fights for me ever again," Sam said.

"Pops would have kicked his ass."

"You ain't Pops."

"Neither are you, Sam."

From the house they could hear Esther calling their names. They replaced their scowls with smiles by the time they hit the table. They explained Karl got called away to bail out a client.

"Never mind. He can be kind of a dick sometimes. I'm glad it's just us."

Brother and sister looked at each other and started laughing.

Midnight found Esther in bed and Sam and Jacob looking into the drainage ditch, drinking rum and cokes.

"I'm gonna say this once. You were kinda badass with Karl."

"Yes, sister, I was." He took a long pull off his drink. "What do you think Candy is doing?"

"Sleeping, or fucking a stranger. Sorry that hurts, but Candy is a free agent. She once told me she only felt fully alive when fucking or running a scam. I don't see the flowers-and-hearts ending you do. I see you getting your heart tore up by my best friend."

"People change."

"Not as much as you think."

CHAPTER 11

"I'd rather be dead than sing 'Satisfaction' when I'm forty-five."

—*Mick Jagger*

FIVE DAYS UNTIL THE HEIST.
KENNY'S SHOE STORE.
NOON.

"Do you have these in a size smaller?" Candy held up a pair of silver stilettos.

"I'll check." White shirt, clip-on tie. The makeup remover hadn't taken off all the eyeliner. There were still little sparks of glitter in his hair.

She let out a quiet but very sexual moan when he put the shoe on her foot.

"Bowie or Iggy?" she asked.

He leaned back on his heels looking up at her, dropping the salesmen drone act. "Bowie all the way. My turn. Queen or Lou Reed?"

"Ooh, that's a tough one. Lou is the godfather. But Queen, I mean damn, did you see them at Winterland?"

"Front row, pressed against the stage."

"No. I was there." She smiled at him, letting it land, her eyes locked on his. "When is your break?"

"Now." He stood up, ripped off his nametag and tie.

"What about the shoes?"

"A gift." He tossed the tie and nametag at the old lady working the register. "Later, Ruth. Get out before they drain your youth—oh hell, they already did."

"What the fuck did I just do?" the shoe salesman said. They were in a coffee shop eating pie. Candy was licking the spoon and taking every opportunity to get his eyes.

"You just set yourself free," she said. "Are you in a band?"

"Yeah, Sound and Fury."

"Like an idiot?"

"Nice, lady knows her *Macbeth*."

"I think I saw you play . . ."

"At the Mabuhay? Have to be. Wild show, jungle theme?"

"You were electric. I better get going."

"We're having a rehearsal tonight, big show coming."

"Sounds fun."

"You wanna come along, to the rehearsal?"

Candy grabbed his arm and let herself be escorted to a VW van. It was spray painted black with *Sound and Fury* slashed across the side in lipstick red.

On the ride he told her his name was Cord. Male form of Cordelia.

"Your nametag said Michael."

"He died when we walked out. Happy liberation day!"

"Vitamin Q?"

"Why the fuck not."

She put it on his tongue and he swallowed. Too easy.

The practice studio was a small warehouse in the Mission. Junkies, drunks, hookers and good old-fashioned bums crowded the sidewalk. Cord eased past them to park in a caged lot next to the rehearsal space.

Taking the microphone, he was stunning, transformed from shoe-selling schlub to a real deal rock star. Three songs in he started to lose the thread, started forgetting lyrics. Then he started mumbling about "the fuck snake rugs. Who let those reptile bastards in?" Amazing what a few drops of LSD would do to an innocent Quaalude.

Chi Chi, the band's cross-dressing guitar player, was losing his shit. "What the fuck is wrong with you? There are no motherfucking snakes. Roaches yes. Snakes no."

"Ahhh." Cord climbed onto a bass speaker box.

Chi Chi wagged his finger in Candy's face. "What did you do to our man?"

"I just met the guy. He seemed cool. I'm Ariana Bend, by the way." She passed Chi Chi a card that listed Candy as a musicians' agent. The phone number on it would be picked up by a service— Bend Agency.

"You for reals, no bullshit?" Chi Chi said.

"Real as they come. You know Fee and The Tubes?"

"Hell yes, we're opening for them New Year's Eve."

"I know. I got them that gig."

"Young chick like you, you manage The Tubes?"

"No. I'm a big fat liar." Behind her Cord was playing with the invisible webs between his fingers. "Why don't I get him home.

Come back tomorrow and hear you guys. If I like what I hear . . .
who knows."

"Yeah, who knows." Chi Chi flounced over to his guitar and let
out a power chord.

Candy drove Cord to the bus station. Bought a one-way ticket
to Wichita. She cleared his pockets of ID and all cash. "I love you,
two heads and all. Kiss me," he said, looking surprisingly sober. This
was not his first trip to weird town.

She offered up a lude. "Take this."

"Only if you will kiss me, let me stroke your scales." She kissed
him long enough for him to grope her breasts. Pulling back she
softened. "OK, baby, Q time." She gave him two more ludes.

By the time he hit the bus seat, he slumped against the window,
out. Watching him go, Candy felt like shit. She had just fucked this
kid's life. Sam's "us and them" wore thin on Candy. During Sam's
two-year absence, she'd had plenty of time to think. In a class at
Foothill Junior College she learned about moral relativism. What
she'd just done to Cord was bad. Robbing a doctor who preyed on
under age girls was good. For her the lines between 'us' and 'them'
seemed permeable.

The next day, Candy returned to the rehearsal space. A band
meeting was in full swing. Chi Chi, dressed as a stubble-bearded
geisha, was saying he knew all the lyrics. The fuzzy drummer said
he didn't give a fuck, he just wanted to play. Chi Chi and the skinny
bassist were about to tear each other apart when Candy cleared her
throat.

"Where is Cord?"

"Good question, chica. Where is he?"

"He dropped me off at my car, seemed better. Said he was going home to rest."

"He never made it home."

"And this is my fault how? He's an adult." She walked around the room, picking up a leaflet for the show. "Four days." She shook her head. "Hate to see you cancel, what I heard was damn good."

"Cord will show up."

"OK, how's this sound? He shows, I hear you play tomorrow, I sign you."

"Just like that?" the bass player said.

"Just like that. You boys ready to take this out of the garage and into the arena?"

"What's in it for you?"

"Fifteen percent." She stuck out her hand. No one shook it.

"Duh," said the fuzzy drummer.

"What if Cord flakes?"

"You boys are fucked and I move on."

"I know the songs."

"You don't look the part. You need a front man if you want to open for The Tubes." Candy turned and clickety-clacked her heels all the way across the room. She stopped dramatically at the door and spun around. "OK, I like you kids. I will send you a singer. You teach him the songs in case Cord is a no-show. Best I can do." She gave them a two-finger salute and was gone.

She spent the rest of the day on the phone calling rockers. New Year's Eve was a hard night to find a decent singer.

CHAPTER 12

"You can't trust anybody, not even yourself."
—Pat Garrett & Billy the Kid

As her plan came together it became clear she would need a demolition man. "I'm thinking of calling Jinks."

"No," Valentina said. "You two are a bad combination."

"That was years ago."

"You broke his heart."

"He broke mine. He was embarrassed to be seen in Chinatown with a *gwai lo*."

"My fab little bunny, it doesn't mater who did who. Do you want to trust him not to blow you up?"

"I trust him. Set it up, please."

"Please? Oh you must want and or need him."

"For the gig, sister, the gig. Period."

"Whatever you say."

Walking into the Golden Pot, Sam spotted Jinks instantly. He was leaning against a fish tank. Black jeans, black Converse high tops, a skintight black Velvet Underground tee shirt that showed every rippling muscle. Sam heard herself gasp, then reeled it in. She strutted to him, keeping her sunglasses on.

"Jinks."

"Sam. You look good, always did."

"So do you." They just kept staring at each other. The chemistry was undeniable. Finally Sam broke the moment with a laugh. "You want to fight or fuck or talk business?"

Jinks let out a laugh, shaking his head. "Man, I missed you." He held up his left hand, a gold wedding band caught the light.

"So that leaves fight or do business, right?"

"Something like that."

"Don't give a girl hope and leave her hanging."

"Business first." He led her into a back room and closed the door. She could smell his scent. She reminded herself to get this done and move on before something bad happened. And it would end bad. Besides, she didn't do married men.

"What's the gig?"

"Your part is to blow up a Pinto."

"A Pinto? Couldn't I just rear-end it?"

"Cute. It needs to go up in flames but not hurt any bystanders."

"A controlled burn."

"Exactly. A distraction."

"What's the job?"

"You get an equal split. Your take could be two grand."

"Could be? I need a guarantee that two is the floor."

"A guarantee?"

"Sorry, doll, way it is." He added a wink, trying to come off more cool and less desperate.

"You don't want in . . ." Sam said, shrugging.

"I didn't say that. What's the job? You can trust me."

Sam looked at his face, searching for any changes, found none. "Taxi Dancer, we're taking down the disco New Year's Eve."

"Oh, bad fucking idea. I hear it's mobbed up."

"Gossip. One of the owners is a closet case, who happens to be related to Jimmy the Hat."

"Mobbed up."

"No macho Italians are going to be involved with a gay disco. If Maurizio gives us any shit I'll threaten to tell his uncle he's a rump ranger who takes black dick up the ass."

"You kiss your moms with that mouth?"

"No, but I used to kiss you with it."

He grabbed a handful of her hair and pulled her face to his. The kiss was a lightning strike, electric, and it just kept going. Sam couldn't have pulled away if she wanted to. His tongue danced into her mouth and she sucked, pulling it deeper. Without stopping the kiss, he lifted her easily onto the table. She had forgotten how strong his hands felt on her waist. She heard him unzip his jeans, felt him lift her skirt and push her panties to the side. She was wet. Ready. He entered her fully in one thrust. She groaned as he pounded in and out. It was furious, a mixture of rage and lust. He came in minutes, ending the kiss with a grunt. He withdrew and zipped up. He left her sitting on the table and started to leave.

"This, um, this mean . . ." Her voice was rough and raspy. "Are you in?"

"Yes."

"Where are you going?"

"I have to pick my kid up at Ma's. Kimmy is working at her father's shop."

"Kimmy? Cute Kimmy? Bleached blonde pageboy Kimmy?"

"Hair is black again. I have missed you." Then he was gone, leaving Sam to clean herself in the women's room. Looking in the mirror, she wondered who was staring back at her.

"You boned Jinks fucking Kang?"

"Yes, little brother, I did. Gonna shoot me?" They were driving back from the city. Jacob had stood lookout in an alley across from the Golden Pot, in case Jinks set them up. It was a long shot, but long shots got you just as bad as sure shots.

"Might shoot him." He'd taken to carrying the .38 wherever he went. He took it out of his pea coat pocket, spun it once then returned it.

"Don't. We need him for the score."

"You brought Jinks fucking Kang into the score?"

"Why did you think I was meeting him?"

"I don't know, catching up, fuck do I know."

"We need an explosion. He's the best."

"You're writing the script, cut the explosion. Problem solved."

"I am writing the script. The plot calls for an explosion. End of discussion."

"Jinks fucking Kang."

"Don't think that's his actual middle name."

"Should be." Jacob had been there when Jinks broke up with her. He'd sat up until dawn smoking Marlboros and listening to her cry and moan too many nights. Sam knew he of all people knew what it had done to her. On the other side of the pain she emerged hardened. She stopped brooking any shit from men, or at least put a time limit on it. She had always been tough, but not with men she was seeing.

"You still love the creep?"

"No, not like that. No hearts and baby cupids bullshit. But . . ."

"You boned him. Was it your way to hook him in to the gig? You have an angle?"

"Look Jake, it just happened. No more than that."

"Whore." He was grinning.

"Prude."

"I'm not a prude."

"Then it's because he's Chinese. Racist."

"Could be that, or maybe, just maybe, it's the fact the fuckhead broke your heart and will do it again if you give him half a chance."

"Then I won't give him a chance."

"Your word?"

"My word." Even as she said it she knew it was a promise she might not be able to keep. Jinks had been her first. Not her first lay—that was Jeff Greenstone under the bleachers at school. No, Jinks was her first real lover. Maybe humans imprinted on their first real love, like hawks. Maybe Jacob would, or had, on Candy. Time would give up the answers when it was ready and not a millisecond sooner.

CHAPTER 13

"The last thing I want to be is some useless fucking rock singer."

—*David Bowie*

"Who puked on my new jeans? Benny Boy? I can't believe this." Brian was junky thin, hair a long black shag, handsome in a rock star way. "A five minute shower and . . . Jan, did you see any—"

"Ariana. Name's Ariana, asshole. 'Ariana, do it harder.' 'Oh yeah that's it, baby, that's it, Ariana.' Ariana." Candy was dressed in a black satin, red-ribboned bra and was pulling on her matching panties.

"No need to scream."

"Just reminding you of twenty minutes ago. I am not Jan." She zipped up her leather skirt and looked for her shoes.

"I know it's Ariana. The puke on my new Sticky Fingers set me off. Ariana, did you—"

"No I didn't. We were a bit busy."

"Aeeeee! Who did it? No. Story of my life. Audition for a gig and I go in smelling of—"

Candy sprayed a double load of Glad Mountain. "You will smell like an alpine meadow. Now run. Already earning my fifteen percent."

Brian struggled into his implausibly tight jeans and the silver lamé shirt he cadged from her the night before. A six foot pink feather boa and zip-up platform boots finished the look. He blew her a kiss and was gone. Candy zipped up her leather jacket over her bra and followed him out.

She walked down the cracked sidewalk, feeling every imperfection through the thin soles of her ballet slippers. It wasn't two blocks before the rocker spun and ran back. She handed him the scrap of paper with the address of the audition and he was gone again.

The night before had been so romantic. He had been singing "I Am Woman" standing on a table at Mabuhay when she first saw him. He had a hell of a voice. Even the band on stage started backing him up. He was doing Helen Reddy proud. When he fell off the table no one even tried to break his fall. Candy helped him into a seat.

"For one magic moment, right?" he asked.

"It was beautiful."

"Then it wasn't. Buy me a drink . . . please?" He gave her that grin, a combination of wolf who just ate granny and a little boy seeing the circus for the first time. The grin that must have had a million girls dropping their knickers.

Candy was no different.

She bought him a drink. A Jack and Coke. Candy was at that tipping point—one more drink and she would be going home with this boy. "Sloe Gin Fizz, please." It was Friday night. He was cute. She was on the pill.

Now she was following him down Mission. Hanging back she gave him space. Nancy Drew would be proud of her tailing technique.

"I found a singer," Candy said into the payphone.

"Just like that?" Sam said.

"He sort of fell into my lap."

"You fuck him?"

"And I enjoyed it."

She gave the band time to audition Brian. When she got to the room the band was on a Top Ramen break. Chi Chi took her outside.

"He smells like puke."

"Fair enough."

"But man can he sing. Fast learner too."

"So are you happy?"

"Close as I get."

"Good. One more surprise. I hired two roadies to load you in and out."

Chi Chi let out a squeal then rushed in to tell the others. Through the door Candy watched them hugging and laughing and wondered what it would be like to really make a person that happy with no rug pull just around the corner.

CHAPTER 14

"You're gonna eat lightnin' and you're gonna crap thunder!"

—Rocky

One day until the heist.

"Play, don't worry." Was easy for Mick Ronson to sing. Sam was up to her ovaries with dread worry. She was driving up the 101, headed for the city with her crew onboard. All but Jinks and Valentina, who would meet them at the Golden Pot. Jinks made sure the back room was open. Candy was riding shotgun. The boys were in the back.

"The new singer?" Sam asked.

"Brian," Candy said.

"Doesn't sound like a rocker's name." Jacob tried not to sound as petulant as he felt.

"Brian Eno," Terry said, "Brian Wilson, Brian May, Brian Jones."

"Shut up, Terry," Jacob said.

"OK, Jake, whatever."

"Is Brian going to keep it together?" Sam said.

"Sure," Candy said, but she didn't look sure.

"You didn't choose him because he was well-hung and made you come?"

"No, although he is and he did, twice. He has a great voice and he'll do what I tell him."

Jacob looked out the window, pretending none of this meant squat.

"Unless he gets too high and misses the gig."

"After the meeting I'll go check out the rehearsal. Make sure he's there. I'll take Jake and Terry with me. Introduce the band to their new roadies."

"Fine. Midnight, we need this junky singer to do his job."

"He'll do it."

"No fuck ups."

"No fuck ups."

In the back room of the Golden Pot, Valentina and Jinks were midstream in a conversation about explosives. They were arguing the relative merits of C-4 versus old-fashioned dynamite. Valentina said C-4 could be molded into a shape charge and was much more stable. Jinks liked dynamite because it was easy to find and hard to trace and he knew exactly what it would do.

Sam came through the door, looked through Jinks, then gave Valentina a warm hug. Candy and the boys positioned themselves around the table. Jacob burned laser beams into Jinks. Jinks gave him a friendly smile then looked at his hands.

"Midnight, they drop confetti, scream and light firecrackers across the city," Sam said. "Midnight, we hit. With force. Shit goes twisted on us, hit the crowd and blend. We'll meet back here if we get separated. Jinks, you pull the Pinto gag and vapor. I'll get you your end next week. That work for you?"

"Any chance we can do it the morning after?"

"Fine, yes, the morning after."

"It's just I have—"

"I said it's fine. Now, one more time, you young dudes and

dudettes." Sam laid the maps of Taxi Dancer on the table. She went over every inch of the plan. Made Terry and Jacob repeat their tasks. No one joked. This shit was serious. Fucking up meant death or jail. It was complicated way beyond Sam's comfort zone.

"Never too late to take a walk away. It don't feel right, we stroll on and live to party another day," Valentina said. She and Sam were in the ladies' room.

"I owe twenty large, no way around that."

"Maybe we kill this Breeze bastard."

"I would, but I'm a thief not a killer."

"You got no idea what you are until you start rock and rolling."

"It's going to be copasetic."

"You say so, I believe it."

Walking out, they saw Candy and the boys had already left. Jinks was waiting.

"I'll meet you in the car, princess," Valentina said. "Five minutes or I come blazing back in. Got that, Jinks?"

"Why don't you like me, Val? Ain't I always been fair to you?"

"You fucked with my girl. Water under the Pont Neuf, but do it again it won't go down pretty." And she was gone.

Jinks looked at Sam's face, fighting to keep from letting his eyes roam over her sumptuous body. "Are we just going to leave it like this?"

"As opposed to letting you fuck me, then you go and pick up your kid? Did you hug your wife with your cock still stinking of me?"

"It wasn't like that."

"It was just like that."

"I never stopped loving you, Sam."

"Marrying Kimmy was an odd way to prove that."

"I got her pregnant first time we did it. I had no choice."

"Still don't. I'm all kinds of bad, but homewrecker ain't me." She leaned in, kissing his lips, let her lips part for a moment then squeezed them closed. "Midnight go boom."

"Yeah, midnight go boom."

"I'll call you tomorrow, set up a meet."

"If I broke up with Kimmy?"

"Give up a sure thing for whatever the fuck it is we have? Dumb move, slick. I better book before Valentina comes back guns blazing." She left him this time. Turned her back and just walked out.

On the rehearsal stage, Brian was rocking out. He still had the lyric sheets in his hands. Candy and the boys were in the corner, sitting in the shadows, waiting for the band to break. The side door swung open stabbing sunlight into the room. A backlit man walked in. He looked ragged. Before anyone could say shit he was across the room. Grabbing Brian by the shirtfront, he ripped him off the stage. The microphone clattered to the ground screaming feedback. The man threw Brian across the room. He was wild, raging. He tossed Brian like a rag doll out the open door, skidding him across the parking lot. Closing the door, he moved back to the stage.

"Cord?"

"Chi Chi, I have had a real weird couple of days. Who was that puke singing my songs?"

"That was nobody. Glad you're back."

"I had to hop trains and hitchhike. Last I remember I was kissing that hot agent."

Candy stepped out of the shadows. "And a lovely kiss it was." She moved up, stroking his sun-blistered face.

"What's your name?"

"She's Ariana Bend, Bend agency?" Chi Chi said.

"That's right. What happened to me?" He stared at Candy for answers.

"You dropped me at my car and were gone. You looked crazed, but said you were fine."

"We found the van in the Kenny's Shoes parking lot," the fuzzy drummer said.

"I always thought acid flashbacks were a joke. Nope. Powerful, wicked, over the rainbow shit. Did you have two heads?"

"You said I did," Candy answered. "Kissed me, scales and all."

"I remember that. That part was cool."

Chi Chi looked over his torn and tattered lead singer. The stubble beard, the twigs in the hair, it was all very not glitter. "Can you sing?"

Grabbing the microphone, Cord stepped onto the makeshift stage. "Kick it and let's find out." Chi Chi counted them in. Cord had a slightly Rod Stewart growl to his voice. It was sexy. It was rock and roll.

"We are so fucked," Terry whispered to Jacob.

"You played ball."

"Yeah, so?"

"So we punt."

Candy walked up to the stage, transfixed by Cord. He left a high school bandleader looking for a break. He came back the real deal. When the song ended she started clapping, the band joined in. Cord looked a bit lost, but happy.

"Billy Joe and Jess, come here," Candy called to the boys. They were wearing matching overalls and Lynyrd Skynyrd tee shirts.

They had work boots. Nothing glitter or cool about them. The perfect roadies.

"You know what you're doing?" Chi Chi asked.

"We're carrying all the crap you're too cool to carry," Jacob said, letting his jaw remain slack.

"Close enough. You a guitar tech?"

"Nope."

"You tune a drum?"

"Nope."

"You really just carry shit for us?"

"Yep."

"Cool, I guess. Ariana!"

Candy came rushing over. "You don't like the Lee brothers?"

"It's just . . . Na, fuck it, they're fine. Rock and fucking roll."

"We'll be here with a truck tomorrow five p.m. ready to load."

"A truck, cool," said the fuzzy drummer. The twig of a bass player was sucking on a Pixy Stix and smiling at the whole fucked up scene.

Terry and Jacob started to leave. Candy said she was staying. "Can I see you outside, Ms. Ariana?" Jacob said, trying to sound subservient.

"What?" Candy said.

"We're counting on you to steal the van," Jacob said.

"That is your purview," Terry said.

"Tomorrow boys. Tonight I want to be sure our lead singer doesn't go walkabout."

"You gonna sleep with him." Jacob played it off best he could, smooth.

"None of your business. Plan is to keep an eye on him. If we wind up doing the horizontal mamba, then that's what needs to be done. We clear? Business."

Trouble was, Jacob saw the way Candy looked at the singer. They'd be making muffins before the night was over. There was nothing Jacob could do about it. Not a damn thing.

"I wish I was in *The Wild Bunch*."

"Yeah, Jake, it is so much easier when the girls are all Mexican whores."

"Fuck you and your white man's logic."

"Come, kemosabe, let's book over to Val's crib."

CHAPTER 15

"We are what we pretend to be, so we must be careful about what we pretend to be."
—*Kurt Vonnegut, Mother Night*

Valentina's flat took up the entire downstairs of a Victorian up the hill from the Castro. It was high enough to be out of the madness of the Polk scene, but an easy walk if you wanted to hang out in gay leather-boy culture. You could always go to Suckers Lickers for a bottle of wine, scotch or amyl nitrate, which was sold semi-legally as Old Locker Room—named after the fact it smelled like week-old gym socks. One deep inhale and your heart roared like two separate gorillas.

They let themselves in with the key from under the welcome mat.

"Make yourselves at home. Mi casa es su casa." Valentina was in the bath. She'd left the door open, so they had to avert their eyes if they wanted to speak to her. "Terr-Terr, there's a bottle of Korbel in the fridge. Would you mind opening it? It's easy, you grab the cork and slowly rock it back and forth until it spews."

Terry went in the kitchen, found the Champagne and three flutes. He worked out opening the bottle with limited spewage. Looking up, his gaze fell on the open bathroom door. In the mirror he could see Valentina's pert breasts. Her skin was coffee and cream. Terry felt an erection start to grow. He shook his head, laughed and walked into the living room. He gave a flute to Jacob. His back was to the bathroom.

"Terr-Terr, come on in here, Momma wants her Champagne."

Terry walked into the steamy bathroom. It smelled of strawberries. He tried not to look, but wherever he rested his eyes he found he was looking into a mirror. Bubbles covered almost her entire body. One long leg draped off the edge of the tub.

"Any chance I might get that before it goes flat?"

Terry sucked up his courage and walked up to the tub. He handed her the flute. Really looking at her, he let out a low involuntary whistle.

"Oh Terr-Terr, you do find me pretty."

"You are a stone cold, wet dream fox. But . . ."

"Butt?" She rolled over in the tub, her perfect ass poking up through the bubbles. Terry whistled again. He gulped down the rest of his Champagne.

"Valentina?"

"Yes, Terr-Terr?" She was pouting slightly, very sexy.

"I have never been with a girl as beautiful as you. Never."

"What a sweet thing to say."

"It's true. But I don't swing the way you do."

"My penis freaks you. I understand. You're not gay."

"Noooo, not gay. Straight."

"See, baby, so am I. I only want to be with men. After this heist, I'm going to Sweden to finish the surgery. Snip snip, no more johnson. So your manhood is intact. You have been ogling a girl, really, that's what I am. Now get out of here while I get dressed."

Jacob was humming The Faces "Silicone Grown" while he rutted around in the freezer. Behind frozen peas, a carton of coffee

Häagen-Dazs and a very cold glass phallus, he found a bottle of Russian vodka. He rounded up three crystal shot glasses. He fired up a joint and took a gulp of vodka. Terry followed suit.

"Did you hear any of that?" Terry motioned to the bathroom.

"Enough to know I don't know shit. Bowie swings both ways and I don't judge him. Valentina is as good a woman as I ever met. Trust her with my life. The rest is whatever it is."

"What are my two stud monkeys talking about?"

"You and how stunning you are," Jacob said.

Dressed in a diaphanous gown that left the important parts to the imagination, she was nothing short of breathtaking. "I see you found my good vodka."

"Your casa and all. Here." Jacob passed her a joint.

She breathed it in, grinning. "That's good shit, Jake. Color me surprised."

"I always pack the best boo."

Terry hadn't said a word. He looked at his drink then glanced at Valentina, then back at the drink.

"Jake, can you give us a moment?"

"Yeah, I need a pack of cigs. Back in a few."

Valentina waited for the front door to latch closed.

She sat next to Terry.

He could feel her heat on his skin.

"Sweet Princess Terr-Terr, what am I going to do with you? See, here is the truth, and I'm not really good at truth so if I get it wrong, be gentle. I like you."

"I like you too, Val."

"Not like that, sweetie pie. I, well since this last fall I started noticing you. You are a good man. You are smart. You hide it, afraid to take Jake's place as the smart guy."

"It's not like that. Jake is fucking brilliant."

"So are you. All I'm saying is, it's more than that rocking sports-hard body of yours. I'm hung up on you. Maybe it's a crush. Maybe it will pass. But I wanted to say it. Now the hard part. I don't think you feel the same way. And . . . that has to be OK. I never want you to do anything you feel isn't right. So drink up and be merry. You dodged a bullet you might not have survived. Yes, lad, I am that good. I have driven grown men mad. I exploded one of the 49ers running back's heart; he couldn't take the wild exertion." Regaining her bravado, she did a vodka shot.

Terry took a joint and wrapped a bill around the cherry.

"Shotgun?" he asked her.

Valentina nodded. Terry put the tube in Valentina's lips and blew at the other end. Rich oily smoke flooded into her mouth and lungs. Their lips were inches apart. And without either planning it, they found themselves kissing. Terry was as tall and just about as strong as Valentina. They were nicely matched. Terry pulled Valentina onto his lap, kissing her neck, nibbling on her ear. Valentina kissed him full and deeply. Terry got his hand tangled in her hair, and suddenly her long blond hair was sitting cockeyed on her head. She started to laugh. Taking it off she revealed a tight Afro underneath.

Terry stroked her Afro. "You're beautiful," he told her.

Standing up, she led him into her bedroom.

Jacob was freezing his balls off when he finally decided it was OK to come back. Creeping in, he realized he needn't be quiet. Terry and Valentina were going at it like wild beasts. Lying down on a sofa, he pulled a pillow over his head. The sixties sexual revolution had spilled into the seventies. Everyone was having sex. All the girls he knew were on the pill. It was consequence-free. Sure, he'd had gonorrhea, but a visit to the free clinic and some penicillin and he was back in the saddle. So all that being said, why was he the only one not getting laid? Was he really holding out for Candy? He kinda thought he was. Not that he would turn down a bunny if she hopped into the room at that moment.

Valentina fell asleep with her head on Terry's shoulder.

Terry had a momentary panic attack. What had he done; what kind of freak was he? Would he fuck a chipmunk if it was cute enough? Valentina snuggled in deeper. He smelled her. He looked at her face, at her breasts pressed against him. He let out a long breath and drifted off to sleep.

Sam was the last to come in. She moved silently, looked into Valentina's bedroom and smiled. She curled up in a big club chair and was almost asleep when Jacob spoke.

"Did you ball Jinks tonight?"

"I don't want to have this—"

"Did you? Simple question."

"Complicated answer. He wanted to go over the exact street location I want for the Pinto gag."

"And then his dick slipped into you?"

"Yeah, it was just about like that."

"Just wanted to know."

"I never lie to you, Jake."

"I know." It was the one rule they had. With all the scams, lies and subterfuges in their childhood, they agreed they would never lie to each other. Even lies of omission were out.

"Candy is banging that Cord guy, right?"

"I asked her to not let him out of her sight, so yeah, I guess odds are real good they bumped uglies."

"Odds are real good?"

"Yes, I'm sure she fucked him. That what you want to hear? Jake, if you really want to love Candy, then you have to see who she is. You have to be OK with it. She hasn't had one boy at a time since we were in the second grade."

"Why, why is she like that?"

"If she was a guy you'd just say he was a healthy teenage stud. Right?"

"Fine."

"Like Bishop said to Angel in *The Wild Bunch* when he's watching his girl go with Mapache: 'Either you learn to live with it, or we'll leave you here.' Can you live with it?"

"Guess I have to. I want to be with her."

"Heartache hotel for us. I'm hung up on a married explosives man. Weird as this sounds, only Terry is backing a winning horse."

"Not that it's not fraught with peril. When he sobers up he may step in front of a cable car."

"Or she might."

"The course of true love never did run smooth."

"What's that from?"

"*A Midsummers Night's Dream.*"

"I must have missed that one."

"The play is a farce, but wrapped inside the comedy Shakespeare was making a cynical statement on love. He believed true love was an illusion. A sprinkling of fairy dust and you could as easily fall in love with a donkey as a man. Maybe lust or chemistry is just fairy dust and he was correct. Dylan Thomas said 'Though lovers be lost, love shall not; and death shall have no dominion.' Right, love that lasts beyond the grave. And he was a philanderer who fucked college students behind Caitlin's back. Swans mate for life. Did you know that?"

"No, I didn't." Sam sparked a Marlboro. "Even high, you really are the brightest bulb in the box."

"I promised Candy I would finish out the year and go on to Stanford."

"Pinky promise?"

"Pinky promise."

"Then there is nothing for it but to go." She took a long pull on the vodka bottle. "Tomorrow, if it goes sideways, I want you to take Terry and get the hell out of Dodge. Lay low overnight and catch the train home in the morning."

"But it's not going to go sideways."

"No, it's not. Gonna be slick as snot on a brass door knob."

CHAPTER 16

"Are you gonna pull those pistols or whistle Dixie?"
—*Josey Wales*

Terry woke cotton headed. He kept his eyes closed, trying to reconstruct the night. Had he made love to Valentina? If it was wrong, why did thinking about it curl his lips into a smile? Was he awake or still dreaming? He heard the low chatter of women. Or was it the low spark of high-heeled boys?

"Get him up," a low voice said.

"Already did, twice."

Was that Valentina?

"His lids are flickering. I think he's playing marsupial." A third low voice.

Terry counted to ten then popped his eyes open. Fuck. Three men stood around the bed, two of them white, one black, all sporting long unkempt hillbilly beards.

"What the fuck do you want from me?" His voice sounded braver than he felt.

"Everything," the black hillbilly said. Leaning down, he tried to kiss Terry.

Terry freaked. Leapt up, darted past the men, hit the first door he found. Pulling it closed, he realized he had just locked himself in the bathroom. No exits.

Laughter filled the hall beyond the door.

"Terr-Terr, open the door, we come in peace." That was clearly Valentina's voice.

Slowly he opened the door. The three hillbillies deconstructed themselves in his mind, reconstructing into Valentina, Sam and Candy, all with long beards and trucker caps.

Candy looked Terry up and down. "Nice bod, Terr-Terr."

"Hands off, bitch, this one's mine," Valentina said.

Sam handed him a robe. "Cover it up, Terry, before we have a catfight."

On the front stoop, Jacob sat drinking coffee and smoking. Fog drifted past, obscuring the city around him. Terry, dressed in a pink bathrobe with a ruffle at the neck, sat down beside him. Inside the women were taking off their costumes.

"Nice look."

"Thanks, I try."

More smoking. More coffee.

"Do you think I'm sick?"

"For going with Valentina?"

"Yeah, I guess."

"No, but it doesn't really matter what I think."

"I feel weird. Kinda free, like whatever I was worried about, what people would think about me, it has or hasn't happened, you know?"

"Not a clue, brother, not one clue. Don't overthink it."

"Do I do that?"

"We both do. But this seems like one of those times to let go of the side of the pool and just swim."

More smoking. More coffee.

"My mother would shit a brick."

"Terry, does your new, um, girlfriend, have a penis?"

"Why yes, Mom, she does."

"She would blow a main bearing for sure."

"I got to shower the drunk funk off. Catch you on the flip side."

"I'll be here. Hey, Terry."

"Yeah?"

"You choose Val, or you decide it was a drunken mistake. We're cool either way. Got it?"

"Thanks."

Terry passed Candy as he went into the flat. Candy sat down beside Jacob. Her disguise gone, she was dressed in short shorts and a glittery tube top. A trench coat kept her warm and gave her the appearance of a smoking-hot flasher.

She took the cigarette from Jacob's hand, had a puff and gave it back to him. "Can't say I didn't see that coming."

"Terry and Val? I guess I should have."

"It's the score tonight. It could go south. Val knows this could be her last chance."

"Like soldiers in London the night before D-Day. Nine months later they had a mini baby boom."

"Really?"

"Really. Explains Sam going to Jinks."

"And me?"

"I guess Cord was what you wanted. Seems like a . . . what the fuck do I know. Did you enjoy yourself?"

"It wasn't un-fun."

"A glowing review. 'Juliet, now that you finally bedded Romeo, how was it?' 'Well, Mr. Cronkite, is wasn't un-fun.'

"Not every time is roses and poison. Sometimes a tumble is just a tumble. Thirty minutes where you don't think."

"Sounds deep."

"Are you angry with me, Jake?"

"No." He sparked a fresh cig, not looking at her. The silence grew, stretching to uncomfortable.

HEIST NIGHT
8:00 P.M.

The rusted-out van was parked on Montgomery near Broadway. Sardine was grinding his jaw rhythmically as he waited blocks from Taxi Dancer. He and Cracker were trading off watching the door with binoculars. Cracker hadn't shut the hell up about his fucking mouth, some bullshit about needing to see a dentist. What the fuck. Even Black Oak Arkansas wasn't calming him down, and Jim Dandy always did the job. The Bolivian marching powder Breeze had fronted them was gone. They switched to whites at the Golden Gate Bridge.

Even this early there was a line down the street—fags, freaks and glitter boys, all waiting to enter the club. It was New Year's Eve and the last day of the bicentennial. Red, white and blue were the chosen colors by many. Leaning against a brick wall, Uncle Sam in star-spangled hot pants was Frenching Abe Lincoln. Sardine felt his stomach go sour at the sight. Fucking out in the open for God and all to see. This shit wouldn't play back home. He wiped the sweat off his brow and scanned the street. Up on Broadway it was even worse. It was a full-on freak show.

Driving in they passed a gook restaurant with punk rockers spilling out the doors. One chick would have been hot even if she did have a crew cut, but she had a fucking line of safety pins running from her pierced nose to her ear. Sick. Next they rolled past the Condor Club, where Carol Doda was shaking twin 44s. Sardine wanted to see her, but business was on and there was no time for gaping at gash. They drove past at least four more strip clubs. In front of the Barbary Coast a skinny barker in a sharkskin suit was screaming at a group of drunken sailors, demanding they come see the hottest chicks on Broadway, telling them if they didn't they was all faggots. Someone once told Sardine that San Francisco was Sodom by the bay. Hell yes, now that was a fact.

On Montgomery, a yellow cab pulled up. Sam got out, all power and swagger, followed by Candy and Valentina. Glitter queens, they were dressed for maximum flash and effect.

"Bingo buffalo chip," Sardine said, passing the binoculars to Cracker.

"Damn, Sam looks good." The girls in their spike heels and plunging necklines were flashing the wrong parts for the mostly gay male crowd standing in front of Taxi Dancer. It didn't matter. They looked so good even gay men gave them a nod as they slid up the sidewalk.

"How'd you like to nail that bitch?" Sardine said, taking back the binoculars.

"Sam?"

"No, not her,you fucking lame bastard. Look what she did to your face."

"The skinny fox with the long hair?"

"No, look. Your fucking eyes, use them. The black chick. The fucking Tina-goddam-Turner bitch."

"Dude, that's a dude."

"Shut the fuck up about my future ex."

"OK, sure. I thought . . . sorry."

"Want me to knock out what teeth Sam left you?"

Cracker disengaged. Eyes downcast he let Black Oak take him

away. After Sam and her friends disappeared into the club Cracker waited a respectful five minutes before speaking.

"This deal ain't going off 'til at least midnight. Think we could hit a Jack in the Crack, I'm hungry."

"Son of a bitch. You're always hungry." On the ride they'd finished off three Snickers, a jumbo pack of Slim Jims, some Fritos, and a six-pack of Bud. Not the feast of kings, but fucking food. The speed killed Sardine's appetite. Nothing could kill Cracker's love of gas station food.

"Breeze paying us to eat, or watch that club?"

"Club."

"That's right. That's what we're gonna do."

"OK. But when this is over, you think we could hang around?"

"You mean like a vacation? Eat gook food, ride cable cars, tour the chocolate joint?"

"Yeah, you think?"

"No, moron. We hit Sam and get shut of this freak show."

Cracker knew better than to argue. One day he would do something cool, tough, show Breeze what he was made of. Maybe he could be in charge sometimes instead of always Sardine. Sardine was family. They'd both flunked fourth grade and dropped out. Sardine always looked after him. Always made sure they ate, got high, and he even got them laid sometimes up at Breeze's motel. At fifteen a poke it wasn't cheap, but the ladies was worth every penny. Maybe some day he would be the big shot. Maybe. It could happen.

Earlier that night, Candy dropped Jacob and Terry off at Sound and Fury's studio. They were back in their overalls and Lynyrd Skynyrd tee shirts. Candy had boosted a U-Haul truck for the band's equipment.

Cord jumped off the low stage and ran to them, pulling Candy into a kiss. "Hey babe, left in hurry this morn, forgot these." He pulled a pair of satin panties from his pocket.

"Those were a gift." She flashed him her sexiest smile.

Jacob shook his head almost imperceptibly and turned away.

"Cord, I need you to do a secret mission for me," Candy said.

"Bond, James Bond."

"Yeah, like that." She spun him a tale of a long-running prank war with Sylvester. Tonight was payback. "At the stroke of midnight, I need you to pull the pin and roll these onto the stage." She slipped two smoke grenades into his jacket pocket, then let her hand slide down him.

"You want me to blow up Sylvester?"

"They're smoke, just smoke." She rubbed her hand playfully up and down his zipper.

"Stroke of midnight?"

"Yes." She cupped his building erection. "After that, you and me will have some celebrating to do."

"Don't you want to kiss me at midnight?" He looked hurt.

"I would love to, but I'll be in the office making sure you get your cut of the door."

Cord wasn't happy for a moment, then he thought it over and started to smile. "Cash and trim, what magic lamp did I rub to get you?"

She flicked his erection. He yelped. She laughed.

At the entrance to Taxi Dancer, Sam dropped three twenties on the cashier, paying cover charges for her, Valentina and Candy.

"You all twenty-one?" The man was dressed in tighter than tight jeans, leather vest and a gold lamé bowtie on his bare neck.

He was buff as hell. "Need to see some ID." Tonight there would be no back door entrance. The bouncers were on high alert for the big night. Tonight they needed to walk in the front. "You girls don't look old enough. Sorry, next."

"Oh, honey child, thank you," Valentina said. "You make me feel young." Then, under her breath, "This here is Lydia Van Horton. Her daddy is a real son of a bitch lawyer. He will sue your ass you pull this ID bullshit tonight. Clear?"

"Sorry, Valentina, packed night. Boss said to keep the bitches out."

"There ain't a bitch in this group. Are we solid, or do I call her daddy?"

"Yeah, we solid." He slapped her upturned palm and they were in. Downstairs, the cabaret was blocked off by a red velvet rope. A stud in jeans and bowtie stood guard over the door. On the stairs leading to the disco the party was already taking off. The Bee Gees' "You Should Be Dancing" was pouring down on them. It was pure stair-strutting music. The three women stepped up, spun their fists in front and bounced their hips in unison. Laughing, Sam grabbed Candy's face and kissed her to the hoots of the men around them.

"Cherry?" Sam asked, licking her lips.

"Of course."

"Yummy."

"You white girls are craaazy."

"Yep." Sam gave Valentina a kiss.

"You fuck up my makeup I will kill you, friend or not."

"I love you, Valentina."

"And I love your silly ass, Princess Samantha." Giggling, the three best friends linked arms and yellow brick roaded up onto the dance floor.

The U-Haul van was parked at the back service entrance. Two massive bouncers with slicked back black hair wearing matching black suits with silver ties guarded the door while Terry and Jacob rolled speaker cabs and amps into the building. They went past the service elevator Sam had diagrammed for them, down the hallway and through a curtain onto the stage. Now that he had roadies, Chi Chi would only lift his finger to point. He was directing the boys where to place the equipment. Three dressing rooms lined the hallway. Sylvester and the Hot Band was written on one door. The Tubes was on the next. The last door just said Opening Act.

"That should say Sound and Fury, right?" Chi Chi said to Cord.

"It don't matter, look where we are. We are about to open for the fucking Tubes."

"It's a respect thing. It should say our name."

Terry was walking through the door carrying two guitar cases. They were heavy. They held the M16s and four clips each.

"What are those?" Chi Chi asked.

"Um, guitars, I guess."

"Not mine."

"Ariana Bend said they were just in case."

"Let me see them."

"What's with the door?" Jacob said, walking up, a green duffle over his shoulder. "Where's your name?"

"Right? I told you, Cord, told you."

Cord looked at the door, trying to will it to change. Terry slipped into the dressing room.

"Get Ariana," Chi Chi stomped a spike-heeled boot. "Tell her this is open disrespect. I won't stand for it."

Jacob took out a fat red permanent marker he had used to mark cables. He wrote in letters taller than The Tubes, SOUND AND FURY. He dropped the marker into his overalls pocket. "How's that, boss? Still need Ms. Bend?"

"You fucking rock," Chi Chi said. "Now get those drums loaded in."

"All over it, boss." Jacob gave him a two-finger salute.

While the band was onstage setting up, Terry slid the special guitar cases and the duffle behind a stained couch.

At the rough insistence of the bouncers, Jacob drove the U-Haul away from the loading dock. Not far down the alley the Firebird sat unnoticed, a dirty car cover kept it from catching the lights. Jacob parked the U-Haul near the mouth of the alley, blocking just enough space so that only one car could make it past.

As soon as the stage was set, Terry and Jacob disappeared into a backstage ladies' room.

"Rock paper scissors," said Jacob. "One, two, three."

"Paper covers rock," Terry said, wrapping his hand over Jacob's fist.

"How can that be? Paper takes rock, really?"

"Really."

"Two out of three."

"No, Jake, you lose. That makes you eye candy, and me muscle."

"Fine. Means you're breaking down the stage when Sound and Fury's set ends."

"I know." Terry went out, heading for backstage.

Jacob stripped off his overalls. Underneath he was wearing

Sticky Finger jeans that were so tight he needed to lie down to get the fly zipped. He had a little kid's tee shirt cropped over his ribs, alphabet blocks spelling out *Brat*. Tossing the trucker cap, he spiked up his hair. He applied eye makeup, combing out his lashes until they appeared impossibly long. Lip gloss. He looked in the mirror. *You sexy beast.* He dumped the roadie clothes into the trash.

When Jacob walked through the cabaret none of the band gave him a second look. Hitting the stairs, K.C. and the Sunshine Band was blasting "Shotgun Shuffle" from the dance floor above. The place was filling up. From the top of the stairs to the giant jukebox that was the DJ booth Jacob got his ass grabbed three times. He was proud. Didn't want to fuck the guys, but proud they wanted him.

"Hi." Jacob batted his eyes at the DJ.

"Hello, hot stuff." The DJ was late twenties, good-looking in his tuxedo slacks and silver mesh tee shirt. "Hold on." He swung around, hitting play on a tape cartridge. Judy Garland's voice filled the room. "Toto, I've a feeling we're not in Kansas anymore."

Then the DJ spun the second turntable and The O'Jays' "Livin' for the Weekend" filled the room. "What can I do you for?"

"I just wanted to see how you do what you do."

"Oh do you?" Only one of them was talking about spinning discs. "Climb aboard, sailor." He reached down a hand and helped Jacob into the booth. Everything was where Sam said it would be.

"What's your name, kid?"

"Billy Two Times."

"Why they call you that?"

"Once is never enough of anything."

"Call me Mr. Magic." The DJ cracked a popper and shoved it under Jacob's nose. One deep hit and the room exploded into flying confetti of color and light. His heart felt ready to rip free of his body and start a band of its own. Sixty seconds later all that was left was the faint gym socks smell. "Ever do one just as you come?"

"No. Amazing?"

"Mind-blowing." He winked not so subtly at Jacob. If only he could get past the fucking men part, Jacob was thinking being gay would be cool beans. Men said what they wanted, went for it. The room vibed sex without the desperation he always felt in straight discos. It was like they all came for the same reason—dance their asses off, have sex, get plastered and head home. It was the answer to the promise the Summer of Love had made.

"Boo?" Jacob said sparking a joint.

"I don't smoke Mexican rag."

"Good. Neither do I." Jacob had been saving these Thai sticks for prom. He planned to take Candy, blow the other students' minds.

The DJ took a deep hit. Held it, felt his lungs expanding, was suddenly coughing madly. Powerful as they were, they had the added kick of being dipped in opium. He pulled a beer out of an icebox under the record shelves. "Damn Billy Two Times, that shit rocks! Hit me again."

Jacob did, and again after that. He wasn't inhaling himself. Much as he hated wasting good smoke, he had a gig to do. Checked his watch—it was ten. Two hours. Down on the dance floor he saw Candy walking through the crowd. "Hey, that's my sister."

"Good-looking kid. Is she a model?"

"Yeah she is. Do you have Donna Summer?"

"Look where you are, kid."

"Right. Will you play 'Love To Love You Baby'?"

"Don't even need a reason. You leaving me the rest of that joint?"

"Yes, but I'll be back." Jacob was out of the booth and moving through the sweat slick crowd. He caught Candy's arm, spinning her around just as Donna Summer started to sing.

"What are you doing?" Candy looked stern.

"Making my big move." Jacob turned up the heat, pulling her into him, rocking his pelvis against hers. Her eyes widened when she felt his growing chubby, then he spun her away and laughed. He was in control.

"This isn't the time," Candy said, but not very strongly.

"Oh, it is so past time." Spinning her back into his chest, he whispered in her ear. "When this gig is done, I will have you screaming the names of gods you don't believe in. There is a deal breaker though; I don't share. Can you live with that?" Before she could speak he spun her away. At the apex of the spin he released his grip on her hand. The momentum took her another few graceful feet. When she looked for Jacob, he was gone, disappeared into the dancing happy mass.

"You and your sister are close," the DJ said.

"Sister . . . it's more of an honorary term."

"Look, cutie, don't care how you swing, long as you swing. Now hit me with another one of your wizard sticks."

Jacob fired a fresh joint. He looked around the packed dance floor and started to laugh.

While Gloria Gaynor sang "Honey Bee," Sam and Valentina were dancing. Moving through the crowd. Eyes scanning for Jo Jo, the big guy in the leather jumpsuit. He'd made at least fifteen cash drops by eleven. The inside man told Sam he never moved less than a grand, often as much as two. This was looking like a solid score. Sam was not relaxed, but she was less tense. This fucker had all the hallmarks of working.

Down in the cabaret, Sound and Fury was finishing their set. The crowd was digging them and their mixture of Queen's fantasy storytelling and Bowie's sexually ambiguous glitter. After two encores the room was still on its feet. The band would have kept playing but the cat at the mixing board dialed them out, effectively pulling the plug. Throughout the set Cord had scanned the crowd, but Ariana never showed. Bummer. Consolation prize was she was handling their business for them, and tonight he would have her all to himself.

Cracker's stomach was growling like an upset lion.

"Can't you shut that thing up?"

"No." He grabbed his gut and made it move like a mouth. "I'm hungry, Sardine. Grrrrr."

Sardine smiled in spite of himself. "How old are you, four?"

"Twenty-three, just like you. Kinda weird you not remembering that."

"It's called sar—never mind." Their rusted-out van smelled of pigs' feet, Slim Jim farts and sweat. Sardine climbed out, buttoning up his Pendleton wool jacket. "Stay. Keep your eyes on the front door."

"Where you going?"

"None of your beeswax."

"I have to piss like a racehorse."

"That's why I brung the milk carton."

"Gross."

"Do it, or don't, just don't leave the van or I'll put a boot up your ass." Slamming the door, Sardine walked across the street. The city was hopping. Music blasted from every car that passed. Bass thumped heavy from Taxi Dancer. Moving between the cars, he was searching for the perfect place. Rounding the building he found himself in the alley that ran behind the disco. He was pissing behind a dumpster when he had an idea. Why would they come out the front if they could hightail it out the rear? It didn't take him long to spot the Firebird. Now it wasn't even a long shot. All this time Cracker had them watching the wrong entrance. Lucky for them, Sardine was on the case.

In the cabaret, The Tubes were pouring out their unique brand of tight electrified rock. Bill "Sputnik" Spooner nailed a clean guitar solo to the wall of sound. Fee Waybill in full Quay Lude regalia teetered around the stage on fourteen-inch platforms and a tawdry silver spandex jumpsuit. He strummed a Q shaped glittery prop guitar. He had an absolutely impossibly large phallus stuffed into his pants. He was singing "White Punks On Dope." The room was packed so tight that it moved as one big amoeba. The Tubes were part rock band, part performance art, part Vegas show. Cord watched them from backstage. In his leather jacket pockets he held the smoke grenades. Would he have the courage to toss them when the time came? He had better not puss out, not if he wanted to make muffins with Ariana again. Taking out the panties she'd left him he sniffed them and grinned.

The Tubes started to play "Boy Crazy." A song about a teenage girl who can't get enough, it hailed her as "boy crazy from town to town." Like all good do-wop morality tales, it ended with her paying a heavy price for her indiscretions. The crowd sang along "Forgot all the names, they're all the same. Forgot all the names."

In the DJ booth, Mr. Magic was getting baked on Jacob's high-end stash. He almost missed a segue bridging Ohio Players' "Fire" with "Love Rollercoaster." He was showing Jacob how to match beats on two turntables. Get them spinning just right and it created a seamless flow of music.

"Twelve-inch singles are for amateurs. I do it live, baby, Billy Two Times." Putting another copy of "Love Rollercoaster" on the second turntable, he was able to extend a song as long as he wanted. And just when the crowd had reached the peak of their sweat drenched, ass bumping, whistle blowing, popper sniffing, frenzy, just as they were about to explode, he would drop Barry White's "Can't Get Enough of Your Love, Baby." Cool them down, give them time to grope and fumble through slow dances or hit the bar for more drinky-poos.

"And then we start to climb the mountain again, this time we climax at midnight."

"You have them in the palm of your hand."

"It's where I like 'em, so to speak." Mr. Magic let out an evil stoned laugh.

ELEVEN P.M.

Sylvester had just taken the stage. He started with "I'm a Steamroller." He was as hot as his Hot Band. Cord stood backstage, hands sweaty. In the dressing room, Terry was starting to pack out.

"Where's your partner?" Chi Chi asked.

"Break."

"Bend paid for two roadies. He better get his ass back here if he wants to get paid."

"You got it, chief." Terry was rolling speaker cabs to the back loading dock. He left them there under the watchful eyes of the two security guards. The wind flipped open one of the guard's jacket, giving Terry a clear view of his shoulder rig and revolver. Fuck. He felt the weight of the .38 in his pocket and wondered if push came to shooting, would he have the balls to fire back.

On the next run he found the small linen closet Sam told him about. Terry dropped off the gun-laden guitar cases and the duffle, then went back to move the drum set. His job was to make sure at twelve-ten there was a clear run to the Firebird. Terry eyed the security guards. If he hit low and hard he would be able to knock them into the alley. Maybe. Or they would go for those guns of theirs and then what? He wished he had lost to Jake. He could be eye candy. Let Jake deal with the variables and equations. He wished he had a joint. Maybe it would go as planned. Or maybe he'd be shot before he had to decide. He flashed on Valentina in a plunging black dress with a veil obscuring her tear-streaked face. Why the hell had he let Jake hold the weed? Why?

CHAPTER 17

"Punch it, baby."
—*The Getaway*

"Look at that dumb bastard." Cracker was pointing to a stalled Pinto in front of Taxi Dancer's front door.

"Piece of shit car," Sardine said. "Now let's get moving, I want to be at the alley when this deal goes off."

It was as if his words had magic power. First, a huge boom. Then a fireball ignited inside the Pinto. The windows blew out and a ball of orange flame rose into the sky. People on the sidewalk started to scream. Jinks folded the antenna on his remote detonator and walked away down the street.

"Gawd damn, Cracker, did you see that som-bitch go up?"

"I heard Pintos did that, but damn. I could feel the heat."

"That weren't an accident. Let's get a move on."

It was midnight. DJ Magic hit the confetti cannons. Jacob spun the dial on the fog machine, turning it far enough to break it open. Fog flooded the dance floor.

"Too much fog, back it off."

Jacob shrugged his shoulders, fighting against the impossible, to stop the building fog bank. The windows along the front of the room filled with a fireball, turning the dance floor into hell for a moment.

In the cabaret, Cord heard Sylvester say "Happy New Year!" and he pulled the pins. The smoke grenades skidded across the stage, landing in the audience, spewing white smoke that quickly filled the air. When they heard the Pinto explode they started screaming. Pandemonium. A true and real disco inferno.

At eleven-fifty, Sam, Valentina and Candy entered a small linen closet. At the booming sound of the Pinto exploding they exited wearing jeans, boots, beards, trucker caps, with trench coats hiding the collapsed M16s and cut-down shotgun. No one noticed them as they took the freight elevator to the second floor.

"Motherfuckers, hit the floor!" Valentina yelled as they burst into the office. Maurizio was hurriedly attempting to shove cash into the safe.

Jo Jo went for his shoulder holster.

Candy racked the shotgun.

Jo Jo froze.

Maurizio started to stand and Valentina slammed the M16's barrel into his forehead. It broke the skin and a small trickle of blood ran down onto his cheek.

"Lock it up," Valentina said.

Candy pulled the door closed, throwing the bolt. Valentina rotated on her left leg and kicked the back of Jo Jo's knees with her right boot. He buckled, hit the floor.

"You dumb hicks. I'm Maurizio Binasco."

"On the motherfucking floor," Valentina repeated. Grabbing his chair, she whirled him around and dumped him onto the carpet.

"You guys are some dead fucking punks."

Candy had Jo Jo on his belly, wrists cuffed behind his back. She moved to do the same to Maurizio. He started to resist so Valentina put her work boots to his gut. He hurled a stream of what looked like clams in a cream sauce.

Candy snapped the cuffs on him. "The combination? What is it?"

"Fuck you."

Candy raised the shotgun butt over the gangster's face, ready to plunge it down.

"Do it. Fuck I care."

Valentina started a stopwatch. "We don't have time for this, gentlemen, we book in ten minutes."

Sam kneeled down, stroking the safe. The Wells Fargo M7721. It was like meeting a new old friend. She knew so much about it she could see the schematics laid over the outer skin. To her it was like looking at one of those transparent men from science class. Stroking the dial, she felt time slipping away. Part of her was in the woods walking with Jinks, another part of her was dancing with the cogs and gears, pins and notches all moving to her touch. Somewhere in the distance Maurizio was saying something. He sounded upset. Sam drifted deeper into the Wells Fargo M7721. It was a fugue state. It was peaceful. And then the loud snapping sound of the final tumbler brought her back to the room. Opening the door, Sam let out a little gasp. The safe was stuffed full of hundred-dollar bill bundles. Big fucking bucks. Fuck. Not the plan. Fuck.

Sam looked to Valentina.

"All of it," Valentina said. No one questioned her. They stuffed the duffle full.

"Do you have any idea whose money you are stealing?" Maurizio said.

They hadn't a clue. The stopwatch buzzed.

"You are so dead."

Maybe they were. But the immediate problem was getting free of the city. Slipping the guns up under their trench coats they walked out. Not running. Walking. The fog had moved into the back rooms. It swirled around them.

The fucking security guards still stood by the rear door. Terry ran out of the fog yelling at them. "They're looting and stabbing and shooting. Ahhhh."

The two security guards charged past him and into the split pea mess. Terry didn't loosen his grip on the .38. He was keeping his options open. His heart hammered and his hand trembled. He fought the urge to bolt.

Jacob met the ladies at the elevator. They rode down in silence, not sure of what was waiting to greet them. They stepped into the linen closet, and in less than two minutes they came out dressed as clubbing girls. Terry pushed the door open. Fog spilled into the alley.

Terry stood sentry at the door until Candy, Sam, and Jacob had jumped off the loading dock. Valentina gave him a kiss on the cheek and went back into the club. Plan was, she would mix with the panicking patrons and become invisible by hiding in plain sight.

Police sirens wailed, coming closer.

Sam tossed the duffle full of cash and guns into the Firebird's false trunk. Her crew piled into the Firebird, Terry riding shotgun, Jacob and Candy in the small backseat. Sam cranked the massive big block over, freeing all four hundred of its horses to run wild in the street.

She floored it, lurching forward, then slammed on the brakes. The windshield was filled with rusted-out metal.

Sardine sideswiped the Firebird. Wrenching the steering wheel, he pinned them against the side of a brick building.

"Fuuuuk. We're fucked!" Terry was screaming, spraying spit onto the window.

"Nope, not this time, you walleyed motherfuckers." Sam flipped on the nitrous and stomped on the gas. Flame shot out the back. The rear tires smoked as the massive load of torque hit them. The Firebird leapt forward, dragging the van with it.

Sardine locked his brakes.

The Firebird dragged the screeching and groaning van down the alley, building speed. They were doing thirty when Sam swerved, sending the van into the band's U-Haul truck. She threaded the Firebird past the wreck and was free. Bouncing onto Kenny, she hung a hard Louie then a Rosco at California. Sam's eyes kept flicking to the rearview mirror. When she was sure they were clear she turned off the nitrous and settled down to cruise mode, drifting in and out of the packed streets. Behind them, fire trucks and police cars converged on Taxi Dancer.

Sam did several loops around the back streets.

"Um, Sam, you missed the 101."

"Chill, Terry, I got this." Sam gave him a wink. She was drifting down toward Market.

Jacob fired his last joint and passed it to Terry. "You want?"

"Oh hell yes I do, thought you'd never ask." The rich smoke swirled around Terry's head. He sank back into the bucket seat, slowly relaxing his face from grimace into a slack jawed smile.

"Better, pal?"

"Much."

"Then why don't you pass the joint back here?"

"Fuck you, Jake. Me and this heady bud are in a committed relationship."

"Thai stick can be a cruel mistress."

"She sure can." Terry took a deep drag and let his eyes droop into slits.

A SFPD squad car ripped past them. Red light from the cherry top floated across Candy's face; she smiled at Jacob. He tried to match her easy expression. This scene was getting fucking surreal fast. Maybe this was that contact high the anti-drug films warned him about. He looked around the car wide-eyed. Just a group of glitter kids out on a lark. Forget the trunk full of cash and illegal firearms. Forget the felonies left in their wake. They were four friends happily rolling down thunder road with no horizon in sight.

Sam pulled up the on-ramp to the Bayshore freeway south. She kept the Firebird to an inconspicuous 70 mph. The San Francisco skyline sparkled in the rearview mirror. No one spoke of the heist, afraid to jinx it. Fireworks were exploding and spiderwebbing the sky over the bay. The radio was tuned to an all news station. A car fire had been reported, but no word of a robbery.

"It always makes me think of Oz," Candy said, watching the city disappear behind them.

"I get that. Magical." Jacob liked this moment. Sitting close to Candy, talking about nothing. He liked feeling the heat of her skin next to his. Smelling her perfume. It was the most normal he'd felt in days. He just had to keep his mind off guns, mayhem and thuggery. Focus on Candy.

"I didn't mean to hurt your feelings. With Cord. I . . ." Candy spoke low so Sam wouldn't hear.

"It wasn't nothing but a thing. I get it. I'm OK with whatever."

His face told another story. He wanted her to himself. In a primal bullshit caveman way he wanted to brand her as his.

"I do like you, Jake. That's the problem. If I don't care then there's no chance in hell I'll get hurt." She let her hand rest casually on his lap. He was instantly hard. She looked up at him, a wicked smile and a twinkle in her eyes.

Jake was about to speak when the window beside him exploded. He couldn't reconcile this fact with any reality. The shower of safety glass was almost beautiful. Then he noticed a small bloody stain on Candy's breast. It was spreading, turning her silver tube top red. She was screaming. Wind howled through the window, drowned out her voice. Beside them a flash filled the cab of a rusted-out panel van. For a millisecond, a grinning man with a rifle was lit by the muzzle flare. He had hay-colored hair sticking up in a rat's nest tangle, several broken front teeth. It stuck frozen in time. Jacob wondered what it all meant. Flames from a second shot leapt toward Jacob.

"You ready?" Sardine asked Cracker. Stepping on the gas, the van rumbled unevenly but kept picking up speed. They finally caught up with the Firebird. As they pulled alongside, Cracker thumbed the safety off the Remington 30.06 carbine. He'd done a hack job to shorten the barrel. The stock was wrapped in electrical tape to cover the crack in the wood. He saw Sam's face. She had always been good to him, except for busting up his face, but hadn't he asked for that, really? She treated him like he wasn't stupid. Talked to him about music. She gave him an album by Bowie.

Sardine trashed it, called it glitter fag music. Cracker snuck it out of the bin. When Sardine was gone to town Cracker would put it on. *The Diamond Dogs are poachers and they hide behind trees.*

He closed his eyes and pulled the trigger.

Sam caught the van on the periphery of her vision before the first blast hit. What was Sardine's piece of shit van doing on the 101? They hadn't followed her, so how in the fuck had those reprobates even found the Firebird? Instinctively she hit the gas. The lurch forward kept the shot from nailing her. The second shot hit the trunk. Who the fuck was Sardine to think he could keep up with the 'Bird? Fuck him.

Candy had imagined being with Jake all summer. Was she worried about rejection, or screwing up a friendship? No, mostly she was afraid of Sam and what she might say. Sam was her best friend. But she was also a mercurial wench. Once, at Jordan Jr. High, that cheerleader, old big-tits-what's-her-name, teased Candy about being flat and skinny. Called her twig, said no boy was ever going to like her. Sam laughed it off, but the rumor was she beat the shit out of the cheerleader in the locker room. Used a towel with some tennis balls in it, like in *The Longest Yard* or some other prison film Sam loved so much. Sam denied it. Cheer-bitch wore long sleeves and jeans for weeks. She wouldn't look Sam in the eye and never spoke to Candy again after that.

When Sam went to Humboldt it was almost freeing. Candy loved Sam, but... dang. Candy found it easy to hang with Jake. When she finally told him she liked him, it had felt natural. She slipped her hand onto his lap, needing to make clear what she meant by "like." His erection felt good. Told her instantly that she wasn't alone in her ardor. As she leaned up, planning to kiss him, there was a flash of lightning and her chest stung. Her wind was knocked out. It was like she'd been hit by a really hard dodge ball. She hated P.E. Blood was spilling down her chest. She struggled to breath. She screamed best she could. She wanted to go home. She wanted to wake up in bed next to Jake. She wanted to laugh at the bad dream.

Terry's eyes snapped open. Pure terror murdered his buzz. This was really happening. Every cell in his body screamed "duck" when he saw the rifle barrel, but fascination overrode it. He watched it all go down. The second and third shots hit metal in the rear with high-pitched pops. The Firebird launched forward, pinning him to the seat. He felt detached, a passive observer to the death race roaring around him. The van seemed to stand still as the Firebird barreled away.

The van let loose a roar of its own. It was coming on fast. Speed and wind buffeted the top-heavy rusted brick, causing it to buck and weave. Sardine didn't let up on the power. Better fiery death then having to tell Breeze he let the cash get away.

The Firebird rocketed down highway 101. The van was keeping up, actually gaining on them. Sam didn't need to look at the speedo to know they were well south of 100 MPH and still climbing. The van rammed them from behind, bouncing the Firebird across several lanes. Sam fought for control. She could feel how easy it would be to flip at these speeds. She hit the brakes. Sardine instinctively hit his brakes. The van slid, its backend whipping around until it was going sideways.

It was nitrous time. Sam flipped the switch, and with a chirp of tires and a deep throaty rumble the Firebird took off.

The car was long gone before Sardine could straighten the van out.

"Sums a bitch!" Sardine pounded the dash.

"She got away."

"No shit, nitwit."

Candy fought for breath, choked, then coughed up a red mist. She was gasping, taking small shallow breaths. Jacob held her, pressing his balled up tee shirt against the wound. "Sam, we need a hospital."

Sam kept her eyes pinned on the highway. "How bad?"

"Bad."

"Fuck."

"She's . . ." He couldn't find words to tell Sam what he saw. He couldn't talk about Candy as if she wasn't looking at him with desperate eyes. He stroked her face, whispered that it would be OK, told her he loved her, told her he always had. He asked her if she wanted to go with him to a new Polynesian tiki bar in Redwood City—they had blue drinks with little umbrellas. It took all her strength to nod. He told her he would complete high school. He would go to Stanford and study theater. He wanted to be an actor, or maybe a filmmaker. He would move to Hollywood. Asked her if she would come with him. He asked if she wanted to go see Iggy Pop in the spring. He just kept mumbling questions—sounded more like prayers. He was afraid if he stopped she would die.

They were ripping past Candlestick Park. Sam's brain was flying.

"Take the next exit," Terry said. "There's a Kaiser up on El Camino."

Sam didn't ask how he knew that. Didn't question if he was right. He had to be. Even a quick look in the rearview mirror told her Candy was dying, drowning in her own blood. Sam took the off-ramp in a four-wheel drift. The Firebird shuddered then found grip. They blew through three red lights in a row. If the cops pulled them over they would all go to jail, but hearing Candy coughing and fighting for breath, Sam didn't care.

"Shhhh, hold on baby," Jacob whispered. "Please don't die. I, fuck . . . Sam!"

"We're almost there." Several blocks away a hospital sign glowed in the fog. "Jake, listen very carefully. When we get there you need to get her inside and then split. If the cops catch you, nothing I can do."

"I don't care."

"I got that, but she will and I do."

"No."

Candy was gasping, fighting for breath. Her pale skin was tinted blue. Jacob knew he was losing her. Sam steered them into the ambulance entrance of the hospital. A young doctor with a large Afro was sitting in a wheelchair smoking. Terry jumped from the passenger seat, folding down the seatback. Jacob climbed out, lifting Candy into his arms. She was as light as a butterfly's wing. She was limp and not breathing. The doctor jumped up when he saw the blood-soaked couple, grabbed a gurney, and rushed to Jacob.

"Put her down here."

"She can't—she stopped breathing."

"I got her." The doctor moved away quickly, pushing Candy toward the electric doors. Jacob tried to follow but Sam grabbed him from behind, dragging him back.

"Let me go."

"No. Get in the car." Shoving her little brother into the backseat she gave him no choice. "Terry, get the fuck in here." Terry numbly followed her orders.

As they rolled out onto the boulevard Jacob stared out the back window. Through the glass door he got one last glimpse of the gurney. Frantic doctors and nurses obscured his view of Candy.

CHAPTER 18

"There's no escape. I'm God's lonely man."
—*Taxi Driver*

The tidal marshland beyond Palo Alto had raised plank paths running through it. It smelled of brine and mud and decay and growth. Jacob stood looking out at the bay. Bare-chested, he'd taken his bloody shirt off, he couldn't feel the cold.

Sam stood behind him. "We didn't have a choice."

"You didn't have a choice. I made mine, but you wouldn't let me stay with her."

"If we're in jail how the fuck am I going to make this right?"

"Make it right? Make it right? What in your mind does that look like? No, tell me. I can't see this right no matter what fucked up angle I peer at it from."

"Little brother, we have a couple of problems. One, the psychotic hillbilly sons of bitches who shot her need killing. Two, Breeze or Callum, or whoever the fuck set us up needs to pay their freight. Problem three? We have a trunkload of cash I'm pretty sure belongs to the mob. They find out it was us took it, we are all dead. All. Moms. All. Terry. All. Got that? We go to the cops, sooner or later they will put us at Taxi Dancer."

Terry sat on the Firebird chain smoking Marlboro 100s. "It was my fault. I know how they knew where we would be heading." He stared at the ground as if his salvation might be there, just beneath the dirt. "Some guy called last week, while we were waiting for Sam. I . . . well, just fuck me."

"What did he say, Terry? It's important." Sam tilted Terry's face up to meet her eyes. "Terry, what did he say?"

"He said they were friends from up North. Said you left a final paycheck behind and they needed to mail it to you."

"You bought that?" Jacob yelled.

"I . . . fuck, Jake, fuck I . . ."

"Dial it back, little brother."

Jacob shoved his sister out of the way. She had an inch and twenty pounds on him. She could kick his ass, but she didn't. Jacob took Terry by surprise, swung hard letting his forward momentum fuel his fist. Terry's head jerked back from the blow, but he didn't so much as stumble. Jacob swung again and again. Terry stood like a redwood and just took it. If he wanted, Terry could squash Jacob. Jacob had never been in a fight. His idea of working out involved riding bikes high on ludes. Terry played football until the day he discovered dope and Jacob and trim. Jacob hit Terry on the back of his head. Pain flared in his hand. He roared. He kept hitting and Terry kept taking it. Snot and tears and blood were smeared across their faces. Terry had blood flowing from his broken nose. Jacob had Candy's blood spread with Terry's across his chest. He looked from the blood to his best friend's eyes and knew he was done. Dropping his arms, he slid down the side of the Firebird. Terry slumped down in the dirt beside him. Back against the cold metal, Terry sparked a Marlboro. They didn't apologize or make up. They had said all that needed to be said.

"It's getting light." Sam, running on survival mode. Do what's next, fuck the past, fuck the future. It was fucking Zen. *Nam-myoho-renge-kyo* was a Buddhist chant a hippy stripper taught her. Supposed to make all things possible or some such crap. *Why not.*

She let the words rattle on in her mind.

Terry passed Jacob a lit cigarette. Jacob inhaled the blue smoke and passed it back. The sun was coming up over the bay, light shimmering on the rolling water. "I'm afraid life will never feel normal again."

"I'm more afraid it will. Jake, man, this, this is . . . fucked."

They passed the cig between them in silence. A great blue heron took flight, gliding out over the bay. Somewhere in the distance a horn honked. Donna Summer sang "Love to Love You Baby" inside Jacob's head.

At the Creekside Apartments, Jacob stood in the shower watching Candy's blood washing away. Moms had been asleep when they snuck in. Small blessing. Jacob didn't know how he would explain the blood and the loss of Candy. Moms still believed he was a non-drinking virgin who had the chess club over when she was gone. Actually, he had no idea what she thought of him. He told her so many lies he had become a shadow-son, a myth of a son. This moment, this one here, is the moment a hero looks at his dead lover's blood, and Travis Bickle or Dirty Harry or the Man with No Name steps up, says he is done hiding, he is going to war. This was that moment. And Jacob saw clearly he would fail the test. Fuck Clint Eastwood. His hands were shaking. He wanted to grab the biggest bud he could find, take Terry up to Foothill Park and smoke this shit away.

From the living room came Pink Floyd's "Wish You Were Here". Terry must have put it on. Floyd was his go-to band. Sam called it hippy crap. Jacob was glad for anything to comfort his friend. He came out of the bathroom, a towel wrapped around his waist. Terry was sitting cross-legged in front of the speaker, eyes shut tight.

"Sam, they'll be coming for us, won't they?" Jacob asked.

"Yes, they will." Sam checked the magazine in her M16.

"Then why aren't we running?"

"Fuck running, I'm ready for them this time."

"We need Valentina."

"Already called her. Cavalry is on its fabulous way."

At that moment Esther came out. "Can I make you all some eggs?" Her cheer-filled face dropped as she really saw the three of them. Saw Terry's bruised and battered face. Saw Jacob's scared face and swollen hand. Saw the assault rifle her daughter held. Esther's face went from cheerful mom to something much harder, something that spoke of her past. "What happened?"

They looked at her. No one spoke.

"Tell me what happened, no lies."

"Candy was shot . . . she may be dead." Tears rolled down Jacob's face.

"Sam? Give me the straight deal, no bullshit."

So Sam did. She told her about stripping for Breeze. About Callum and the rip-off, the twenty grand she owed Breeze. The threats to their family. She told her about promising her father to go straight. She told it all in a flat, emotionless voice. Emotions were for once they were safe. Emotions would get them killed.

"This Cracker and . . . ?" Esther asked.

"Sardine."

"How long before they show up at our door?"

"Could be minutes, hours, I don't know."

The phone started ringing. Jacob jumped.

"Don't answer it," Esther said. "Keep them guessing as to where we are." She opened the duffle, took out the cut-down shotgun. "Terry, dear, I need you to take this and cover the back door."

"Sure, Moms." Terry walked back into the kitchen. Sitting on the floor he leaned his back against the stove and aimed at the glass section of the back door.

Jacob was holding his snub-nosed .38 in his lap.

"You know how to use that?" Esther asked.

"Yes."

"Are there a lot of things you know I don't know you know?"

"Yes."

"I'm sorry."

Sam dumped the cash onto the coffee table and started counting out the stacks of bills.

"Whose money is it?" Esther asked. "Sam, rule one: before stepping on stage know whose money you're taking."

"Name is Maurizio Binasco."

"Who is he?"

"He owns Taxi Dancer."

"Mob?"

"I don't think so."

"You don't know? Is this how your father taught you to set up a show?"

"No. No, it's ... fuck." She let her voice trail off and finished counting the bills.

"How much is there?"

Sam let out a long breath. "Two hundred and forty thousand dollars. We figured, based on door and booze, max we would clear was thirty or forty grand."

"You were set up," Esther said. "If they just wanted the twenty large you owed, why not wait for it, meet you here? No reason to start shooting. Who tipped you to taking off the disco?"

"Breeze. Son of a bitch."

"Their plan? Take the cash and kill you all. Leave not even a whisper to connect him to the heist."

"I'm going to kill Breeze."

"If it comes to that. But now you're going to eat some eggs and toast. Jacob, get the coffee going. Samantha, keep an eye on that front door."

Jacob watched his mother put breakfast together, stunned by her transformation from Polly Sunshine to General Patton. Both he and Terry watched her every move like she was an alien. "Boys, Grandpa Bloch, the thief, he was my father. I worked with him. Your father was a thief. I chose him, married him. We ran a crew. Wasn't until you kids came along that I gave it up. Now some Humboldt pimp wants to hurt my family? No. That won't happen."

Eating an egg sandwich, Sam let a plan form. First things first— she needed to hide the cash. It was their only leverage. Replacing it into the duffle, she went outside, scanned in a wide circle. The sun was up. Maybe Sardine was smart enough to wait for dark to come after her. Popping the trunk on the Firebird, she unlocked the false bottom and hid the cash. To be sure no one stole the car, she flipped the kill switch and then, as an afterthought, detached the distributor cap and took it inside with her.

"What do you want me . . . ?" Jacob asked.

"Nothing. You, Moms and Terry need to go to a motel until this crap is shut up tight." She tried to ruffle his hair but he stepped back out of her reach. "She was, is, my best friend, Jake. I didn't mean for this to happen."

"Yeah, but it did. It did happen. I'm not leaving."

"Yes, you are. You stay, you'll get Valentina and me killed."

"You set this up. You brought this to us. You got Candy shot."

"All true. Now it's on me to find our way home."

"Fuck home. This changes nothing, Sam. Get yourself killed, or don't, I don't give a fuck. I love Candy. I'm not walking."

"I'm in," Terry said, eyes still on the back door.

"Thirty-six hours of labor to have you." Esther gently pushed Sam's hair up off her face. "That's what it took. I'm not letting you go this easily. Nope. I'm not going anyplace."

Sam looked from resolute face to resolute face. Immovable.

Her family.

Her blood.

Jacob and Terry were witnesses to the shooting, maybe a murder. No way would Sardine let them live.

She had to end it.

If she got this wrong they were all dead. Alive they could feel their feelings and whatever.

Not now.

CHAPTER 19

"You don't make up for your sins in church. You do it in the streets."

—*Mean Streets*

"Bitch, you do nothing by halves do you?" Valentina was in the kitchen. She had arrived in her Galaxie, which was waxed to a mirror as always. She was dressed for action in culottes, white tennis shoes and a low-cut argyle sweater that showed a healthy amount of her estrogen-enhanced breasts.

The boys were lying down in the bedroom. Sam had given them each a Quaalude. They needed to be awake for the night. At least that's what she told them.

"Jacob?" Valentina asked.

"He hates me. He looks mind-fucked. Terry's not much better."

"That, princess, is normal. That is how normal people react to seeing a friend get shot."

"You think I'm broken?"

"Do I look like a shrink? Baby, we are all broken one way or another. Like the man says, 'Life ain't nothin' but a funny, funny riddle.'"

"John Denver?"

"I dated a cowboy for about a minute."

After Sam told Valentina where the cash was hidden she said the hillbillies would recognize the Firebird, best to hide it in the trunk of the Ford Galaxie. Made sense.

In the carport, Sam opened the hidden compartment.

It was empty.

She blinked. Closed trap door. Took a deep breath and opened it again.

Still empty.

No duffle bag full of cash.

No hope in hell.

Sam's gut felt like she was in a freefalling elevator.

Fucked. They were totally fucked.

"Jinks? Did you tell him about the hidey-hole?"

"No, while boning on a table the subject didn't come up. Just our crew knew."

Valentina flicked her eyes around them, searching. "Those inbred hillbilly cousin fuckers?"

"Maybe. If it was, they may be flying up the coast. Or . . ." Sam said turning slowly around, scanning for danger.

"Or they have sights on our bodacious ta-tas."

"I'm kinda fond of my ta-tas."

"They are dazzling, princess."

"What's the play?"

"We do nothing. If they're looking to do us harm, I'd rather meet them on our ground." Valentina slipped fluidly between disco queen and hardcore soldier.

Jacob stepped out of the shadows. "Whole lot of ifs and maybes floating around."

"I don't have a script for this part of the show, Jacob."

"Those fuckwads had a small window of opportunity between

when we got home and when Valentina showed. I think they head-ed for Humboldt."

"You think, little brother? For all we know they could be head-ing south, going to fuck rich Malibu beach bunnies. Maybe west to play in the Half Moon Bay tide pools. Or, and this is real likely, they showed, grabbed the cash and were heading in to kill us when Valentina rolled up. Right now they could be lying low, watching."

"They went north, trust me. If Breeze controls the inside man, I assume he also controls a clear line to Maurizio," Jacob said.

"You assume—"

"Fuck off. Breeze can feed us to the Italians. But he'll want the cash in his hand before selling us out. We have however long it takes them to get the cash to Breeze."

"You done, little brother?"

"For now."

"He just laid out a very solid scenario," Valentina said.

"If you're right, what's our countermove?"

"Get in the goddamn car and chase down the sons of bitches."

"One problem."

"What's that?"

"What if Sardine and Cracker didn't blow town?"

Esther got their attention by clearing her throat. She held the twelve-gauge nestled in her arms. "They come here and we will send them crying to their mommies or to a shallow grave."

Valentina looked at the plump, little mother with a big gun. Jacob was a skinny high school kid, more heart than ability. "I'm staying, princess. You take Jake."

Sam wanted to argue, gain back her eroding power, but she couldn't see her way around the logic of it. "Come on, Jake, let's saddle up."

A couple black beauties, a couple roadies of rum and coke and they hit the 101 heading north. Jacob shoved *Aladdin Sane* into the 8-track. Solid driving music, and Bowie, so he knew Sam wouldn't complain. Bowie, Mot the Hoople, T-Rex, Iggy, The New York Dolls—as long as it glittered she would love it. Stray into Pink Floyd or Rundgren and she might toss the tape out the window. When "Panic in Detroit" came on, Sam sang along, beating out the rhythm on the steering wheel. "He looked a lot like Che Guevara, drove a diesel van. Kept his gun in quiet seclusion, such a humble man."

In South San Francisco they passed the place where Candy had been shot. It sucked the air out of Jacob. "Do you think she's alive?"

"I don't know." Sam chewed on her lower lip. "How do you take that much life and just make it disappear?"

"Maybe we could swing by the hospital, just check and see if she's breathing. We owe her that."

"What the living owe the dead is to keep fighting to stay alive. We don't catch these pukes, they'll sic the mob on our whole crew."

"Dead? You think she's dead."

"Yes, I do. If she was alive she would have called Mom's crib. You know that."

"Moms wouldn't let us answer the phone."

"Right, so maybe she's fine, recouping it up in a satin nightgown. We go poking around the hospital we will get our asses locked up. And we'll be sitting ducks for any hitter trying to make his bones."

"We don't know anything. The cops could have her under surveillance. She could be in a coma. We don't—you don't—know."

"No I don't, kid. I do know we have a gig to do if we want to survive. If she is alive they will come after her, same as us. So, no, we won't be heading to any hospitals today."

"You're not—"

"The boss of you? What are you, ten?"

"I wasn't going to say that."

"What? What were you going to say, smart boy?"

"Drop it," Jacob said, then went silent.

They rolled up the bay and into San Francisco. Traffic kept them at a reasonable speed. Not a problem. The way Sam figured it, Sardine and Cracker were driving a van full of instant felonies. Add one nosey cop and they were headed to big-boy jail. If the mob didn't have them killed in lockup, they would still go down on a firearms beef and the bag of cash would connect them to the Taxi Dancer heist. Surely they were bright enough to keep the needle pinned at five miles over the limit—just enough to show they weren't scared of being stopped. She, on the other hand, didn't give a fuck. She was driving to save her family.

Once she cleared the Golden Gate Bridge Sam let it rip. She told Jacob to keep a steady lookout for CHP. All of her attention was on flying past or around anything in front of her. Roaring along she scanned for the van.

"All they have to do is stop for gas or to take a piss and we'll blow past them," Sam said.

"This Breeze fucker?"

"Yeah?"

"Is his office on the main highway or up a smaller road?"

"His office is a strip club with a brothel just across the road. Why?"

"Is it a ways off the main road? Yes or no?"

"Yes, it is. Why?"

Jacob explained that they might get lucky and catch the hillbillies out on the highway, but then what? On a country road in Humboldt they could easily spot them and bushwhack the sons of bitches. Sam looked at her brother, then back out the window. She was proud of him, but she wasn't about to show it.

It was after five when they arrive at the Humboldt County line. Fog was coming in when they passed through Eureka and Arcata. Crossing Mad River, they took the North Bank exit. They drove twenty minutes into the hills and found themselves on a gravel road surrounded by giant redwoods. Three miles of sliding around tight corners, Sam found the dirt road she was looking for. It was several miles before Rapunzel's strip joint. She backed behind a thicket of Scotch Broom. The yellow flowers screamed color in the green and red forest. She popped the trunk, unlocked the hidden compartment and took out the M16 and Jacob's .38. "Something has been bugging me," she said. It was the first they'd spoken in three hundred miles.

"Just one thing, huh?"

"The trunk. How did they unlock it? How'd they find the hid-ey-hole?"

"That is a conundrum, maybe—"

Tires speeding on gravel and the low rumble of a Detroit V8 breathing through glass packs ended their conversation. Sam knelt by the front fender, motioning Jacob behind her. She took aim at the road. The plan was simple: when the van crossed in front of them they would open fire.

In Mountain View, Valentina blew the steam off her coffee and took a sip. "Just the way I like it, Esther, black as night, hot as hell and rich as a woman's love."

"That's an old John Wayne line. What film?"

"I don't remember. My father loved him. 'Courage is being scared to death but saddling up anyway.' He had that quote on a framed poster of the Duke in our living room. Dad was a real man's man."

"Was? When did he pass?"

"Seventy-two. I was back in the world, but a mess. Anywho, I haven't been home since. Don't think those fools in McLennan County Tex-ass would know what to do with all this amazing fabulousness."

"I don't guess they would. Their loss is our gain."

"Thank you, Esther." She drank another sip of coffee. Terry had fallen asleep in the living room, his gun aimed at the door. For reasons only he knew, he hadn't been able to meet Valentina's eyes. She tried to talk to him but he wouldn't. It was as if now, here, what had happened between them was a ghost in his closet. Valentina didn't push it. It hurt, but she refused to be anyone's dirty secret. Besides, she had her hands full trying to keep them alive.

"Esther?"

"Yes, Valentina?"

"I really want you two out of the way. If they come for us, they may need killing. I don't want Terry caught up in this mess."

"They're coming after my kids, Terry included."

"True. But best way to keep them all safe is for you to take Terry out of here and let the queen of bad-ass put in some work." Valentina's flippant flamboyant ways were gone. She was steel now.

HUMBOLDT.

On the gravel road in the redwoods Sam moved her finger onto the trigger. Jacob was pressed behind her, revolver in hand. "Don't shoot me in the excitement."

"OK."

Aiming at the road, Sam focused on where the car would be. The tires could be heard spitting rocks as they rounded a corner, close.

Sam was ready. Just a few pounds of pressure on the trigger and she would empty the 30-round magazine in seconds.

A competition yellow 1970 Mustang matte black racing stripes flew into view.

Sam swung the M16 down. With her free hand she motioned for Jacob to do the same. No good killing some civilian just looking to drive out to the whorehouse and get his hood ornament polished.

Turning back, Sam saw the driver, mustache and all. Callum. He was fully concentrating on wrestling the brute of a car down the road. Only at the last moment did he see the Firebird and his ex with a machine gun. He stomped on the gas. Gravel and dust roaster-tailed out behind the Mustang, spraying Sam. Before she could wipe the dirt from her eyes the Mustang was gone.

"Son of a goddamn bitch." Sam pulled a full-on Starsky, jumping and sliding over the hood. Landing on the driver's side, she was in and cranking the key before Jacob was even in the passenger seat.

"Who the hell was that?"

"A dead man." She nailed the gas. The car powered onto the road, the back end fishtailing wildly. The rear end slid and clipped a tree. There was a screeching thudding noise. Sam hit the gas and kept going. All that was left of the Mustang was dust that hung in the air, killing the visibility. Pushing way past safe, Sam hit a tight switchback. The Firebird left the road and careened into the brush.

Sam locked the brakes, slammed the Hurst pistol grip shifter into reverse.

For two miles Sam played bumper-pool with the flora. It wasn't until she hit the wide spot in the road that lead to Rapunzel's parking lot that she saw the Mustang. Callum wasn't in it. Sam started to pull in when a big, bare-chested man in overalls came running out of the club, a lever-action Winchester 30/30 in his hand.

Sam blew on past the strip joint.

Over the roar of the engine a rifle fired.

The rear window blew out.

Sam kept the car careening down the road.

She didn't let up until they were deep in the forest, down a fire road and headed back down the mountain. She looked over at her brother for the first time since the chase began. He was ashen white.

"That was fun, sis."

"Wanna go again?"

"No. Your boyfriend is a dick."

"Very true. He's a dick who has our money."

"Had. Your ex-boss has it by now."

"We are well and truly screwed."

"Yes we are."

"Callum never stole any of Breeze's product."

"Who's Callum?"

"The dick with a mustache."

"Then, no, he didn't. Breeze set you up from the jump."

"I'm a fucking idiot."

"That would be my assessment."

"What are we going to do?"

"Hell if I know."

CHAPTER 20

"Dolemite is my name, and fuckin' up motherfuckers is my game!"

—*Dolemite*

Jacob sat at the counter in Paterson's coffee shop on the square in Arcata. He had to convince his sister that they needed food. He wasn't hungry, but it had been twelve hours and low blood sugar was making his thinking fuzzy. He fought to keep from thoughts of Candy. He had called the hospital, but they wouldn't give him any information. He said he was her brother, but that only got him an offer to speak to her parents. He hung up fast. He needed to focus on the present situation, to come up with a plan. Sam was little to no help. She was in the parking lot, chain smoking, talking into a payphone and pacing in tight circles. Jacob closed his eyes and wrote imaginary notes in his head. No cash, they had no hope of clearing their names with the closeted mobster. Even with the cash he might kill them, but at least they had a shot at bargaining. Kill the mobster? Nope, that would lead to more mobsters and death. They needed the cash. They needed a lever.

The clatter of dishes opened Jacob's eyes. A skinny Mexican busboy was picking up several plates he had dropped. The coffee shop was old. Hell, the grease on the walls was probably older than he was. The patrons were a mixture of hippy stoner college students and loggers, the latter identifiable by their uniform of jeans, lug boots and Pendleton shirts. The sawdust on their trucker caps and smell of fresh-cut wood also tipped Jacob off to their vocation.

The waitress, an aging Earth momma stuffed into a 1950s diner uniform, set down two burgers then topped off his coffee. "You alright, sunshine?"

"Fine, yeah. Burger looks good."

"You don't look fine, you look like a scared, unhappy, white rabbit. Alice break your teacup?"

"I'm good, just been a long couple of days."

"If you say so." She stepped in close and whispered. "If you need some weed to calm you down, I have joints for sale. Maui Waui."

Jacob shook his head, while his brain screamed yes.

The waitress moved down the counter refilling coffee mugs and joking with the locals.

A small bell rang when Sam came in from the parking lot. No one took much notice of her. She sat down beside Jacob. Her eyes roamed the crowded room.

"What did Valentina say?"

"I warned her that we hadn't seen the nitwit cousins up here. She said all was quiet on the home front, but if it got loud she was locked and loaded. She sounded . . ."

"What? Scared."

"No, never. She sounded butch."

MOUNTAIN VIEW.
CREEKSIDE APARTMENTS.

Valentina was dressed in a tight tank top. She'd taken off her sweater. Cute as argyle was, she needed freedom of movement more than style. She never showed bare shoulders; she was embarrassed by her thick biceps and the tattoo of a bulldog with U.S.M.C. on its collar.

"What's the tat about?" Terry asked two nights back, when they'd been in bed.

"It's a Marine thing, baby doll."

"You were a Marine?"

"I was a lot of things. Now crawl back over here and give momma some sugar." They made love again and didn't speak of her past anymore. She respected Terry for letting her keep her secrets. Then again, maybe he was just too freaked out to ask any more questions, or too lust-driven to care.

Now in the silent apartment, Valentina's mind strayed back to Saigon.

Girls in long white dresses and black pants rode their bicycles through the crowded streets. Henry, as she had been called back then, and Jerome took a scooter-powered rickshaw to the red-light district. The tattoo artist used the cherry of his cigarette to sterilize the bamboo needle. By hand he drove the needle in and out, leaving black lines in Henry's puckered flesh. He wanted to scream. He wanted to smack the guy causing him the pain. Instead, he took it like a man. The bar girls sat drinking Number 333 from the bottle and watching. They giggled when Jerome winced at the tattoo needle. No one laughed at Henry's stoic expression.

Things Henry did to prove to his dad he was a man:

Played football, Pee Wee league on through high school.

Dated a cheerleader. She'd thought it noble that he never tried to have sex with her. It was the Summer of Love, but that was in California. In Texas in 1967, only bad girls and boys were doing it.

Joined the Marines. In boot he learned to channel his frustration into rage. He was an animal.

Gone to Nam.

Killed the enemy.

Got a tattoo.

Gone with a bar girl to a room only big enough for a mattress. The door was hanging beads and did nothing to block out the busy street beyond. Through thin walls he could hear Jerome's rhythmic grunting. Henry was flaccid. The bar girl, who said her name was Jane, took him in her mouth, but nothing. He felt a rage growing. She put her small breast in his mouth, letting him suckle her nipple while she stroked his cock. He felt nothing but anger. When he heard Jerome's victory yell at orgasm, Henry wanted to smash the girl's face, wanted to smash his own face. He paid the girl. Ashamed. Sad. Furious.

Back at base he drank himself to sleep.

In the jungle he let the beast out to play.

The close, wet heat. The smell of rotting vegetation and un-bathed men. He was black in a mostly white unit. He walked point. He would have volunteered for it if they hadn't ordered it. Men walked point. Men rocked 'n' rolled full auto. Men turned their enemies into pink mist. Men killed until the jungle was silent except for the buzzing of flies as they lit on the dead. Men refused R&R leave. Men stayed in the battle until they became one with it. After a month in the bush, Charley, booby-traps, malaria, gonorrhea and dysentery had taken over half their unit. Henry didn't really care. He wore the ears of his victims on a cord around his neck. He didn't cry when Jerome was blown apart by a Bouncing Betty. Henry was a man.

By his nineteenth birthday Henry was a skilled life taker. Gun, knife, rock, fist—all the same to him. It won him medals and the respect of his leaders.

Until it frightened them.

They found him in a hooch having an argument with the

severed heads of six Viet Cong regulars. If several of them hadn't been women, if he had saluted his sarge, if a reporter from the *Times* hadn't witnessed it, they would have kept him in the jungle. Killing was their business and he was good at it. Problem was, he was twenty-four-seven crazy. They section-eighted his black ass and shipped him stateside.

The MPs delivered him to the VA hospital in San Francisco. They doped him to the gills. They put him in therapy. They slowly decompressed him. In a drug-slurred voice he shared in group with other soldiers. He was not alone they told him. He was not a bad man. He didn't believe them, but it felt good to hear them say it.

The country around him was divided. The promises of Martin Luther King Jr. had been pushed back. The black power movement scared the hell out of Richard Nixon and his cronies.

Henry knew he couldn't go back to Texas. It held nothing but bad memories.

As he returned to semi-sanity, they cut his drugs.

And then on Saturday, June twenty-fourth, nineteen seventy-two, his life changed irrevocably. At daybreak he received a telegram informing him his father was dead. He didn't cry, or even feel sad. He felt numb, with a strong undercurrent of freedom. He spent the morning wandering the streets of San Francisco. He drifted into the Haight. The Summer of Love was well and truly over. LSD had been replaced by heroin. By ten that morning he was near Market Street. The closer he got the more people he saw. Without knowing it, he was being swept up into the second annual Pride parade. The first was held in Golden Gate Park—four hundred people attended that one. But after the Stonewall rebellion all bets were off. The queer community had had enough of hiding in the shadows. A crowd of fifty thousand came together to march, listen to speeches, sing and dance. It was colorful. It was a giant street party. It was a blast. Henry stumbled through the crowd feeling like Dorothy arriving in Oz.

Watching a man in biker leathers kissing his boyfriend, Henry knew he should feel revulsion. But what he felt was released from a bondage he didn't know he had been caught in. He was turned on. It would take a year of therapy to fully integrate that day's feelings.

Valentina didn't arrive fully formed. She was birthed in a slow and sometimes painful process. But once she was there, she was never going back. She had put Marine Private Henry Calhoun away in a tightly sealed footlocker.

Until now.

Valentina left the lights off, letting the apartment slip into shadows with the setting sun. She sat in an overstuffed easy chair in the living room. An M16 sat on her lap, the fire selector set to full boogie auto.

At ten thirty-two Valentina heard someone break the glass in the back door. She knew the exact time because she had been meditating on the mantle clock since dark. Her eyes had focused on it while her mind tripped back to the jungle. It was time to let the beast off its leash. Silently, she rose.

Sardine and Cracker crept into the kitchen, cocksure no one could hear them. Sardine was first through the doorway into the living room.

This was his bad luck.

Valentina grabbed his shirt with one hand and punched his throat with the other. She landed six blows before he knew what was happening. One moment he was walking, the next he was on the floor with a bruised throat, a broken wrist and a fucked knee.

Sardine looked at Valentina in stunned amazement. "Who the rabid-fucking-dog are you?"

"Valentina Creamerosa. Confused because I just kicked your filthy ass?" From the corner of her eye she saw a second man coming on. He had a hunting rifle held at hip height. It was aimed at Valentina's stomach. From five feet he wouldn't miss.

"Step away from cousin Sardine."

"Honey pants, you wouldn't shoot a lady would you?"

"I might. And I sure as fuck will shoot a she-male."

"Kill her, Cracker." Sardine was pushing his back against the wall, sliding up it to stand. "Kill her."

"Him."

"What?"

"Him. It's a him." Cracker's back was to the bedroom door. He didn't hear it swing open.

Sardine tried to yell.

Valentina dropped to the floor. As she landed on her ass her foot shot up. The kick landed hard into Sardine's balls. The force lifted him up into the air. Sardine fell into a moaning lump.

Cracker heard a footstep behind him. He was spinning around when the butt of a twelve-gauge shotgun connected with his cheek. Esther gripped the barrel and swung like a major leaguer hitting for the fences. Cracker stumbled back, blood running down his face. Valentina was up and on him. She ripped the rifle from his hands and tossed it across the room. Then she set in pounding his face, landing several punches into the exact spot the shotgun's butt had hit. He was staggering when she dropped down and swept the back of his knee. He went down hard.

Valentina was raging. She stomped the man's head. He rolled over and tried to crawl onto his hands and knees.

"Oh, fuck this noise," Valentina said as she grabbed the M16 off the chair and took aim. "Body bag time, bitch."

"No, Valentina, no." Esther was moving to get between the M16 and the man on the floor.

"These bastards shot our Candy. No way they get to walk out of here."

"I didn't say let them skate. But think about it."

"I am, and I think they need to go. Now, eeny meeny miny moe." She moved the front sight from one cousin to the other and back again. Sardine covered his face with his hands and started to weep.

"What if we need them to bargain with their kin up North?"

"Candy demands blood."

"They are bleeding. The one over there is never going to have children, from what I saw. But enough."

Valentina let out a long, slow breath. She looked at the two pitiful hillbillies. One was crying like a little girl, the other was moaning and holding his pulpy cheek. Henry would have killed them. Henry would be wearing their ears as he rode into Humboldt. Henry wasn't here, Valentina was. "Fine, Esther. For you they get another day above ground. But if Candy is dead? These no-style motherfuckers go. Regardless of any trades you may think we can pull off."

Cracker let out a long-held breath.

Sardine kept crying—apparently he was too far gone to hear he wasn't going to die.

Esther leveled the shotgun at the prone men.

Valentina went to the kitchen for a roll of clothesline.

Terry stood in the bedroom doorway, wide-eyed. Valentina had told him and Esther to stay hidden no matter what they heard. Told them if they wouldn't leave then they at least would stay out of the way. She said Sam would kill her if she got Moms or Terr-Terr killed. Esther hadn't taken direction very well. Thankfully.

Terry looked from Valentina to the beaten men and back to her. He felt a combination of pride, arousal and revulsion.

CHAPTER 21

"So, you wanna play with knives, huh? Well you picked the wrong player!"

—Coffy

ARCATA.
MIDNIGHT.

Sam and Jacob knelt in the shadows behind a dumpster across the street from Callum's apartment building. It was close enough to the bay to smell the salt in the fog that swirled around and obscured them. Jacob was sucking on the last of a roach. He bought a couple of joints off the Earth momma waitress. It wasn't what she advertised. Wasn't bad, but wasn't that.

"Maui Waui? Hell no, little bro, you got taken."

"It is definitely not Maui Waui, but it's not bad."

"Shouldn't be, that's Breeze's pot. Calls it Hustlers Gold. Said it was the soil or the redwoods or some bullshit. Said one day these hills will be filled with pot farms."

"In the States? Bullshit. Hasn't he heard of the DEA? Nixon may be gone but we are stuck with his drug goons."

"Word is Breeze owns the local cops."

"DEA is federal."

"I guess his farm is either well hidden, or not on their radar."

"Exactly. But that will change." Jacob was grinning.

"You're high."

"Yep." Whatever else he had to say was lost in a deep engine rumble as the yellow Mustang rolled up the block. It parked in a loading only zone and Callum climbed out. He turned from right to left, scanning the surrounding area. His black leather blazer flapped open, giving Sam a quick glimpse of his Colt Python, a massive .357 magnum revolver. Feeling secure he headed toward his apartment.

The apartment building had exterior stairs and walkways. Sam didn't want to brace Callum out in the open. She and her brother stayed hidden until he was inside. Jacob lifted the lid on the dumpster.

"What are you looking for?" Sam asked.

"Don't know yet. Wait, here you go."

Callum hadn't slept in thirty-six hours. He was spent. Hearing the knock on his door, he rolled his eyes. Who the fuck was banging around this late? Arcata rolled up the sidewalks at sundown. He pulled the Python, holding it down beside his leg he went the door and looked out the peephole. A young man stood holding a pizza. "What?"

Jacob smiled a pot-addled smile. "Johnny's pizza delivery. If ain't hot, you pay naught."

"I didn't order a pizza, so shove off." The voice was muffled through the closed door.

"Dude, um, is this apartment 2C?"

"Yes."

"Dude, you didn't order a medium works?"

"No, now blow before you piss me off."

"Damn Jerry. That stoner prick got it messed up. Sorry." Jacob turned to go, then looked back at the door quickly. "Oh, damn. Hope you don't drive a yellow Mustang."

Callum ripped the door open. "What are you—"

Sam was against the wall and she swung into the doorway. She drove the snub-nosed .38 into Callum's gut. He coughed a spray of spittle, doubling over. Sam slammed her fist up into his jaw. The revolver made a brutal set of brass knuckles. Callum stumbled back, tripping over his own feet. He went down painfully. The Python skidded across the floor. Jacob followed Sam in, closing the door. He stepped past his sister and plucked the revolver off the floor. It had a six-inch barrel with a rib running from the cylinder to the front sight. Heavy and shiny blue-black, time and hard use had not removed much of the bluing.

"Sam, whoa." Callum was gasping, a hand up protecting his face.

"Why don't I shoot you, asshole?"

"I get you're angry with me. Hell, I'm angry with myself. Fucking Breeze said he would have Big Bob, Cracker and Sardine feed me to their pigs if I didn't go along."

"You are so full of shit." She kicked him in the ribs. "Where is my cash?"

"Whaaat the hell, Sam?"

"Where?"

"I don't know."

"Wrong answer." She pointed the snubnose at him. But her heart wasn't in it and he could see that.

"Quit screwing around. You aren't going to shoot me."

"I will." Jacob flared his nostrils. "I fucking hate guns. Hate. Because of your bullshit a girl I love had a bullet rip through her chest. She may already be dead. She may die tomorrow. Point is, your life means nothing. Not one thing to me. Fuck it. I may pull the trigger just to see what you look like with a sucking chest wound. Yes, I think I will."

"Sam, who the hell is he?"

"Young man about to put a hole in your chest, looks like to me. We call him Crazy Jake. Wanna guess why?"

"One." Jacob aimed the .357 magnum at Callum's chest. "Two. Three." He pulled the trigger. Callum tried to scream but no sound came out. The hammer landed on an empty chamber with a metallic clunk. A wet stain started to spread on the crotch of Callum's jeans.

Jacob held up a bullet. "I forgot, took one round out. Sorry. Take two?" Opening the cylinder he slid the round into the one empty chamber. Snapping it closed he pulled back the hammer. "Now where was I? Yeah, one. Two—"

"Stop. He, um Breeze, he put the cash into a safe in his office."

"What about your share?" Sam asked. "Ten percent I bet."

"I didn't get—"

"Three." Jacob aimed down again.

"OK, it's in the paper bag on the coffee table. Call him off."

Sam lifted the bag. It was stuffed with bundles of bills. She showed it to Jacob, who went sanpaku. He stabbed the Python at Callum.

"Call him off. I did what you wanted."

Sam shook her head. "Oh, sweetheart, we aren't done. Not near done."

"What?" Callum was pretty sure he was a dead man.

"Was there ever a drug deal?" Sam asked. "Did you lose Breeze's twenty grand? Remember, you are hanging on by a frayed goddamn thread."

"I know. Please have him point that gun another direction."

"You feel like pointing that another direction, Jake?"

"No."

"Sorry, he doesn't want to. Talk fast."

"OK. There was never a drug deal. Breeze found out I was on probation and he threatened to have the sheriff violate me. I had to go along."

"You told me you'd done your full bit."

"I lied, I didn't want to scare you off."

"And now you're telling the truth?"

"Yes, I swear."

"You better be. Now time for the biggie. Did he come after you before or after we met?"

"I can't go back inside."

"Before or after?"

"Before."

Sam lost all steam. Her shoulders slumped. She turned away from Callum.

"We done with this piece of dog brown?"

"Yeah, Jake, we're done." She picked up the cash and walked out.

Jake knelt down beside Callum. He didn't show any emotion, let his mind go blank. Just looked at the piss-stained man.

"What, um, what are you doing?"

"Deciding."

"Please don't. I'll disappear, just get in my ride and be gone."

"Do that." Jake eased the hammer down on the Python and walked out.

Sam was in the parking lot writing down the license plate on the Mustang. She'd popped the lock on the passenger door with the flexible metal ruler she'd stashed in a hidden pocket in her leather jacket. She asked Jacob for a joint and the Python. She planted them in the springs under the driver's seat. She relocked the door and walked away.

"I'm sorry, Sam," Jacob said as they climbed into the Firebird.

"What is wrong with me, Jake? Why do I choose the most fucked up guy in any room?"

"I don't know, sister, really I don't. What was that last stuff back there?"

"Payback."

From a payphone at a Shell station Sam made two calls. First was home. Esther was overjoyed that her kids had survived. She started crying. Valentina took the phone. She and Sam agreed Sam should come home. Maurizio Binasco was their most immediate problem. If Breeze sold them out to the mob, they would quickly run out of holes to hide in.

"You called Pahk? Why? In a hurry to meet your jailhouse wife?" They were back on the highway pushing north.

"Pahk's the only cop I know, other than Sheriff Winslow who's bent so far he can kiss his own ass."

"Pahk's not?"

"He's a solid gold turd, but he's not on Breeze's payroll."

"Why call any cop?"

"I left him a message. Told him I was a concerned citizen. Gave him the plates and location of a yellow Mustang. Told him it was driven by a dangerous felon who was selling pot and guns to school kids."

"You dimed Callum?"

"Sold that lying prick out. The name I left, and you're gonna love this, Judy S."

"The fu—oh, Judy S. Judas. Not bad actually, pretty good."

"Glad you approve."

"You feel better?"

"Not much." Sam pursed her lips. "Fuck it, maybe I'll feel better when he's in the joint snuggling up to Bubba."

Jake leaned his face on the window; the glass was cool and refreshing. He closed his eyes and tried not to think. They drove in silence, the road empty around them.

Sam looked at her brother with a mixture of sadness and pride. "Back there, with Callum, you did good. I even thought you'd gone cuckoo's nest."

"'He won't let the pain blot out the humor no more'n he'll let the humor blot out the pain.'"

"What? Time to lay off the weed, bro."

"Ken Kesey."

"Whatever. I'm trying to compliment you. Stanford is getting one hell of an actor."

"Wasn't acting with Callum. He got Candy shot. He set you up. He started this whole ugly ball rolling."

"You wouldn't have shot him."

"I almost did." He looked out the window at his face reflecting back with the guardrail blurring through it. He didn't recognize himself.

Sam waited until they were well shed of Humboldt County before looking for a motel. It was a Motel 6, cost six bucks and was relatively bug free. Neither of them thought they would sleep. Sam took a shower, and when she came out Jacob was asleep on top of the blankets. She covered him up, but didn't wake him. He looked like a kid again.

CHAPTER 22

"If they move, kill 'em!"
—The Wild Bunch

SOUTH SAN FRANCISCO.
KAISER HOSPITAL.

Jacob walked through the electric doors. He had a bouquet of roses stolen from a van parked by the hospital loading dock.

"Fifteen minutes, then I book," Sam told him. She couldn't risk getting caught by the cops. Using a payphone she found out that Candy was in the ICU on the third floor. She gave Jacob the room number. "Hey, Jake?"

"Yeah?"

"Tell her I love her. I'd be there if I could."

"You sure this is how you want to play it, Sam? Come with me."

"No can do, kid. Fifteen minutes. Get going."

The roses did the trick. Holding them up, Jacob cruised past reception and the rent-a-cop guarding the front door. Stepping off the elevator onto the third floor he stopped. The door to the ICU was locked. Nearing the entrance he set the roses on the floor and knelt to retie his shoelaces. When a young doctor went through, Jacob was up and moving, catching the door inches before it closed.

"You can't bring those in here." The nurse standing behind the station looked Jacob over, clearly not liking what she saw.

"Sorry, what?"

"No flowers on this ward. Who are you?"

"No flowers? I was told—"

"No, you were not. Now who are you?"

Looking past the nurses' station he could see through the windows into room 315. He knew it was Candy, though her face was mostly covered by an oxygen mask. Tubes ran fluids into her arm. A spiderweb of wires connected her to the monitors. She looked tiny in the face of all that medical technology.

"Who are you?" the nurse asked again.

"Is she . . . is she going to make it?"

She picked up the phone. "I'm calling security."

In room 315, Jacob noticed Candy's parents. He hadn't seen them in several years, but their pain marked them unmistakably as her mother and father. Candy's father sat crumpled over in a plastic chair, elbows on knees, face in hands, staring at the floor. Her mother stood beside him, her hand resting on his back, eyes unfocused.

"Security, this is ICU one, send someone up here." The nurse looked past the phone at Jacob. He knew his time was up.

"Forget it, please." He gave the nurse what he hoped would pass for an innocent face. It didn't.

As Jacob was exiting the ICU he ran into a security guard coming on fast.

"Catch!" Jacob yelled and threw the roses at the young man in a gray uniform. The guard instinctively grabbed for the flowers, giving Jacob time to dodge him. Hitting the stairs, Jacob took them three at a time. By the time he made it to the lobby the guard was closing in fast. Both young men were panting hard. Jumping past an empty wheelchair Jacob hooked his hand on it and sent it spinning in his wake. The young guard was moving too fast to stop his momentum and hit the wheelchair at a full run, tangling up his legs. He went down. Patients, nurses, doctors, all watched Jacob as he sprinted out the electric doors.

Sam was just getting ready to leave her brother when he burst into the parking area. He jumped into the Firebird and they were gone.

"Cops?" she asked.

"No. Rent-a-guys."

"How did she look?"

"Bad. Her parents—"

"Bob and Jen."

"Is that their names?"

"Yeah. Clueless, but not bad people. They told Candy they thought I was a lesbian and was trying to corrupt her."

"They were half right."

"Shut up. Was she . . ."

"She was . . . she looked bad. I don't know." Jacob stared out the window. They hit the 101 and headed home. Seeing Candy's parents had shifted something in Jacob. Made it more real. Made it hurt more. He'd been running on a romantic notion of what being a member of Sam's heist crew would be. Somehow it always seemed like Sam lived outside the laws of nature. But that was bullshit, a little brother's vision of his sister. The truth was . . . the truth was Candy in that room with tubes and wires. The truth was her parents' anguish.

It was early afternoon when they reached the Creekside Apartments. In the visitors' parking sat a year-old, black Lincoln Continental. It had a black vinyl roof, opera window in the back and deeply tinted glass. It looked to Sam like a shark waiting to feed. Pulling into the carport, she looked at their apartment. "I don't like it."

"What, what don't you like?"

"Any of this. 'Trust the gut' Pop used to say. I want you to creep around back and come in the kitchen door." She passed her brother the .38 and relocked the trunk.

"What about you? Won't you need a piece?"

"I come through that door with an M16 and someone is waiting, it's likely to escalate to bloodbath before you can say boo. But it goes sideways, I'm counting on you, Crazy Jake."

Jacob gripped the snubnose in his pocket and started around the building.

Sam waited five minutes, giving him time to get in position, then she moved up the walkway. The front curtain moved almost imperceptibly as she reached for the door. The living room was dark with the curtains drawn, but even in the gloom she could see it had been ransacked. Feathers dusted every surface, sofa slit open. In her periphery someone moved. She started to turn toward a huge shadow. Something roughly the size and hardness of a two-by-four slammed into her right cheek. Pain exploded down her nerves. Her knees went out and she was falling, then she was on the floor. Blood was coming off her cheek, running into her mouth. A boot slipped under her belly, lifted her up, flipped her onto her back. Jo Jo towered over her. His huge fist was wrapped by a set of brass knuckledusters. Out of his leather jumpsuit, dressed in a dark jogging suit, he looked a lot less silly and a lot more menacing. He roughly searched her for weapons then stood back up.

"She's clean, boss."

"She's anything but clean." Maurizio Binasco was sitting in the easy chair, drinking from a coffee mug. "Your mother's coffee sucks."

"You suck—"

A boot nailed Sam in the side. She coughed, trying to pull air in.

"Espresso. I had a machine imported from Italy. It is the cocaine of coffee. This swill . . ." He poured the remains of the cup onto the floor. "Wait, I remember you. You said you were Bruce's sister. Some story about your mom being a whore."

"I lied."

"Clearly. Is my head bartender in on this? Don't answer that, it's a stupid question. Obviously he is. You were casing my joint. Where is my cash?"

"Where, where is my mother?"

Jo Jo the giant cocked his boot back, ready to kick her again.

"Before he kicks you into the emergency room, maybe I should explain how this works. I ask. You tell. Or Jo Jo kicks the living shit out of you. Capisce?"

Now would be a good time to come through the door. And as she thought it, Jacob did come through the door. *Where is his gun?*

Something from behind propelled Jacob into the room and he stumbled and caught himself before falling onto Sam.

"Looky, looky what we found snooping around out back." Sardine limped into the room, a makeshift splint tied to his wrist with a bandanna. Behind him was Cracker, his face a blooming mess of lumps and contusions.

"He had this." Sardine held up the .38.

Maurizio looked from the gun to Jacob. He smiled and licked his upper lip ever so slightly. "You're the brother, um, Jake, right?"

"Sam?"

"I'm OK, Jake. And, yes, he's my brother."

"Nice to have family time." Maurizio nodded to Jo Jo. The giant slugged Jacob in the gut, doubling him over. Jo Jo was about to nail

Jacob in the mouth when the boy plopped down onto the floor. He looked up at Jo Jo, then squeezed his eyes shut. Jo Jo felt any rush of battle leave him. He didn't want to hit this kid. He looked to his boss, who shrugged. Jo Jo relaxed, relieved.

"For the moment, and it may be a brief one, I have decided not to crush your brother's face."

"He doesn't have anything to do with any of this."

"Oh, but he will pay the price if you don't get me my money."

"I don't have it." Sam flicked a look at Sardine. "I don't know what bullshit these duplicitous hillbillies been feeding you—"

Sardine raised his voice, trying to drown her out. "You lying bitch. She took—"

"What, you inbred sister-fucker? I took—"

"Bitch shut your—"

"Stop!" She put her palm up at Sardine, then looked at Maurizio. "They have your cash." She quickly crossed her heart, trying for what she hoped was a cute sexy smile.

"Liar! Black liar!" Sardine was red faced and spitting when he spoke. "She's a fat liar, Mr. Binasco. See what she did to my cousin Cracker? Knocked his teeth out and near took his face off with a blowtorch."

"OK, I did do that, but look at them; they are an invitation to be beaten."

"Enough." Maurizio looked from Sam to Sardine then back to Sam. "Jo Jo?"

"Yes boss?"

"Next one speaks, take a finger."

Jo Jo nodded. Sam started to say something but stopped herself.

"Sam? Is that short for Samantha?" She nodded slowly. "OK, here is how this plays out—we searched their rolling troiaio. No cash." Sam's lips went white from clamping them closed. "I know, you'll say they hid it. But, and this matters, if they had it, why hang around?"

Sam raised a finger, but Maurizio shook his head. "We'll have time to talk in a moment." He smiled at Sardine. "And you, inimicus inimici mei amicus meus est."

"Huh? That French?"

"Latin. The enemy of my enemy . . ."

"Ain't your enemy?" Cracker spoke up.

"Close enough," Maurizio said, standing up. "Just a couple of innocent weed dealers?"

"Yep, sir. Like I told you, this bitch here and her crew was ripping us off."

"Bullshit," Sam said. "They—"

Maurizio nodded and Jo Jo grabbed her pinky and waited for his boss to give the order. Maurizio thought about it. After a long moment he shook his head. "Ribs."

Jo Jo kicked Sam in the side, driving the air from her lungs in a painful grunt. Jacob trembled with impotent anger. He wanted to attack the giant, but he also wanted not to be beaten to death, so he stayed still. Sam slowly sucked air in. She was able to inhale without screaming so either the big man pulled the blow or, for once, being big boned saved her ass.

"Careful, she is a wily wench. You seen the way they had us trussed up. You hadn't come along, she and hers would have killed us for sure."

"Where did you say you gentlemen were from?" Maurizio asked Sardine.

"Mountains above Arcata."

"Where is Arcata?"

"Humboldt County." Maurizio looked confused, so Sardine

took another stab. "Way up north near the Oregon border. You know, logging country?"

"No, I don't. But I trust you know your way back home."

"Sure do."

"Then shoo." Maurizio motioned with his hand, sweeping them out of the room. As they walked out, Sardine gave Sam an evil smile. Cracker couldn't look at her at all. And then the door was closed and they were gone.

Maurizio stood over Sam, smiling. "I could have Jo Jo play kick the human can all day long. Much fun as that might be, it will also get messy."

"I swear, I do not have your money."

"That is a real shame. Grab the kid." Jo Jo did as told. Gripping Jacob's biceps he lifted him onto his feet. He vised down on Jacob's arms making movement impossible. "This is how it will play out: I get my cash, all my cash, in twenty-four hours or I send your pretty little brother home a chunk at a time."

"But I don't—"

"Too bad. After him I come back for your mother, then anyone dumb enough to have ever known you."

Jo Jo stiff-armed Jacob out of the apartment.

"Twenty-four," Maurizio said and walked out into the afternoon sun.

CHAPTER 23

"The money's the key to whatever this is."
—All The President's Men

Sam fought to stand. Stumbling out the door she saw the Lincoln Continental sharking its way out onto the street. She would never make the Firebird in time. Didn't mean she wouldn't try. Fumbling with the keys she stabbed at the lock several times before opening it. She fell into the driver's seat, cranked the key over and drove after them. She blasted down Rengstorff but the Lincoln was nowhere. They were long gone. She drove up the 101 for several miles until it became clear her brother was gone. Pulling off at University Avenue she parked. She shook, tears rolling down her cheeks. She got angry seeing herself crying in the rearview mirror. She slammed her fist on the dash. She screamed. She stuffed it all back inside and drove home.

Jacob was surrounded by dark. When Jo Jo placed him in the trunk he had whispered to keep still or Maurizio would make Jo Jo hurt him. Jacob could see the giant didn't want to do that. He also knew he would hurt Jacob if he was ordered to. The highway thrummed under the tires as they floated along on soft luxury cruiser shocks. *Sam will find me. She will.*

Sam walked back into the apartment. She sat down on the sofa, ignoring the down she kicked up. The feathers danced in the shaft of light coming in through the open door.

Valentina filled the doorway. "Where did the goombah squad go?"

"They took Jake."

"No. Bastards. Where did they take him?"

"I don't know, Val. Said they'll kill him if they don't get their money."

"Then we better get their cash, and fast." Valentina said she had seen Maurizio coming, but she didn't know how many boys he had with him so she grabbed Esther and Terry and lit out the back door. She stashed them at the Glass Slipper Motel on El Camino.

"I'm all out of ideas, Val."

"Fuck that, princess. Climb out of that hole, we ain't got time for it. You gots to move that pretty fanny and figure out how to get Jake back and us clear of this mess."

"I screwed it all up."

"I don't care. Don't. I need you fully functioning, so clean up your thinking and get it together."

"Oh, shit."

"What?"

"Val, Breeze didn't tip them to us. Maurizio hadn't heard of Humboldt, but he knew this address. Knew my name, Jake's. How?"

"We screwed this up somewhere. Where?"

Something was gnawing at Sam's mind. Something she didn't want to face. But once it hit the surface, it had to be said. "Jinks knows where we live."

"He sure does, baby."

"He wouldn't sell me out."

"You willing to bet Jake's ass on that?"

"Let's jet."

They took the Ford Galaxie and headed to the city. Not knowing if Sardine and Cracker would return, they decided it was best for Esther and Terry to stay at the motel. Sam promised to call that night.

"You didn't tell her where Jacob was," Valentine said, arching a perfectly plucked eyebrow.

"No need to worry her."

"You say so." Valentine felt the lie, but let it drop. Truth was, Sam didn't want to deal with her mother finding out she'd lost Jacob.

They parked off Grant Avenue. They wanted to be able to keep an eye on the Golden Pot. When Jinks finally arrived he was walking slowly up the street, limping. Sam was out and moving and reached him quickly. Grabbing his shoulder, she was about to punch him when he spun around. "Jinks, you backstabbing—"

When he turned she saw his ruined face. One eye was swollen shut, his upper lip purple and torn. He spoke through broken teeth. "Sorry."

"Who?"

He looked at her and then down at the pavement.

"Maurizio?"

He nodded slightly. "I . . . he knows about my son. Kimmy. So sorry."

Sam's face softened.

Valentina walked up behind them. "Get in the car, Jinks."

"Val, I couldn't . . . They . . ."

"Fuck them. It's me you have to worry about. Here or at my crib? Here it gets ugly fast."

"Yes."

"Yes what, Jinks? Spit it out."

For an answer he climbed into the back seat of the Galaxie.

No one spoke until they were moving up the steps to Valentina's flat. "Are you going to kill me?" Jinks asked.

"All signs point to yes."

Sweat was beading on Jinks's brow. His arrogant stance and rakish bravado were gone.

"She's not killing anyone. Tell him, Val."

"It'd be a lie. I don't get some truth, this man will be chum in the bay by sundown. Keep him here." Valentina left them standing in the entryway.

"They took Jake. The motherfuckers took Jake."

"Sorry." Jinks wasn't able to hold her gaze. He looked down at the floor. Valentina came from the bathroom carrying the shower curtain. Dropping it on the kitchen floor, she took a chair and set it on the vinyl. "Bring him."

Sam nodded her head and Jinks moved into the kitchen. Sitting, he closed his good eye. Valentina slammed a butcher knife into her cutting board. Jinks jumped at the sound, his eye popping open. Sam started to speak, but one look at Valentina's face shut her down. Valentina pulled the blade from the wood and moved on Jinks. "Scared?"

"What?"

"Are you scared?"

"Yes. Please, I'll tell you—"

"Be clear. Comes to it, I don't have any qualms about slicing you up. Clear?"

Jinks looked at her, steadying the building tremor best he could.

Valentina flicked his swollen eye with her finger. He let out a high squeak. Sam had to turn away.

"We clear, Jinks?"

"Yes. I'll tell you what you want."

"Yes, you will." From a drawer she took an extension cord and looped it around Jinks's arms, tying him to the chair back. "Where are they holding Jake?"

"Don't know, swear."

"Fair enough. Easy one then, how did they find us?"

"I didn't have a choice."

Valentina slapped him across the face, opening a scab on his upper lip. "How, not why."

"Fuck. I don't..." Blood was running into his mouth, reddening his broken incisors. "My uncle, he's a tong soldier. Bought the black powder for the Pinto from him. Sold me out. Swear."

"So you gave them us."

"Had to."

"Or they would hurt your wife and baby. I got that. Where?"

"What?" Jinks braced for a blow. Valentina raised the butcher knife. "Don't, Val, just tell me what you want me to say."

"Where did they take you?"

"The club, Taxi Dancer."

"OK." Valentina buried the knife once again in the cutting block. "Don't go anywhere."

On the front stoop, Valentina plucked the Marlboro pack from Sam's front pocket.

"You don't smoke."

"I also don't torture men in my kitchen." Putting the cigarette between her ruby red lips, she waited for Sam to strike her Bic. Taking in a deep lungful of smoke she let it dribble out. "I was on the other side of the world last time I had a cigarette. Still tastes like shit." She pulled another deep drag.

"What do we do with Jinks?" Sam asked.

"You buy his story?"

"Seems scared enough. Why would he lie?"

"Whole deal sounds wrong. Uncle tells Maurizio? How did the uncle know what he used the explosives for? Uncle sells out nephew, why? What are the odds some street tong knows Maurizio in the first place? No, not buying. If that's bullshit what else is?"

"You think he knows where they took Jake?" Sam's face went stone.

"Maybe. I just don't know."

Sam's anger bloomed. She marched into the flat. Her first punch landed on Jinks's jaw with enough force to topple him and the chair. She kicked him in the guts and air flew out his mouth in a fine spray of pink mist. "Enough going easy, asshole. Truth, or I take you apart one joint at a time."

"Sam, it's me." It hurt when he spoke.

"Hell yes it's you, you scheming son of a bitch." Sam kicked him again. "How much did they pay you to sell us out?"

"They didn't . . ." Looking into Sam's hard face he rethought what he was about to say. "Samantha—"

"Jinks? We're almost out of time here. I don't think you'll survive much more." She sank the steel toe of her Red Wing Engineer boot deep in his gut. He fought for air, panicked. Gasping, he struggled to form words. "Ribs go next pal," Sam said. "Probably no coming back from that."

Valentina leaned against the wall, smoking a fresh cigarette, watching Sam impassively.

"Nnnnno. Sam. Had to," Jinks said, every word costing him precious air. "I owe them."

"You gambling again? Stupid question, of course you are." She shook her head. For a man who prided himself on control, Jinks had always been weak when it came to cards. His ego told him he was a better player than he was. Sam could see now why he had been so anxious to sign on for the heist. If he had planned to sell them out from the jump or it had come to him later didn't matter. He had, and now his only value to Sam was if he could lead them to where Jacob was being held.

"You want to see that kid of yours again?"

Jinks nodded.

"Good. I don't find Jake, you die. We crystal on this?"

Jinks nodded again.

"Where do I find Maurizio?"

"The disco?"

"Cops have it shuttered. Where did you meet with him, you know, when you sold us out?"

"Wasn't like that. His gorilla snatched me coming out of work."

"Right. You didn't call him?"

"No."

"And you have no idea, no clue where I can find him. Too bad." She hovered her index finger above Jinks's face, deciding where to strike. "Eye?"

"No, no."

Sam stabbed her finger down stopping so close she could feel his eyelashes. "Wait. Why you? If you didn't call him . . . then?"

"Jo Jo knew I did demo. Put two and two. They snatched me.

Said Kimmy, my kid, we were all dead if I didn't rat you out. Didn't even clear my debt. Swear."

"He screwed you hard and dry. Val, the knife."

"Whatever you say, Sam." Valentina pulled the butcher knife and handed it to her. Jinks went pale.

"Last chance. Where."

"Shit, um, shit . . . I heard he lives in North Beach, swear it's all I know."

Sam gripped the knife, took a breath then leaned down and slipped the blade under the extension cord. With one smooth move she freed Jinks from the chair.

"Sam?" Jinks said, rolling over to stand up.

"Don't say my name. History gets you a walk away. Can't promise the same if I see you again."

Jinks looked from Sam's cold eyes to Valentina's. He started to say something, shut up and walked out. Sam followed him to the door and locked it behind him.

"Should have killed him."

"You're a thief not a killer, remember?"

"Losing Jake changes everything."

"I know, baby."

"Who do we know?"

"Nobody that runs with the black-hand boys." Valentina went to the built-in alcove that held her phone and phonebooks. Grabbed the white pages.

"Really? He won't be listed."

Valentina thumbed rapidly through the names. "Bingo, big boy, busted."

"What?"

"Maurizio Binasco, douche, lives over on Chestnut Street in

North Beach. Man has big balls, lists his number because who would have the stones to front him?"

"We would." Sam grabbed her leather jacket and was out the door before Valentina had her purse.

"Slow down, little sister, we have to play this smart."

"Or we kick in the door and shoot anything that moves."

"Good as that might feel, might not get us Jake back."

"You got a better plan?"

CHAPTER 24

"Is it safe?"
—Marathon Man

"Your name's Jo Jo, right?" Jacob asked the huge man looming over him.

"They call me that. Name's actually Clarence."

"Last name's not Odbody is it?"

"No. Who's Odbody?"

"Clarence Odbody. No? *It's a Wonderful Life*? No? Nothing?"

"I'm not supposed to talk to you."

"Yeah, I get that, but what am I going to do? My hands and feet are tied. I'm blindfolded."

"Still . . . boss would have my ass, he finds out."

Jacob heard the refreshing pffft of a beer bottle opening. "Brewski? Can I have some? 'Swear I'm so dry I'm spitting cotton.' *Bus Stop*?"

"You're weird, kid, real space case."

"A thirsty space case. Come on, one sip. What's the harm?"

The bottle clinked against Jacob's teeth as Jo Jo tried to give him some. "Sorry, kid."

Jacob took a deep chug. "No biggie. Thanks. Hey, you smoke boo?"

"I guess."

"You guess? You call me weird. I'll make you a sweet deal. Take off my blindfold and I'll share some Panama Red with you. Good, blow your mind, Class-A grass."

"I'm not even supposed to talk to you."

"So someone comes, you put the blindfold back. Right?"

"Ummm, I don't know."

"Pussy." A hand hit the back of Jacob's head. "Ow."

"Sorry. Promise you won't tell Mr. Binasco?"

"Scout's honor."

When the blindfold came off, Jacob couldn't see all that much better. A dim overhead light revealed an industrial-looking storage room. Jacob was on the floor with his back against the cement wall. Jo Jo sat in a metal folding chair a few feet away.

"Front shirt pocket, Bugler," Jacob said. Jo Jo reached in and pulled out the tin. Plucking out a joint he sniffed it. "It's good shit, trust me."

"We'll find out in a minute," Jo Jo said, flicking his Bic. He took a hard hit, holding it in. He leaned back on the hind legs of his chair and tilted his head back.

"What about me?" Jacob asked. Jo Jo looked down at Jacob then leaned forward, putting the joint between his lips. Jacob held the smoke in like a pro, not even a tiny cough.

"Fuck," Jo Jo said, leaning back again.

"Told you it was good shit."

"You didn't lie, little man." Polishing off the beer, Jo Jo opened a fresh frosty. He gave Jacob the first gulp.

Jacob noticed a line of scabs and bruises on Jo Jo's knuckles. "What happened there?"

Jo Jo looked at his fist. "That Chinese dude from your crew."

"Jinks?"

"That'd be him."

"You kicked his ass?"

"Mostly his face. Cut myself on one of his fucking teeth."

"He is a total scumbag," Jacob said.

"Tried to trade you for a marker."

"See? Scumbag."

"He'll be eating his egg foo yung through a straw."

"Good."

As they finished the joint and the mellow set in, Jacob got Jo Jo talking about his childhood. He'd grown up in South Bend, Indiana. "While the other guys were playing with cap guns I was dressing up my sister's Barbie. That should have tipped my folks off to something."

"When did you figure out you were into dudes?"

"I always knew. I mean, I didn't have words for it. But yeah, I knew. I didn't have anyone to be gay with."

"Truth, Jo Jo, some days I think it would be easier to be gay. I, um . . ." Jacob let it trail off.

"Tease, that's what you are, little man. But I got a newsflash."

"Yeah?"

"Yeah. I ain't into boys. Men are what springs my pole."

"Did you just say 'springs my pole'?" Jacob was laughing.

"Yes, um, I did." Jo Jo started laughing and the laughter took on a life of its own. Soon their eyes were watering and they were howling. Slowly it subsided. By then, neither could remember what had started it.

After Jacob caught his breath he looked up at Jo Jo, serious. "Jo Jo, if Binasco tells you to kill me, will you?"

"I'd have to. That's how this works. I'd feel like shit though."

"I don't want to die."

"Then you shouldn't have robbed Mr. Binasco's disco."

CHAPTER 25

Maurizio Binasco's address was a three-story white with black trim Victorian. Black iron scrollwork supported handrails leading to the second floor entrance. It had one door, making it clear it had never been broken up into flats. From the earliest days North Beach was San Francisco's little Italy. Joe DiMaggio grew up there, lived there in the '50s with Marilyn Monroe. The beat generation flocked to its coffee shops. In 1964 the Condor Club opened on Broadway. It was reported to be America's first topless and bottomless entertainment venue. None of this history meant jack shit to Sam as she sat in Valentina's Galaxie with an M16 on her lap. Looking up she could see a sofa and part of the living room through the sheer curtains covering the second floor bay windows. A pretty, middle-aged woman was helping a ten or twelve-year-old boy with his homework, or at least that's what it looked like to Sam.

"We go in and snatch the wife and kid, trade them for Jake," Sam said.

"You really want to play chicken with a mobster? You willing to shoot an innocent kid? The wife?"

"For Jake? Maybe."

"No you're not, neither am I. We don't bluff with Jacob's life, deal?"

"Deal. Man, I hate waiting." Thirty painfully slow minutes later Maurizio emerged from the back of the house dressed in a suit. He kissed his wife and then put up his dukes like he was going to box with the boy. The boy threw a stage punch. Maurizio snapped his head back in exaggerated slow motion. They both laughed. Maurizio tousled his son's hair then walked out the front door. Coming down the stairs there was a spring in his step. Sam and Valentina crouched down in their seats. Through the open window they heard him whistling Diana Ross's "Love Hangover." Sliding behind the wheel of the Lincoln Continental he pulled away from the curb. Valentina gave him a two-block lead before she followed.

"Where are you going, Mr. Binasco?" Sam asked as the Lincoln rolled up onto the 80 heading toward the Bay Bridge. They followed him across the double-decker bridge. Curving at the tollbooths, he took the 580 into Berkeley. He was driving slow, casual, like he had nowhere to be. It was Monday night and traffic was light. At University he exited. Near the freeway off-ramp he took a left into an industrial neighborhood. Valentina had to hang well back as there was no other traffic to hide behind. At a small warehouse he stopped. Sam slipped down below the window as the Galaxie cruised past Maurizio.

By the time Valentina circled the block Maurizio had disappeared. Parked beside the Lincoln was a cute little red Alfa Romeo Spider. "'Mrs. Robinson, you're trying to seduce me,'" Valentina said pointing with her nose at the sports car.

"What?"

"The Alfa, it's what Dustin Hoffman drove in *The Graduate*."

"Val?"

"Yeah, Sam?"

"Weird time to bring that piece of trivia up."

"Agreed."

"What are the odds my brother is being held in that building?"

"Good."

"What do you say we go get him back?"

"Little sister, there is nothing I'd rather do." They were parked two doors down. Each had an M16 with a full magazine and a spare taped to it upside down, jungle style. "Time to take it to them full rock and roll, baby."

"You got it," Sam said, switching the rifle's selector to full auto. Quietly they circled the building. No back entrance. The roller door in the front was locked down. A steel-clad wooden door was the only other way in. It had a Schlage deadbolt with a thin metal pick guard, enough to keep most out. Sam wasn't most. In thirty seconds flat the door clicked. Sam swung it silently open and Valentina moved into the room. Spinning in a quick 360 she cleared the small inner office. From the Snap-on calendars on the wall with babes in bikinis humping tools to the grease-stained invoices on the desk, it was clearly a machine shop of some kind. From beyond the office walls drifted the sound of a cello. A second door seemed to lead to the main floor. Valentina motioned with two fingers for Sam to take the left side of the room when they breached the door.

Stealth was over.

It was time for shock.

Valentina hit the door with her shoulder at a dead run. The hollow wood splintered in. Valentina aimed right, sweeping the room with her M16.

Sam was behind Valentina, sweeping the left side of the room. At first her mind couldn't catch up to what she was seeing. Instead of a machine shop she saw a grand living room. Several crystal chandlers hung from the rafters lighting the room in a warm glow. Kilim Persian rugs littered the floor. Large canvases hung from the walls, some blank, others dripping Daliesque cityscapes in various stages of being painted. The cello was coming from a high-end hi-fi with a reel-to-reel tape player and glowing tube amplifier.

Something moved in the middle of the room. Sam took aim. Through the rifle's sights she saw Maurizio sitting on a pile of pillows, back resting against a chaise lounge. He wore a floral kimono. In his hand was a Champagne flute. On his lap rested a pretty young man's head.

Maurizio's mouth formed an O but no sound came out.

The young man sat up, pulling an afghan over his naked chest.

Valentina kicked open a side door, discovering a kitchen and dining room, both empty.

Sam kept the front sight planted squarely on the middle of Maurizio's forehead.

In the back of the space Valentina found a bedroom, also empty. She moved back into the carpet-strewn main room and studied the tableau.

"He's not here," Valentina said in a soft voice, not wanting to startle Sam into action.

"Where?" Sam said, walking forward, keeping the sight on Maurizio, her finger on the trigger. "Where? Where?"

"Fuck this." Maurizio stood and a Walther PPK, slick little automatic, appeared in his hand. "You two bitches want to dance? Let's boogie."

Valentina shouldered her M16, dialing in on the mobster. "No way you walk out of here."

"Ha! You chicks kill a made man? How long before my associates find you? Hours, days if you're lucky, which you aren't."

"I just want my brother back. Where is he?"

"Bottom of the goddamn bay if you don't put that piece down."

"Don't do it, Sam." Valentina moved in, taking aim at the pretty young man on the floor. "The twist goes first. Can you dig it, old man?"

"Ricky? He's got nothing to do with this."

"Please." Ricky started to cry softly. "I'm just a painter."

"Collateral damage, babe." Valentina was in full-on jungle mode. "This shit gets wet nobody's going to stay dry. Sam, you got the greaseball?"

"He twitches and he's a smear on the rug," Sam said, readying herself to pull the trigger. Hesitation would get them killed.

"Do I look even vaguely like I care if I die?" Valentine let her eyes droop to bored slits. "Even if you somehow kill us both, on full auto we will rip you both to shreds before we hit the floor."

"Popi, do what they say. I don't want you to die," Ricky said.

"Shhh, Ricky." Maurizio opened his hand and let the automatic fall out of it. "I'm talking to a couple of ghosts. Kill me and there will be nowhere to hide."

"Let's do this thing, Val, screw him and his threats."

Maurizio looked from Sam to Valentina. "Be a god damn shame to punch bullet holes into a beautiful woman like you. Why not put the guns down and talk. See if we can get you home in one piece."

Valentina slowly lowered her rifle. "Yeah, alright, talk. Sam, keep a bead on him."

"You got it. Scratch your balls without giving me fair warning and I will punch your timecard."

"Understood. Ricky, get us some coffee. Cappuccino, you gonna love it." Ricky stood up, shaking. He started to move to Maurizio for comfort but the older man shook his head ever so slightly. "Go on. Alright, gorgeous, pull up a chair." He motioned Valentina to a chair in front of one of the paintings. The mobster sat on the end of the chaise lounge. "What a fucking mess, right?"

"Fubar," Valentina said in a flat voice. "And you are just as fucked as we are."

"How you figure that?"

"Your associates OK with a fanook for a soldier?"

"No, but I ain't no fanook. I got a wife and kids to prove it."

"I think you might believe that. Walks like a duck, fucks like a duck, it's a duck."

"Ricky, he's an artist. I'm his patron."

"You haven't told your uncle Jimmy that you lost his two hundred grand."

"I handle my own business."

"Word gets out on the street that you got rolled by three girls and a couple of high school kids, well, you can do the math."

Ricky came back in. He'd changed into a tight tee with Andy Warhol's Marilyn Monroe silk-screened on the front. He had a tray with two cappuccinos. He knelt at Maurizio's feet, serving him first. Maurizio didn't look down. He took the cup while keeping his eyes on Valentina.

"Um, thanks." Valentina blew on the steaming liquid. "You're right, it's good."

"Dark roast, caffè nero, ground fine, that's the trick. You?" He raised a cup to Sam. "Not thirsty?"

Sam kept her finger on the trigger and slowly shook her head.

"You made a huge mistake when you took her brother. Sam is a stone killer when it comes to family."

"I think you're right, about the mistake part. I misjudged you two. That won't happen again."

"Wait a fucking minute," Sam said lowering her rifle. "I don't have to threaten your Guinea ass. Nope." Leaning down she took the cup from Valentina and took a sip. "You're right, that is one hell of a cup of coffee."

"Sam?"

"I got this one, Val." She turned to the boy on the floor. "Ricky, this goes sideways and I don't walk out of here, you'll need to line up a new sugar daddy."

Ricky looked up at the older man. "What is she talking about?"

"She's blowing smoke up my ass."

"Think about it, big guy. I am the only one in this room who has any idea where your two hundred grand is, and I'm the only thief here good enough to get it back. You lose all that bread, no place in the world you can hide. Now, shitbird, where the fuck is my brother?"

"Girly, you and me, we're Siamese twins, sharing the same heart." He smiled at her. "You think if they come after me yours won't be the first name they hear? Clip me now and Jo Jo does your brother and then hands your name over. We are appaiato significato. Partners. Only way we make it out is together."

"Partners." Sam reached out and Maurizio took her hand. "Now, get me my brother back and I'll start figuring a way to get your bread back."

"He's at the disco. Basement storage room."

"You gonna let Jo Jo know we're coming?"

"He'll know. I'd lend you the key to the back door, but with you that seems both redundant and insulting."

"True. Let's jet, Val."

"Right behind you, princess."

As they left, Ricky sat down on the chaise, sticking out his lower lip in an obvious pout. Maurizio waited until they were gone before he moved to appease his comare.

CHAPTER 26

"Sometimes you have to lose yourself 'fore you can find anything."

—*Deliverance*

"Boss said I'm supposed to roll with you," Jo Jo said to Sam.

"Not going to happen, big guy."

"Mr. Binasco said you'd be resistant. He said you should think of me as your surrogate Siamese twin."

"And if I say fuck off?"

"Then I'm supposed to hunt you down and take out someone you love. I don't want to do that. But . . ."

"You will," Jacob said.

"Come on, Princess Samantha, our own personal queer ogre is just what this freaky luau needs."

"Fine. Anyone else want to climb onboard the suicide train? Toot toot, all aboard, next stop, the gates of hell."

Squeezing into the back of the Galaxie, Jo Jo smiled at Jacob. "I really am glad I didn't wind up having to kill you. Friends?"

Jacob looked at the large outstretched paw. "Why not. Just don't break my hand, I may need to use it some time."

It was after 2 a.m. when they arrived back at the Creekside Apartments. The headlights sweeping across his windshield woke Detective Pahk. "What a freak show," he said to Sam as he looked at Jo Jo and Valentina.

"Jacob, take our friends inside, get them something to drink."

"You got it."

Sam waited until the other three were in the apartment before she gave Pahk her attention. "What is it this time, Detective, you come to tuck me in?"

"Cute trick, Judy S."

"I have no idea what you're rambling about."

"The Humboldt address tipped me. I don't like being jerked around. I had the state boys check out your paroled felon."

"They didn't find him?"

"They found him. He was clean. Doesn't have a record. Not even a jaywalking ticket. They don't like being jerked around any more than I do."

"Well shit, take me in then." Sam held out her hands to be cuffed. "Arrest me or walk away, I mean it."

"Oh, you mean it. Well that's a horse of a completely different color. You mean it. I think I'll go for door number three."

"What?"

"Yes, it gets better. I put your whole crew on the wire. Got flagged. Your girl Candy is in the hospital. Took a high-caliber round to the chest."

"You think I shot my best friend?" Sam kept her face neutral.

"Could be. Doc thinks I can talk to her tomorrow. You and I both know that bullet in her chest leads back to you and that he-she Amazon."

"You have nothing." Sam sounded less than sure.

"Accessory to a felony or two I'm sure. From where I'm looking, you are circling the drain. Want a hand? Talk to me now and we'll see, maybe we can swing a deal with the DA. Once Candy starts spilling, it's out of my hands."

"This is bullshit. I'm calling my lawyer." She started to turn away. Pahk grabbed her biceps, pulling her close.

"You don't walk away until I say so." She could smell the whiskey on his breath. "Be smart. Don't think I'm above bending the law to nail you. It gets dirty, your smart-ass little brother may get splashed." He released her with a shove that sent her stumbling back. "You got my number. Clock is ticking."

In the apartment, Jacob was passing around rum and Cokes. He handed one to Sam when she came in. "What did Detective Dick Weed want?"

"Candy woke up."

"Is she OK? Is she going to—"

"I don't know. And, yes, it could be total BS, but Pahk said he was going to interview her in the morning."

"But she's awake? Fuck yes. Fuck. Yes. I'm going to the hospital."

"Pahk, cops, they all may be there."

"Stealth is my middle name."

"It's nice to see you smiling. Take the Firebird. And Jake?"

"Yes?"

"Tell Candy Pahk is coming after me. He wants to lay her shooting at my feet."

Jacob's smile fell. "Should I be sure she has her story straight before or after I say how glad we are that she's still breathing?"

"That's not what I said."

"Kinda is. But forget it. You're in triage battle mode, that justi-fies everything, right?"

"I'm trying to keep us all free and above ground. Got a problem with that?"

"No, we're solid." Jacob walked away without meeting her eyes.

Behind the wheel of the Firebird Jacob's shoulders relaxed. Candy was alive. She of the captivating smile, the intoxicating fra-grance. She of the one perfect kiss. Her lips soft, inviting, and tast-ing of cherries. She was alive. Everything else was crap he could deal with later. She was alive. A goofy grin spread across his face. With a deep rumble he pulled out onto the 101.

"OK, princess, what's the real skinny?" Valentina asked Sam.

"I'm just beat."

"Tell that to some ordinary girl. This is me, your ever-fabulous human lie detector. And you're lying."

Sam looked over at Jo Jo, not wanting to be overheard. Jo Jo's full attention was on the black and white TV, where ABBA was playing on Don Kirshner's Rock Concert. They were performing "Dancing Queen." Sam kept her voice down. "Pahk has our scent like a mad bulldog. Threatened to fabricate a case against us."

"Think he'll do it?"

"Maybe. He was sloshed. That man needs to get laid, or some-thing."

"That man needs to have a bullet parked behind his ear," Valentina said without a smile.

"It may come to that." Taking the glass from Valentina's hand she took a long drink, then handed it back. "We sleep in shifts. Jo Jo you take the first shift." He smiled and nodded but his eyes never left the glittering Swedes on the TV set.

Valentina and Sam rested on Sam's bed. Neither were sleepy. Both were exhausted.

"This shit's over, I'm going to Aruba," Valentina said, "lie on a beach and have some cute cabana boy bring me drinks that look like a fruit cocktail and kicks like a mule."

"Over? You really think there's any such day?"

"I hope so, girl."

"You wonder who we'll be when the credits roll on this one?" Sam asked.

"All the time. Valentina? I fight to keep her here. Keep me here. Seems sometimes I'd, hell, we'd all be better off if I let the lady go and went back to being Henry. Bitch is, I know he ain't me, not now. I'm a mess."

"You are a stone cold, beautiful mess, Valentina."

"Thank you, princess."

Sam took Valentina's hand, squeezing it. There was nothing left to say. They would or wouldn't survive the building war. And if they survived, there was no telling how intact they would be.

CHAPTER 27

"It's all bullshit except the pain."
—*Mean Streets*

A thick fog blanketed the Kaiser hospital. Jacob was glad an alarm didn't blare and rent-a-cops didn't swoop down on him when he entered. An older Chicano man was pushing a floor polisher in swirls around the lobby. If he noticed Jacob he didn't show it. A yawning woman at the information desk told Jacob that Candy had been moved out of the ICU to an intermediate room.

"What does that mean, intermediate? I thought she was getting better."

"She may be." The woman looked down at a binder. "It just says she was moved last night. An intermediate room is for seriously ill patients who don't need as close supervision. It is better than ICU."

"Where is she?"

"It's too early for visiting. You her brother?"

"A friend. I, we, thought we were going to lose her. Then I heard she was going to make it. Now this intermediate shi, um, stuff."

"I'm afraid you'll have to wait until after ten." The lady was older, her long gray hair loose down her back. She wore a simple muslin dress and chunky Navajo jewelry.

"I get it's your job to tell me that. Normally I would smile like Eddie Haskell, say I understood, then sneak up the back stairs. Fact is, the girl up there? She is the most amazing thing in my life and I didn't know if I would ever see her again. I just want to look in on her, see her. Can you understand that?"

"You love her, this girl?"

"Like the moon."

"Room 247."

"Thank you."

"Love matters," the woman said, then looked back down at the papers on her desk.

Jacob took the elevator up. Candy was in the first bed in the room. Curtains hid the bed behind her. She looked pale, but now there was less of a gray tint to her skin. A tube ran from an IV bag down to the needle taped to the top of her hand. Wires snaked from monitors to her, spreading out into a spray of small sensors taped to her chest. A tube entered her ribs just under her arm and a pump hummed and gurgled as it sucked fluid from her chest cavity. An oxygen mask covered her mouth and nose. Jacob stood watching her chest move up and down. Even with all of this, she was still the most beautiful girl he had ever seen. It wasn't that he didn't see the sweaty sheen on her skin, or her oily hair or the tubes and wires—he could. But superimposed on her in the bed was every smile she'd ever given him. He saw her on the dance floor spinning in his arms. He could feel her breath on his ear. She was still alive and that meant anything, any future, was possible. Even one where they went out to the tiki bar for blue drinks and drove home eager and hungry for each other. After fifteen minutes he became aware he'd been lucky not to get caught by a nurse or security guard. He started to go, then turned back and took her hand. He needed to touch her, feel her warmth.

Candy's eyes fluttered open very slowly. She looked dreamy and doped as she worked to focus her eyes. Recognizing Jacob, her eyes widened. When she first spoke, her voice was a dry, raspy whisper.

He couldn't hear her words. Leaning down, he put his face very close to hers.

"Jake, I'm sorry," she said, floating from the painkillers.

"Oh, Candy, what could you possibly be sorry about?"

"I must look terrible." She rolled her eyes and tried to smile.

"You look amazing. What are you sorry about?"

"Everything. I thought . . ." Her voice dropped to a low mumble. ". . . and all I wanted was . . ." She reached up and touched his face.

The curtain slid open, startling Jacob.

Candy's mother was puffy with sleep and surprised to see a young man standing over her daughter. "Who are— I know you. You are Samantha's brother."

"Jacob, Mrs. Harmon."

"What are you doing here?"

"I had to see Candy. I heard—"

He felt Candy squeeze his hand weakly.

"Do you know who shot, what happened to my daughter?"

"No. I just heard she was in the hospital."

"You're lying. If you care about Candice—that is her name, Candice—if you care about her at all you tell me what happened." She was moving closer to Jacob, a hard edge in her face.

"I love your daughter." Jacob looked from Mrs. Harmon to Candy. "I love you."

Candy smiled and then her lids got heavy and she drifted off.

"You're no better than your sister. I know you were involved." She was hissing to keep her voice down. "Trash, your whole family. I warned Candice. Said sooner or later Samantha would ruin her life. Look at her. Look at my baby girl." Angry tears rolled down her cheek.

Jacob gave Candy's hand one last squeeze. She had retreated back into her drug-induced haze. Turning, he walked out.

"I will prove you and your sister did this. I will."

Mrs. Harmon's voice was cut off as the elevator doors closed. Jacob could see himself reflected in the stainless-steel walls. He looked rough as hell. He'd been tied up and tossed in a trunk, hadn't slept in twenty-four hours and he needed a shower. He looked like the trash Candy's mom accused him of being. Even if he'd cleaned up and put on a suit before going to the hospital, it wouldn't change the fact that if Candy hadn't come with Sam and him on this ride she wouldn't have been hurt. In the park, when she told him about Berkeley, he should have insisted she give up the heist and go to school. Was he selfish? Was the reason he hadn't stopped her his desire to be with her? Or was it worse? Was he weak? Had he been afraid she wouldn't think he was cool if he told her to stay away from the robbery? A man would have kept her safe.

Driving the Firebird out of the parking lot, Jacob took good measure of himself and found himself wanting. He hid in remembered sentences, phrases stolen from master wordsmiths. Wild Bill Shakespeare: *Frailty, thy name is woman.* No, frailty, thy name is Jacob the miserable pussy. *A coward dies a thousand times before his death, but the valiant taste of death but once.* Fuck Shakespeare.

Dylan Thomas: *I know we're not saints or virgins or lunatics; we know all the lust and lavatory jokes, and most of the dirty people; we can catch buses and count our change and cross the roads and talk real sentences. But our innocence goes awfully deep, and our discreditable secret is that we don't know anything at all, and our horrid inner secret is that we don't care that we don't.* Thomas was no better.

Jacob's mind skipped to movies, struggling to avoid feeling by creating the distance of insignificant thoughts.

"I'm God's lonely man," Travis Bickle said in *Taxi Driver.*

"The pain in hell has two sides. The kind you can touch with your hand; the kind you can feel in your heart." Charley in *Mean Streets*.

Words.

Mountains of words as he bounced from one thought to the next.

"I'm mad as hell, and I'm not going to take this anymore." Paddy Chayefsky wrote that in *Network*. He also wrote *Marty* starring Ernest Borgnine, who played Dutch Engstrom in *The Wild Bunch*. They died like men. All of this knowledge, this trivia, did him no good. It was noise. His ability to remember and synthesize facts earned him a 1450 on the SAT. He was smart enough to get into any college he wanted. And that did not one thing to help Candy.

"Man, you look spent," Terry said. Jacob picked him and Esther up at the Glass Slipper motel. Entering the apartment, they found Sam crouched behind a sofa aiming an M16 at them. Sam laughed it off, saying she heard them coming. Jacob couldn't deal with any of it. He took Terry back outside.

"I am spent, Terry. Burnt crispy fried," Jacob said as he sat down on one of the crossbars of the high-power tower. The freeway was full of cars stuck in morning rush hour. Terry fired up a joint then tried to pass it to Jacob, who shook his head.

"Come on, this is no kind of day to give up the boo."

"I need to keep my head straight."

"Why exactly do you need to keep straight? Huh?" Terry licked his finger, touching the joint where it was burning unevenly.

"Our shit is well and truly fucked up, Terry. Fucked. Up."

"No shit, Sherlock. So you want to think our way home? That it?"

"Something like that."

"Ain't going to work, man, no way. I mean it will, but not like this. You are the smartest cat I know."

"Then?" Jacob asked.

"We need you. How long have I known you?"

"Ninth grade—three and a half years."

"Three and a half formative years," Terry said through tight lips, smoke escaping with every word.

"I'll give you that. Point?"

"Point is, I know you better than any motherfucker, right? And I know when you've got your chain wrapped around your axle. You want to sink into your poor fucking me bullshit self-pity?"

"Candy is in a hospital bed because I didn't stop her, didn't tell Sam to fuck off and solve her problems without involving everyone I love."

"History, all of that. 'I never saw a wild thing sorry for itself.' We need a wild thing about now."

"D.H. Lawrence? Dropping the big boys on me? OK, here." Jacob took the joint from Terry and sucked in a deep toke. "Happy? I'm still thinking of jumping."

"Take another hit."

Jacob inhaled and held it. Slowly he jetted out the smoke. "I hate to admit this . . ."

"What's that, Jake?"

"Fuck. You're right. We need to find our way home from this shit." He took a last hit, then ate the roach. "And I do my best thinking high."

"Truth, man. Now let's go save the world. Only first we need to climb down without breaking our necks."

"That would suck dolphin dick." Jacob started to climb down. "D.H. Lawrence. Surprising choice."

"You're not the only honor student stupid enough to climb a high-power pole."

Jacob let the pot and morning sunshine work their magic on his tense muscles and mind. Terry was correct; they'd both written most of their truly inspired papers high. The only difference here was people died or went to jail if they got it wrong. No need to sweat that. Jacob's foot slipped on the dew-slick girder. He stumbled into space.

Terry grabbed Jacob's wrist, stopping his fall. "Dipshit. You die now, up here, it's tragic or ironic, but not heroic."

"All places are alike, and every earth is fit for burial."

"You almost die just so you could lay some Marlowe on me?"

"No, I don't think so. Good freakin' weed, brother man."

"You got to feed your brain." Terry kept Jacob in hands' reach as they continued their descent.

"Time to di di mau up North and start putting heads on pikes," Valentina said, sitting at the breakfast table finishing a plate of Esther's fine pancakes.

"He's got a hillbilly army up there," Sam said. "And he owns the local law. We can't go in blazing."

"No, you're wrong on this." Valentina didn't notice Terry and Jacob come in the front door. "We roll in and light them up. Kill anything that moves, grab our cash and be gone."

Terry watched Valentina, shaken, unsure of whom she had become. A gorgeous woman with an angry soldier's voice coming out of her.

"That is not the way. Not our way. Your father never owned a gun," Esther said.

"Esther, I love you and all," Valentina said, "but comes to this you ain't got a vote."

"But I do," Sam said, drawing patterns in the syrup on her plate with a fork. "Best case we don't get killed, but we do go to jail for the rest of our lives. Massacres just don't fly, even up North in Hicksville."

"OK, Sam, what's your plan?" Valentina stared at Sam, waiting for an answer. None was coming. "You are always the glam-dam with the plan so toss it out there. We go all ninja? Black pajamas and throwing stars? What?"

"I'm working on it."

"Well tick-motherfucking-tock, princess. Maurizio called huge and silent over there. Gave us a no-shit-they-will-start-dropping-bodies-in-the-bay deadline. He needs that cash in forty-eight hours."

"She's right," Jo Jo said from the living room, where he was watching *Scooby-Doo*. "Jimmy the Hat don't get his cabbage Wednesday night, he'll start stacking bodies up."

Turning to see Jo Jo, Valentina saw Jacob and Terry. Her voice softened, went up in pitch. "Terr-Terr, Jacob, you missed breakfast."

"We're good," Jacob said.

"I know you're good. Hell, you two are fine."

"The bread is north." Jacob spoke to Valentina, keeping his back to his sister. "So while we figure out the play we should burn up miles."

"There you have it, even the brainiac agrees with me," Sam said. "Eat up, me hearties, we sail north this afternoon."

"Why not now?" Jo Jo asked.

"Because I said so, and I run this crew." Sam shut the room down. Chaos came from no leadership. Sam hadn't a clue in hell what they were going to do, not one idea how to pull it off. She only knew the next step and hoped like hell it would lead to the path that would take them out of this monumental jug fuck.

Motioning with her head, Sam led Jacob out the back door, closing it so they couldn't be overheard. She leaned against the chalky stucco wall and sparked a Marlboro.

"What?" Jacob stood defiant in front of his big sister.

"Want a butt?"

"No."

"You still pissed at me?"

"Yes."

"I don't blame you. I'm pissed at me. We survive this brutal road trip, I'll buy you a case of Mickey's and you can tell me all the ways I fucked your life."

"If hillbillies don't kill us in the hills above Arcata. If the goombah squad doesn't drop us off the Golden Gate on principal. If that psycho cop doesn't nail us to the wall. If by some miracle of miracles we live through this suicide run, you want to do some ESTian primal scream kumbaya circle jerk about why I'm pissed?"

"You're angry, got it. You need to grow the fuck up. You need to at least pretend to respect me around the others."

"Aye aye, mon capitaine." He gave her a snap salute. "The helm is yours."

"Cute. A crew needs to know who is in charge, or things go sideways fast."

"Sideways? Like the man said, I been down so long it looks like up to me."

"I didn't ask you in on this." Sam turned to him, locking her eyes on his for emphasis. "But in you are. So slam the brakes on the petulant teen boy bullshit. I need you one hundred percent in."

"How many ways do I have to say I'm in? J'en suis. Ich bin dabei. Jeg er med dig."

"Stop. I get it."

"No, I seriously doubt you do." Jacob leaned against the wall, looking out into the puffy clouds drifting happily above them. How dare the clouds be happy? He spoke quietly, eyes remaining on the sky. "Growing up, when we were kids, I wanted to be you, wanted to fit in with our family. I remember lying in bed fantasizing that you were all Russian spies and I was the only true Stern."

"That's one screwed up adoption fantasy."

"Remember asking me how I got good grades?"

"Good? Freakishly stellar, create a new ceiling, blow-the-curve-for-the-rest-of-the-class grades."

"Right. And I said being smart was only part of it. Not the big part even. Other part, the key, is I listen to the teachers, figure out what thing they want me to do, then I do that thing. Whatever gene that you got that says fuck authority, I got one that says fit in and keep your head down."

"That's not a gene, Jake. 'Keep your head down' is our family mantra."

"Point is, the point I'm trying to make, I don't have any illusions about you. But that doesn't mean I won't follow you on a one-way flight to hell if that's what is called for."

Sam looked at Jacob for a long moment. She wanted to say something profound or something that might win him back over to her side. Words evaded her, she was in free fall. No backup chute. Fuck it. It was one more thing she probably wouldn't survive to have to deal with.

CHAPTER 28

"And these children that you spit on as they try to change their worlds . . ."
—David Bowie

They divided up into two cars, agreeing to meet at Callum's apartment. He was long in the wind by now and no one would expect to find the crew there. Terry and Jo Jo rode in the Firebird with Sam.

Jacob saw the way Valentina's face fell when Terry asked to go with Sam, so he asked to ride with her in the Galaxie. As a bonus, he got to get away from Sam. His feelings were raw, near the surface. He was afraid of what he might say if he was stuck next to her for five and a half hours.

Esther said she wanted to go with them, insisted on it. Sam sent her to the store for food and drinks for the road. As soon as Esther's VW bug drove away, Sam loaded up and rolled out. "This mean no road snacks?" Jo Jo asked.

Sam threw him a hard look.

"I was just asking. I didn't have lunch, was looking forward to some beef jerky and Fritos."

"You want a snack?" Sam asked.

"Yes, I'm hungry."

"You, the guy who would have killed my brother if you got the word, are hungry?"

"That was business. No choice, you know?"

"No, I don't. Shut the fuck up or I'll feed you the barrel of my piece. Want a lead sandwich, asswipe?"

Jo Jo sucked air through his teeth. He rested his hand on the pistol holstered under his arm, but said nothing.

"How about you, Terry, you hungry, need to take a potty break, make a boom-boom?"

"I'm solid, Sam." Terry dreamily watched the glowing tendrils growing off his fingers.

"How stoned are you?"

"Pretty stoned," he said in a bad Monty Python accent. "If truth needs be told, I'm mad as a stick but not sick as a parrot."

Sam banged her head twice on the steering wheel, then drove on in silence.

Valentina parked near the freeway entrance, giving Sam time to get up the road. If one of them got busted or hit by Breeze's boys, the other promised to finish the gig.

"One way or another, this thing ends," Sam said before they left.

"One way or another," Valentina echoed.

"There's a rumor going around I don't care about anyone but myself," Sam said.

"Jacob?"

"Kid hates me."

"No one likes seeing a hero fall off the pedestal. You'll always be my Princess Samantha, if that helps."

"More than you could know."

Before pulling onto the freeway, Valentina had Jacob light her a Marlboro. She let the smoke dribble out over her full lips. "Tastes like shit."

"So you keep saying." Jacob took a drag on his cigarette.

"How is Terry holding up?" Valentina tried to sound casual.

"Solid, just ask him."

"Does he talk about . . ."

"You? Does he like you? Maybe we should find a buttercup or make one of those paper thingamajigs with the numbers. A cootie catcher? You put them on your fingers and count off, find out if he loves you. Or a Magic 8 Ball?"

"You have one?" Valentina smiled. "I know I'm ridiculous. Maybe this is what an estrogen overdose looks like. He makes me crazy."

"Truth?"

"Please, Jacob."

"Terry is down the rabbit hole and stumbling in a land not of his making. Two weeks ago, he and I were hanging in the parking lot at Truman with the other smokers, arguing over whether Bowie or Rundgren would stand the test of time, trying to decide if we should go to trig or to Foothill Park and get stoned." Jacob lit a fresh cigarette off the ember of his current butt. "Terry's life is strange because he's my friend, and being near our family makes shit weird. But it is the fucking Brady Bunch compared to where we are now. Is he freaked out? Yes. By you?" He mimed shaking a Magic 8 Ball and reading it. "Reply hazy, try again."

Valentina relaxed, breathing slowly in and out. "I read this book, *Zen and the Art Of Motorcycle Maintenance*," Valentina said. "It was about how it is only when you stop and look back that the road makes any sense."

"Yeah, but 'we can't stop here this is bat country.'" Jacob quoted *Fear and Loathing in Las Vegas*.

"You're an odd lad, Jacob. But I do love you."

As the Galaxie crossed the Golden Gate Bridge and the Emerald

City receded in the rearview mirror, Valentina wondered if she would ever see the sparkling womb that gave her life again.

It was just after six when the Firebird hit Arcata. The sun was down, streetlights haloed in a fine layer of fog. It wasn't thick yet, but it was getting there. Parking in the alley behind Callum's apartment building, Sam told Terry and Jo Jo to wait in the car while she checked it out. Moving up the exterior stairs she walked with a confident stride—she belonged there, no question. Through the blinds she could see that Callum left in such a hurry he didn't even turn the lights off. Slipping a diamond-shaped pick into the lock she moved the pin. With a second skinny tool about the size and shape of an icepick, she rotated the tumbler. The deadbolt was a Schlage; a good enough lock, but for Sam it was too easy to be an enjoyable distraction.

Entering the apartment, she relocked the door behind her. No need to be surprised by an unwanted guest. On the coffee table sat an open beer with a small pool of condensation leaving a ring in the wood. She moved to the bedroom.

A man stepped out from behind the door and dropped an arm over Sam's neck. She struggled but he was stronger than her and had her in a headlock.

Instinctively she brought the heel of her Red Wing down on his arch.

He howled and released her.

Sam spun, saw her attacker.

Callum.

She swung a fist, but he blocked it and grabbed her wrist, pulling her in too close to strike again. "Stop," he said. "I don't want to hurt you."

"Funny, I want to hurt the hell out you, you duplicitous bastard."

He hugged her against his chest, lifting her off the floor. "Sam, listen, it's not what you think."

"Let me go, douchebag."

"No, listen. I'm not who you think I am."

"No shit, really?"

"I'm a cop."

This information winded her. She stopped struggling.

He released her, setting her down. "I work for the Drug Enforcement Administration."

"Prove it."

"Wait here." He moved to the closet and dug into a messy suitcase and slid open a hidden compartment. Returning, he handed her his Federal ID and badge.

"At least your name is Callum, you lying pig."

"I know it doesn't do any good, but I hated doing it."

"Means zero. You going to arrest me for the heist?" Sam was fighting to sound like she didn't care one way or the other.

"One, I work for the DEA—drugs are my only purview. Two, I set you up to pull the heist—that's called entrapment. You would skate."

"Then why, dickweed, did you sell me down the river?"

"I did it to get close to Breeze. He's my target."

"Now that makes me feel so much better. You fucked me to get to him."

"Not exactly. I fucked you because you drive me crazy. I set you up to get next to him."

"Now I should what?" Sam flipped her hands in the air in exasperation. "Trust you? Forgive you? What? Come on handsome, you tell me."

"Let's start with calling a truce and see where that leads." He stuck out his hand.

Sam looked down at the hand. "We're not there yet."

"So inviting you to bed would be an overreach?"

"Massive." Sam couldn't help a small smile from escaping.

"OK, we've established you didn't come here looking for a tumble, so why are you here? You taking Breeze down?"

"No. You first. Why haven't you busted the son of a bitch yet?"

"He promised a pile of dope to help set you up, only he never said exactly that. He spoke around it. Cautious and wily. He used an intermediary to deliver my stash. I don't have a solid link to him."

"Why not plant the weed on him?"

"Like you tried on me?"

"Found that?"

"Some Highway Patrol officer did. Nice trick." He winked. "My boss in D.C. had to chill them."

"So, why not set him up? I know you're not a Boy Scout."

"When I take him down, I want to make sure he stays down. And I was a Boy Scout, but that was a long time ago. Your turn. You here to take him down?"

Sam took a long breath. She looked in Callum's blue eyes, then looked away before her hormones did the talking. "I need your word you won't come after my crew."

"Then don't tell me about anything outside of the disco robbery. Keep to that and you're covered. You decide to kill anyone, like say, Breeze, I can't know about it."

"It may come to that."

"Really?"

"Don't worry, I won't tell you about it."

"Good. Be better you didn't do it in the first place."

"I'll keep that in mind."

A knock took Callum to the door. Through the peephole he saw a muscular young man. His eye makeup and sparkling Velvet Underground shirt gave him away as one of Sam's glitter crew, so he opened up.

Jo Jo stepped in front of Terry, pointing his Smith & Wesson .357 magnum at Callum's face.

"Jo Jo, this is Callum." Sam stepped between them. "He's a cop. Callum, this is Jo Jo. He's a . . . what are you, Jo Jo?"

"A handyman. A mechanic. A soldier. You choose," Jo Jo said.

"I think I'll go with enforcer," Sam said. "Put the piece away. We won't be shooting any cops quite yet."

"You say so." Jo Jo slid the revolver back into his shoulder holster. Finding the TV, he turned it on and settled into a bean-bag chair. *Welcome Back, Kotter* was midway through. Horshack mugged for the camera. Vinnie Barbarino said "Up your nose with a rubber hose." The audience cracked up.

Terry sat cross-legged on the shag carpet next to Jo Jo. He smiled at the innocence of the show and lit a joint. "Billy Holiday always knew when she was strung out because she could stand to watch TV. Clean she couldn't take it," Terry said.

"Yeah," Jo Jo said, his eyes not leaving the screen.

"It's a fact, I think."

"Hmmm?"

At the kitchen table Sam and Callum drank a couple of cold Heinekens. "I got no reason in the world to trust you," Sam said.

"What you don't have is a choice. Trust me or not, I may be your only ally in the straight world. This goes wrong, you will need a friend."

"Goes wrong? Man, that was three stations ago." After threatening to scalp him if he screwed her, Sam told Callum about the robbery and exactly whose money he had turned over to Breeze.

"You stole Jimmy the Hat Binasco's cash from Maurizio Binasco? Breeze knows whose cash it was?"

"Had to. You were backup. He sent Sardine and Cracker to take us off the board. He was looking to remove any link between him and the robbery."

"Balls. Cast iron balls on that guy. What's your plan to get to him?"

Sam struggled to come up with an answer, finally settling on a shrug.

CHAPTER 29

"A bit of the old ultra-violence."
—*A Clockwork Orange*

When the first gun went off it brought on a volley that sounded across the hills like thunder. Twelve hours earlier, Jacob swore his plan would be free of gunplay.

"Getting the cash is step one, and relatively easy," Jacob said, "compared to getting free of Humboldt alive." The crew was sitting around Callum's apartment. The coffee table was littered with pizza boxes, three large 'kitchen sinks' from Johnny's. Callum provided Heinekens all around. Jacob had been in favor of shooting Callum, cop or no. Sam took him outside.

"He may wind up being our only safety line if this deal goes Hindenburg on us," Sam said.

"You mean that, or you just hung up on the guy?"

"What?"

"Don't play innocent, Sam. If you bone or want to bone some cat, it's a clear sign they are wrong."

"Not always."

"Pretty much always. We could use you as a schmuck dowser."

Sam started to argue then thought better of it. "So, little brother, let's say you're right. What do we do? He's a fed."

"And thanks to you he knows we're planning to take Breeze down. We either use him or have Jo Jo drop him in the mighty Pacific. Me, I'm favoring plan B. You?"

"Breeze owns the local cops," Sam said.

"So you've said, more than once."

"Jacob, you need to let me off the hook and stop being such a dick."

"No, I actually don't. Get back to your point, local cops et cetera."

"If we get busted we may need our own cop, a fed, to clear our names."

"You sure . . . wait, that's not half bad."

"What's not?"

"My plan." Jacob thought a moment, then added, "You're going to need to call Maurizio Binasco."

Rapunzel's parking lot was half empty when Sam pulled in. Jo Jo sat in the passenger seat. "Remember, you keep quiet and look imposing," Sam told him.

"And if these punks want to fuck us up?"

"Then you go all mob thug on their asses."

Big Bob stood leaning by the door. The Winchester 30/30 looked small cradled in his huge arms. He stepped in front of Sam and Jo Jo. "Sam, you know I got orders to shoot you on sight."

"Hi Bob, you're looking . . . big."

"Who's he?" Big Bob nodded to Jo Jo.

Jo Jo moved up into the hillbilly's face. Neither man was used to being confronted by someone their own size. Jo Jo smashed his forehead down on Big Bob's nose, grabbed the Winchester and threw it skidding across the parking lot. Big Bob stumbled back but didn't go down. Blood ran down his face. He smiled, curling his hands into fists. Sam stepped between the two giants. Putting a palm on each, she tried to push them apart. It was like trying to move blocks of granite.

"Bob, this is Jo Jo. He works for the Binasco family. Breeze is going to be really pissed off if you fuck him up. Trust me on that."

Big Bob cocked his fist back.

"No shit, Bob, Binasco family," Sam said in a calm, almost friendly voice.

Big Bob slowly relaxed his arms and let them hang at his side. "Wait here. Lots of guns inside. Surprise Breeze and this gets bloody."

"No one wants that," Sam said.

As Big Bob turned to go, Jo Jo spoke under his breath. "Pussy."

Big Bob spun, ready to swing.

"Bob?" Sam said.

"All right, all right. But Breeze gives me the go ahead, I take this city boy apart."

"Leccami il culo."

"What the rat fuck does that mean? Huh?"

Jo Jo said nothing. His eyes were dead cold.

Big Bob stared back, muscles and veins popping from restraining his rage. "What did you say?"

"He said, get your ass inside before I lose my shit and tell Breeze you make the crib girls give you and your trucker buddies free tug jobs."

Big Bob twitched to that. "How you know that?"

"Girl talk. Jump now."

"OK, but no more wop talk. We speak American here. Got it?"

"He gets it." Finally Big Bob let Sam push him back. After he was gone through the door, Sam turned back to Jo Jo. "What did you say to him? I have to know if it was worth us almost dying."

"Lick my ass."

"Excuse me?"

"Not you. I told that redneck to lick my ass."

Sam almost smiled, almost said yeah that was worth it. Instead she kept an indifferent tone. "You fucking nuts, is that it, big man?"

"Guy's a punk. I don't like being pushed around."

"You a sensitive big poofta?"

"No, I . . . he just rubbed me wrong."

"Here on in, no one else gets hurt. You want me to tell Maurizio you, um, queered the deal?"

"That wouldn't be good for any of us."

"No, it would not. No more provoking the natives?" Sam stuck out her hand. Before Jo Jo could shake it Big Bob stepped out of the club. He was pressing a bar towel to his bloody nose. He told them Breeze was in his booth. He said he needed to search them. Sam raised her arms and let Big Bob do a quick pat down. That he copped a feel didn't surprise her. When he turned to pat down Jo Jo, things got tense again.

"I have a .357 magnum under my arm, a stiletto in my sock, a sap in my left jacket pocket, and a Walther .380 holstered to the back of my belt. Touch me and you get to see them all real close," Jo Jo said.

"This screwhead for real, Sam?"

"Real as a bullet in the brain, Bob. I wouldn't touch him."

Big Bob let out a long sigh. "I'll be back." He went into the strip club. They could hear the Allman Brothers Band's "Ramblin' Man" playing inside. Big Bob came back out the door. "OK, here's the deal. We got plenty of guns in there. You even fart too fast they will rain down on you."

"I can live with that," Jo Jo said.

"Or die, your choice." Pushing open the door, Big Bob stood back and let them enter.

Blond and freckled Angie was prancing around the stage. There were a few actual customers sitting at the rail. Rough-looking hillbillies occupied most of the shabby club. Sardine and Cracker cleared out of Breeze's booth. Breeze was dressed in black leather jeans, a white silk tee shirt and a half jacket. He got up and made a show of kissing Sam's hand.

"You look good, Sam, real good," Breeze said.

"Yeah? Not near as dead as you planned, right?"

"Ancient history, girl. Sit."

Sam sat, as did Breeze. Jo Jo stood, his back to them, scanning the room. He was ready to reach for his piece if needed.

"Drink?" Breeze asked.

"I don't think so. This ain't that kinda visit."

"Yeah, what kinda visit is this?"

"Kind that will either get you rich or get you killed."

"Sam, look around. You really want to threaten me?"

Sam shook out a Marlboro, calmly tapped the filter on the table, then stuck it in her mouth and looked at Breeze. He looked at her, smiled and flicked open his Zippo.

"You got some stones, girl."

"Funny, same thing Maurizio Binasco said about you. He also said you were dead meat."

"And yet, here I sit, handsome as ever."

"True. Question is . . ." Sam took a drag, then blew smoke into the room. "Question is, and this is important, do you want to go to war with the Italians?"

"The big guy is here to prove you speak for Binasco, right? What am I supposed to do, get all quivery and hand over a bag of cash? You really think that will happen?"

"It would be the simplest way."

"I'm a complex guy. How about this? What I could do, and this is a real option, I could chop you and the jolly giant into little chunks and send you back to the greaseball. Up here, I am the biggest swinging dick. So fuck Binasco where he breathes."

"Breeze, you are emperor up here, no doubt. I think I found a way we all walk away alive."

"Spill. And hurry, I'm getting bored with this crap."

"I convince Maurizio Binasco the money is gone—"

"That's true, or might as well be."

"—then instead of killing me and you and everyone we know, I tell him that you have something he could use. Pot. Your sinsemilla, in fact. If it is as good as you say, he'll take a hundred and fifty keys and call it even."

"One fifty!" Breeze slammed his hand onto the table, spilling his bourbon. "Get the fuck out of my face."

"Fair price." Sam dropped her cigarette butt in the spilled drink, where it sputtered out.

"Bullshit, bullshit, bullshit. He wants to buy my product with money I already have? Bullshit."

"Not bullshit. It's a way to stay alive and, as an added inducement, Breeze, he could become your preeminent customer. Wanna break into the San Francisco market? The Binasco family opens that door."

"Small carrot and zero stick, far as I can see. It was good seeing you, Sam. Sorry about what comes next." He motioned for Sardine to join them.

"Breeze, mouth to God, you are going to regret this. Wanna know why?"

"Not really." Breeze looked from her to Sardine. "Cousin, looks like the lady and this gentleman are—"

Jo Jo's first punch was an uppercut, landing under Sardine's jaw. The power of the blow lifted the hillbilly into the air and sent him tumbling back over a nearby table.

Cracker and six of his walleyed cousins stepped off from the bar, all reaching for pieces.

Sam reached up under the back of Jo Jo's blazer and pulled his Walther.

Big Bob ran across the room, head down like an angry bull, aiming straight at Jo Jo.

Sam took aim at Breeze's head.

Breeze put his hands in front of his face, shielding himself.

"Fucking flinch," Sam yelled. "Any of you motherfuckers fucking flinch and the boss man dies!"

Big Bob was moving too fast to stop his bulk from slamming into Jo Jo. Both men went down, shattering the corner of the booth. Breeze jumped up, scurrying away from Sam.

The gun in Sam's hand popped and spit a thin line of flame into the dark room.

Breeze froze, then realized she'd missed.

Sam fired, missed Breeze again. The third slug caught him in the thigh. He went down clutching his leg.

The boys at the bar all had guns out.

Sam took aim at Breeze's chest. "Tell your mutants to drop 'em or you're having dinner in hell." She had to shout to be heard over "If You Wanna Get to Heaven" by Ozark Mountain Daredevils. A redhead with huge tits and a skinny waist stood frozen on the stage. "Shut that fucking noise off or I kill him on principle." The needle scratched across the tracks and the room went silent, save Breeze's quiet whimpering.

"You fucking shot me."

"Next one is a killer. Ready to die, Breeze?"

"No. Boys, put your guns on the bar." The hillbilly hit squad didn't move. They kept their guns trained on Sam.

"'What we have here is a failure to communicate,'" Jacob said. He and Valentina stood just inside the door. Their M16s swept the boys at the bar.

Still on the floor, Sardine held an old single-action Colt. He started to turn his gun on the new arrivals.

"Do it," Valentina said, targeting him. "Let's get this bloodbath started."

"Breeze, talk to them," Sam said. "This shit is about to become irreversibly fucked."

Breeze used a chair to pull himself up until he was standing. "Boys, put that shit down."

"That crazy bitch will shoot me," Sardine said, eyes locked on Valentina.

"Or I will," Breeze said. "Do it now or incur my full fucking wrath." Slowly the hillbillies set their guns down. Sardine was last. He put his on the floor, in close reach if he needed it.

Jake stepped past Sam, his rifle aimed at Breeze. Moving close to the older man, Jacob spoke in a near whisper. "Breeze, right? Dumb name."

"Look, boy, my leg is killing me. I need a drink, so go play with someone else. Sam?"

Sam looked at Breeze and slowly shook her head.

"Who are you? Sam, who is this punk?" Breeze asked.

"He's my pissed off crazy brother.'

"And, I'm your last prayer," Jacob said. He nodded at Sam. She turned and helped Jo Jo to his feet. Jo Jo gave Big Bob a kick in the head, then pulled his revolver and moved to stand near Valentina. Sam walked past them, heading for the door.

"Sam, Sam, come on," Breeze said.

"Got to jet, Breeze," Sam said, then winked and walked out.

"That's better, no distractions," Jacob said. "Now about that drink. Make mine a Cuba Libre. That's a rum and Coke with lime to you."

"I know what a Cuba Libre is."

"Good, didn't mean to imply you were ignorant. What are you drinking?"

"Drinking? Who the fuck are you, boy?" Breeze asked, starting to raise his voice.

"Shhh. Take a seat, have a drink with me," Jacob said. "Valentina, what are you having?" he called over his shoulder.

"You think they know how to make a Grasshopper?" Valentina said.

Jacob looked at Breeze, who shook his head.

"Doesn't look like it."

"How about a Blue Moon? They have any Blue Curacao?" The bartender shook her head at Valentina. "I guess I'll pass then."

"How about you, Breeze—really is a dumb name—what are you drinking?" Jacob suddenly shouldered the M16 and took aim at Breeze's forehead. "Order a fucking drink."

"Fine. Shelly, Jack straight up and a Cuba Libre."

Jacob didn't say a word, just aimed at Breeze and waited for the cocktails to be built. Only after the bartender set them on the table and Jacob had taken a deep gulp did he speak. "This—we—are just the first wave. Binasco's people come up here? It will be scorched earth. Like Sherman, they will march you to the sea and leave only ashes in their wake."

"Who the fuck is Sherman? Sherman and Peabody, the cartoons? What?" Breeze asked.

"Not a fan of history, are you? Never mind. You'll hear from Mr. Binasco tomorrow." Jacob paused to take another pull off his drink. "He'll want to know where you'll be delivering his weed. I was you, I'd have a location all set up. Or, one hell of a hiding place." Jacob finished his drink, taking his time, relishing it. "It's the lime that makes it." He smiled, then backed slowly toward the door.

"I don't need to warn you, you hick bastards, not to step out that door, do I? Didn't think so," Valentina said as she and Jacob exited the bar. After a moment they heard Breeze shout something and "Gimme Three Steps" by Lynyrd Skynyrd started to thump through the walls.

Deep in the forest, Valentina pulled the Galaxie off the fire road they had been bouncing down. She killed the engine and lights and waited for Sam to join them and lead them out the back roads. If Breeze had been crazy enough to call his pet cops, they wanted to stay way off the main roads. Ten minutes and two cigarettes later the Firebird arrived in a cloud of dust. It flashed its lights twice and drove on. Valentina pulled out behind her. It took several hours, but finally they arrived at Callum's apartment.

Terry was sitting on the floor by a portable stereo. On a folddown turntable an LP was spinning. Terry was listening through a pair of headphones, his eyes half-lidded and brick red. The room reeked of pot smoke.

Sam pulled one of the earpieces away from Terry's head. "Where is Callum?"

Terry looked up at her, his eyes focusing. "You made it. Valentina, Jake?"

"Everyone is good, fine. Where is Callum?"

"Good. Yeah, good." Terry smiled in a far off way.

"Callum?"

"Out. Said he had something to do."

"He say what it was?"

"Nope, and I didn't ask. He has mostly shit taste in music. I did find some Roxy Music." Terry held up a black album jacket with art of a woman in implausibly tall heels and a beyond skintight Visqueen dress walking her pet panther.

"It's mine," Sam said. "So is the T. Rex."

"Makes sense." Terry put the headphones back on, closing his eyes.

Valentina looked at Terry for a long moment, then turned away. From the fridge she got a beer, took a long pull off the bottle. In the living area was a white, plastic, spherical chair. Valentina turned it to face the front door and sat down. Resting the M16 across her lap, she drank in silence.

Jacob looked from Valentina to Terry to Sam, who shrugged.

Jo Jo broke the silence. "What'd I miss? Seems to me we just showed a room full of punks who's boss. A celebration wouldn't be too far out of order."

Jacob looked at him and walked out.

"What's with Jacob?" Jo Jo said to Sam.

"A whole lot of none of your business."

"Fine, fucking weirdoes." Jo Jo turned on the TV and started clicking the channels around the dial. News, news, reruns, reruns. He settled on *The Six Million Dollar Man*.

Behind the apartment building, the Firebird was shrouded in fog. Jacob sat in the driver's seat singing along with Ziggy Stardust. "I'm an alligator, I'm a mama-papa coming for you. I'm the space invader, I'll be a rock 'n' rollin' bitch for you." Bowie brought some semblance of normalcy. He had traveled so far from Foothill Park. A little over a week ago he and Candy had been in her car singing and talking about going to college.

Now it felt like it was forever ago and a million miles away.

In the strip club, confronting Breeze, he had just been playing a roll, an improv like in drama class. An improv like De Niro and Keitel in *Mean Streets* or *Taxi Driver.*

"You talking to me?" he said into the rearview mirror. "I'm the only one here, who the fuck are you talking to?"

He felt like crying. His heart was pounding. He felt like running away. He felt like driving down the coast to be with Candy. He felt like following Terry's lead and getting massively stoned. What he did was turn up the music and try to let his mind go blank.

"I shot Breeze," Sam told Callum.

"Did you kill him? And if you did, I don't want to know."

"In the leg. He'll live. But how fucked up is that? I shot him, would have killed him I think, if it went that way." They were sitting at his kitchen table.

Behind them Jo Jo was laid out on the couch snoring. A rerun of *Gilligan's Island* hummed on the TV. Terry was lying in a fetal position, headphones on, eyes scrunched shut. Valentina hadn't moved from her vigil guarding the door.

"Looked in the mirror a minute ago and I scarcely recognize myself," Sam said. "That's kinda bullshit. I can see me—I know it's me—but in the eyes . . . I don't know her. Fuck it. Maybe I'm just tired."

"Kid, no one plans to grow up and shoot someone. No one. It don't make you bad or evil or broken or whatever story that lovely mind of yours is cooking up. Just means you did what you had to do to stay on this side of a dirt nap."

"Dirt nap? You're so hard boiled."

"Yes, ma'am, I am. Tough as nails and twice as sharp." Callum winked.

"You ever shoot anybody?" Sam asked.

"Yes."

"Kill them?"

Callum paused for a long moment. When he spoke his voice was flat. "Once. Nogales. A counterfeit ring. I was FBI then. A good old boy decided he'd rather try to kill my partner than get arrested. Shot him twice in the back. He bled out before the medics arrived. It was him or my partner. I made the right choice."

"You ever think about it?"

"Not much. Time helps."

Sam reached out and took his hand, squeezing it. "I still think you're a duplicitous dick."

"Fair enough." He looked from her eyes down to her lips and back to her eyes. "You take the bed."

"I will." She released his hand and stood up.

"Any chance I can join you?"

"Not a one." At the door to the bedroom she turned back to him. "We'll talk again, if we survive tomorrow."

"Yes we will, kid, you're not shed of me yet."

Sam kissed him on the cheek and slowly closed the door.

Lying on the bed she pulled a pillow to her chest. She could smell him in the sheets. She wasn't screwing him, that had to be progress. His rich musk called to her. She would be strong. She would prove Jacob wrong.

When she opened the bedroom door Callum was still standing

there, as if he knew she would cave in. She found his self-assured-ness very sexy. That and his damn Burt Reynolds mustache. He was no Thin White Duke, he was . . . a man. She needed to lose herself in need. She led him to bed. He started to speak but she put a finger on his lips.

"One word and the fuck's off," she said without even a hint of a smile.

CHAPTER 30

"Here she comes, you better watch your step."
—*The Velvet Underground*

Sunrise found Jacob in the Firebird, his sweaty face pressed against the glass, clearing a face-sized space in the condensation that blocked the rest of the windows.

In the dream he was in a dark forest. He had the M16 and was turning in a circle trying to see where the danger was coming from. An animal screamed behind him. He spun and let rip. Bullets lacerated leaves and branches, tore into a shadowed form. Candy fell from the brush. A bullet hole in her chest gushed blood. Jacob dropped the gun and tried to run to Candy. His legs were stuck in quicksand, unmoving. He fought to scream but he couldn't make a sound. He was forced to mutely watch as Candy bled out into the rotting leaves that covered the jungle floor. Behind him the animal growled again.

Jacob's eyes popped open. Where was he, where was Candy? Fuck. Dead. No. He was in the Firebird. As the dream receded his heart slowed. His neck hurt. And then reality set in. He remembered the day before, and the day ahead, his heart started to pound again. He dug a crumpled pack of Marlboros from the pocket of the brown velvet blazer Candy had stolen for him. He straightened out a bent cigarette. Rolling down the window, he sparked his Bic and sucked in the blue smoke. Slowly, the nicotine calmed his nerves and brought on the numbness that made reality almost bearable.

Jacob was on his second cigarette when the Humboldt County Sheriff's car pulled to a stop in front of the apartment building. He slid down in the seat. A potbellied older officer in a khaki uniform and campaign hat lumbered out. He reminded Jacob of Ernest Borgnine in *The Wild Bunch*. Climbing the single flight of stairs winded the lawman. At Callum's door he adjusted his Sam Browne gun belt. One hand on his pistol, he used the other to knock. Even from across the street Jacob could hear the powerful blows on the door.

Jacob turned over the Firebird's engine. He was about to lay on the horn, figuring he could draw the cop off, hoping he could out-run him. Before his hand hit the horn, he looked up and saw the apartment door open. Callum stepped out dressed in only a pair of jeans. They spoke for a moment. The lawman jabbed Callum in the chest and he raised his hands in a sign of placation. After a short conversation Callum went back into his apartment. The law-man waited on the balcony. Five minutes later Callum came back out, dressed and carrying his leather jacket. They didn't speak as they walked down the stairs, got in the police car and drove away. Jacob waited until they rounded the corner, then stepped out of the Firebird.

"I don't trust him," Jacob told Sam. She was in Callum's bed, a sheet pulled up over her naked body.

"I do."

"You trusted Jinks."

"This is different. He's a cop."

"Oh, he's a cop, right. When exactly did you start trusting cops?"

"He's . . ." Sam struggled to find any logic to back up her gut.

Jacob looked down at her and the bed. "You boned him. Un-fucking-believable. He has a goddamn mustache."

"Jake—"

"No. Don't want to hear it. Don't care. Where did he go? I care about that. That is germane to digging our way out of this massive shit pile you put us in. Boning him, not germane. So, where did he go?"

"To Rapunzel's, to see Breeze. The phone was off the hook, so the sheriff came to take him up there."

"Leastways that's what mustache told you."

"I got the number that will get us clear of this clusterfuck." She plucked a matchbook off the nightstand and tossed it to Jacob. The matches had a silhouetted girl bending over on the cover.

"Brass Rail. A strip club. This helps us how?"

"Inside."

"Oh."

"For a genius you can be kind of thick."

Under the flap Jacob found a handwritten number. "And?"

"For the DEA, Callum's field office. Once we know where and when the meet is, I'll let him know. That way he can be there, watching. We put Breeze with the dope, he'll ride in with enough feds to sew the whole hillbilly crew up."

"But he'll let us skate, right?" Jacob gave a mirthless laugh.

"We'll be his CIs."

"What about Binasco? He doesn't get his weed, we're still on the hook."

Sam flashed her bother a smile. "Got it handled."

"If mustache doesn't show?"

"We play out the deal with Binasco and Breeze, hope neither are holding homicidal grudges."

"I don't like it," Jacob said, "but I'm out of ideas."

"You? You are out of ideas?"

"Shooting blanks. So . . ."

"We trust Callum."

"No, we hope like hell that you have made a correct assessment," Jacob said, then pointed out they were no longer safe in the apartment. Sam had to agree. It wasn't worth risking their lives on her gut feeling. While Sam got dressed, Jacob woke Terry and Jo Jo. Valentina hadn't slept and looked a little crazy around the eyes.

Breeze, Callum . . . hell, any of the players out there would recognize the Firebird, so they all climbed into the Ford Galaxie and headed down the highway. Jo Jo bitched about wanting breakfast, but no one paid him any attention so he let it go.

Terry rolled a joint and fired it up without a word. When Jacob suggested he ease off on the dope Terry just asked him to turn the radio up and took another deep toke. Elton John and Kiki Dee were singing a love song when they drove past the Humboldt County line marker.

At a payphone outside the Ukiah Natural Foods Co-op, Sam called Maurizio Binasco.

"You got a lovely mother," Maurizio said. "Shouldn't leave her all alone."

"Do you go a day without threatening someone's family?"

"No threat, Sam, just pointing out a simple fact of life. You got my pot?"

"Soon."

"You gonna screw me?"

"No."

"Right. You even gonna think of screwing me?"

"Never." Sam pushed the receiver down, killing the connection. Through the window she could see her crew eating and drinking coffee in the Co-op. She dropped a dime and dialed the number for Rapunzel's. It took less than a minute for the bartender to give the phone to Breeze.

"Just got off the phone with Binasco, deal is set."

"And by deal you mean you getting to rape me, right?"

"Actually, Breeze, that was the original plan. May still be, let's see how this plays out. 'Cash, grass or your ass,' his words."

"I think I heard that before someplace."

"Me too. What'll it be?"

"I think, and I mean the wop bastard no disrespect, but I think he can blow me. Unless you want to do it for him?"

"Breeze, no shit now. You do not want to go to war with these guys."

"I was just fucking with you, girl." Breeze let out a pinched laugh. "You know the upper meadow off that fire road, leads past Jenny Tyrell's place?"

"Yeah, middle of goddamn nowhere."

"Close to it. Tell him to be there at five, I will make him a happy man."

"Him? That's not part of the deal. You go through me."

"Trust you, right? Some humungo greaseball shows up and you say he's from Binasco, and I what? Roll over and give you a small mountain of sinsemilla? Never, ever happen." Breeze finished speaking and let the silence hang between them.

"I'll see what I can do. No promises."

"Only way this works." Breeze hung up.

Sam looked in again through the glass. Terry was staring at an onion bagel, stoned to the gills. Valentina was arguing with Jo Jo. Jacob was stoic. All Sam had to do was keep them together until they had the pot in hand and this would all be over. It should be a simple transaction. Should. The word rang in her head like a death knell.

Terry was numb. He knew he had a body, just couldn't feel it.

"I know you want some peach pie." The hippy chick waitress slid the slice down in front of Terry. Her nametag said Star. She had long, shiny, chestnut hair in a thin braid with beads in it.

"Thanks." Terry forked a piece into his mouth. "Not bad."

"You have a nice smile," Star said. "You wanna smoke?"

"Oh, hell yes." Terry followed Star through the store.

Valentina watched as Terry disappeared past a row of granola, down the cereal aisle. Her eyes were stone cold.

"I'm sorry, Val," Jacob said.

"I'm not. Great guy, hope he gets what he wants."

"He's so wasted he has zero clue about what he wants."

"He's pretty clear about what he doesn't want." Valentina took a drink from her coffee mug. Jacob wanted to say something, but Val was gone to some faraway private place.

Star sat down on the small loading dock. She patted the spot beside her and Terry sat down. "You are running with a very, um, different group."

"They're alright. My friends."

"Oh yeah, totally, like, cool." Reaching into her bra, Star took out a skinny joint. "Sinsemilla, like, takes you home. Almost better than sex, like, almost." She giggled.

Terry took out his Bic and sparked the joint for her. After a deep hit, she passed it to him. Terry looked at the joint. A pure connoisseur, he rolled it between a finger and thumb, sniffed the smoke, took a lungful and let it expand in his chest. He didn't choke or cough. "Smooth. Where's it from?"

"Joey Shark. You, like, know him?"

"No. Where was it grown?"

"A dude up in Humboldt. It's, like, amazing, right? Mellow and powerful, kinda like you."

Terry smiled and took another hit.

Star looked at him, very serious. "We can do it if you, like, want. I have a station wagon."

Terry held the smoke in. Looking her up and down he smiled. She was hot and looking hotter with every hit.

Sam sat in the restaurant. Picking up a fork, she carved off a piece of the peach pie.

"That's Terry's," Jacob said.

"I don't mind sloppy seconds." Sam took a big bite and smiled. Gulping it down with a swallow of Terry's coffee, she turned to Jo Jo. "I need to know, for real, does Maurizio have any men, other than you?"

"Have or can get?" Jo Jo said.

"Access to, is that clearer? How many could he have up here in say, the next seven hours?"

"Um, yeah, that would be mostly me."

"Good to know." She looked at Valentina, shaking her head subtly. "Good news is, I don't have to worry about him trying to take us down. Bad is, we are fucked if Breeze goes bush bandit on us. Consolation prize is, we won't go down alone." Sam stood and walked back outside. On the payphone she called Maurizio again. She gave him the address of the Co-op, told him he needed to be there by four if he wanted his weed. Yes, he bitched. Yes, he threatened. But faced with not coming up with the cash for his uncle he agreed to come.

Sam made one more call, this one to the Drug Enforcement Administration. She left a message for agent Callum Stark, letting him know where the deal would go down. "Upper meadow, above Jenny's place. Near where we saw the red-tail. And tell him I'll signal once I'm sure it's not lawn cuttings or bricks of oregano."

Having Binasco in on the deal was a big complication, but she was good at solving on the fly. The pieces were in motion now.

No turning back.

No calling quits.

Olly olly oxen free.

Win or lose no middle ground.

All that was left was waiting.

Maybe Terry was the only sane one. Maybe they should all get blazed to ride this wild pony of a plan home.

Or die trying.

CHAPTER 31

"Cry 'Havoc!' and let slip the dogs of war."
—William Shakespeare

Deep in the Humboldt Mountains, Sardine and Cracker moved through the woods. They were dressed in hunting camo, rifles slung over their backs. They left the van on a fire road two miles downhill.

"Poison oak." Cracker pointed at the oily, bright green plant on the side of the animal trail they were walking on.

"I can see that. I seem stupid to you?"

"I was just tryin' to . . . never mind."

"No, say it. You were trying to what? Help?"

"Yeah, but no good deed . . . right?"

Sardine stopped, snapped off a thin branch from a Scotch Broom and used it to scratch between his shoulders. "Why the hell are we tramping through the woods like a couple of hobos while Big Bob, Clem and them is riding with cousin Breeze?"

"Maybe he blames us for not taking care of Sam and her people."

"You think? Been colder than a polar bear's balls ever since we got back. He treats Big Bob like family and us'n like we was the help."

"We best get moving," Cracker said, slapping a gnat on his neck. "Don't want to piss him off more than he is."

"I ain't his bitch, you know. We move when I say we move."

"When would that be?"

Sardine waited for ten seconds, looking at the trees, casual. Then he started to walk again. Cracker followed without saying anything. Twenty more minutes and they came to the upper meadow. Sardine took out his pocket watch, which was strung with a leather thong to his belt loop. He tapped the watch's crystal as he spoke. "Thirty minutes early, just like I said we would be. Think cousin Breeze will think to give us a nod for that?"

"I don't know, maybe."

"No, Cracker, he won't. This deal jumps the track, they start shooting, we should let him and Big Bob fry. Don't lift a finger. That's what we should do." But even as he said it he was looking for a good tree to fire from.

Five on the dot, the black Lincoln and the Ford Galaxie entered the meadow from the east. The Galaxie pulled up and stopped beside the Lincoln. Sam stepped out of the driver's side. Maurizio and Jo Jo joined her. They leaned on the hood of the Lincoln and waited.

Somewhere in the tree line behind them Valentina was moving into position.

Jacob knelt by the Ford's trunk, rifle in hand.

Terry checked the snubnose. Finding the cylinder loaded, he snapped it closed and slipped it into his pants, pulling his tee shirt over it. He joined Sam and Maurizio.

No one said a word.

A '63 Dodge Power Wagon carryall bounced up a rutted mud track, entering the meadow from the west. It stopped a hundred feet away. Breeze climbed from the Dodge. He and three men in overalls and Pendleton shirts leaned on the hood of the Dodge, mimicking Maurizio. The men all held hunting rifles.

Valentina wrapped the M16's sling around her forearm. Leaning against a massive redwood's trunk she took aim at Breeze. Cut down their boss and these hillbillies would fall apart. Least that was her thinking. Seemed right in theory. The redwood forest looked nothing like the Indochinese jungle, but it sure felt the same. The air was cool, yet beads of sweat bloomed on her brow and soaked her underarms. She flicked the fire control from safe to burst. A pull of the trigger would release three rounds at a time, conserving ammo in case the enemy didn't head for the hills and instead stuck around for a firefight.

Big Bob said something to Breeze then, with Winchester in hand, walked east through the tall grass.

Sam stepped off and walked out to meet Big Bob.

"That should be me," Sardine said, watching it play out in the crosshairs of his scope.

"Needs be, you want me to take Sam or the big Italian?" Cracker also had his scope to his eye.

"The bitch is mine." Sardine targeted Sam's head.

Sam looked straight at the huge man coming toward her, then flicked her eyes down to scan the ground. If she tripped in a gopher hole, carnage and destruction would paint the meadow.

They stopped a few feet apart.

"What do you say, Bob?" Sam sidled to the left slightly, giving Jacob a clean shot.

Jacob tasted bile. His stomach hurt, had been knotted from the moment he picked up the M16. A cold wind pressed against his back, blowing his long hair forward. He didn't dare take his hand off the trigger long enough to sweep it back. He kept the iron sights planted dead center on the huge hillbilly. At this distance, even with a clear shot he wasn't sure he could avoid hitting his sister. She'd told him she would make it simple—if she went down he was to throw the entire clip at the fat fuck. His heart was pounding like a frightened jackrabbit. *This is when you discover just what kind of man you are. Travis Bickel or Richie Cunningham? Bullets don't lie. Fuck.*

Big Bob looked past Sam to the Italians and spat a stream of brown tobacco juice. "See you brung the asswipe coward that sucker-punched and kicked me in the head."

"Bob, you aren't harboring any ill feelings are you?"

"Not *harboring* anything. I hate the guy."

"That's what—"

"I get a chance, I'm gonna shove my boot so deep up his wop ass he can wear it as a hat."

"The boot or the ass?" Sam asked.

"What?"

"Which is he going to wear as a hat?"

"Um." Big Bob blinked two, three times. "I'm gonna fuck him up, all I'm saying."

"Got it. How about we leave that for later, and you, Bob, tell me how Breeze wants to handle this."

Big Bob told her to send her punk brother over to them. When they had him, Breeze would meet with Binasco. "Anyone fucks with Breeze, we cut the kid down."

Sam stared up at the monster hillbilly. "You hurt my brother, I'll kill you."

"You kinda have to say that, don't you? Him being kin and all."

"I will."

"OK." Big Bob just stared at her. He waited while she walked back through the grass.

Jacob didn't relax his stance as Sam moved toward him. The huge hillbilly had the rifle resting in the crook of his arm, still a threat. Jacob kept his finger on the trigger until Sam was safely behind the Galaxie. He set the gun down, rubbing his sweaty hands on his jeans. He listened while she explained they wanted him as a hostage before Breeze would come out in the open.

"Val will have you covered the whole time." Sam lit a cigarette, took a hit and passed it to him. "I wouldn't ask you to do it if she didn't."

"Yes, you would, because you don't see any other way this plays out. We don't know where Val is or what she'll be covering."

"Callum and the feds are out there too, watching. He won't let you get hurt."

"Again, maybe si, maybe no. He is or isn't out there, and he will or won't act. Variables. Lots and lots of variables."

"Don't do it then. Your call, Jake. We can pack up and jet right now." She took back the cigarette and inhaled.

"No, actually, we can't. You and I know that. We run, they will give chase. Either Maurizio's family or these *Deliverance* rejects or the feds will nail us. I wimp out, we all pay."

"Or we choose door number three, little brother."

"Three?"

"Yeah, there's always a door number three—we draw down on these pricks and blast away. Any luck Maurizio and Breeze will kill each other, and the feds will clean up the rest."

Jacob stood. "How about, no one gets shot today." He leaned the M16 against the Galaxie's trunk and walked out into the open.

"I will get you out of this, Jake, I will."

"Our wills and fates do so contrary run," Jacob said.

"Shakespeare?"

"*Hamlet*. You will try, and then what happens, will happen. No deus ex machina, I fear."

"Will you settle for deus ex Valentina?"

"Sure." Fighting the trembling that threatened to take over, Jacob walked past his sister and into the meadow.

"Don't do nothing stupid." Big Bob aimed at Jacob's belly.

"I'm cool." Jacob kept his hands away from his body and let Big Bob pat him down.

"Let's get to it." Big Bob shoved the Winchester's barrel between Jacob's shoulder blades and pushed him toward Breeze. At the touch of the steel it got real. Jacob's stomach lurched. Involuntarily he bent over and puked up a mixture of organic muffin, coffee and bile.

"Son, that's disgusting."

"Said the man with shit-brown teeth." Jacob's fear was driving his words, as if he thought speaking would keep him alive. Knew it was bullshit. Couldn't help it.

"The hell you say?"

"Nothing." Jacob wiped his mouth on his shirtsleeve. "Just that people with not only shit-brown teeth but brown drool staining their beards really shouldn't throw stones. Glass houses being what they are."

"I hope Sam screws this up and I get to pop you." Shoving the barrel again, Big Bob marched Jacob to where the other hillbillies were standing around the Dodge 4x4.

"It's the little man with the big words," Breeze said, then looked from Jacob to Clem, a walleyed man holding a Ruger Blackhawk. "If they even look like they want to play us, make him into a stain in the grass."

"A grass stain?" Jacob tried to shut up, really he did, he couldn't help it. "I bet that sounded much tougher in your head."

Breeze grabbed the carbine from Big Bob and cracked the butt against the bridge of Jacob's nose. Pain flooded in. Jacob's knees buckled and he fell to the ground, holding his face. Blood ran through his fingers. Oddly, now that it was happening he felt some relief. The pain was real, but not as devastating as he thought it would be.

"What, nothing funny to say now, huh? Nothing?"

Jacob slowly shook his head.

When Sam saw Breeze hit Jacob, she started to move. Maurizio put out his arm stopping her. "Think about it, girl. Your brother has some stones, let him play his hand."

"Fuck that."

"No, fuck us if you get emotional and blow the deal. You sold me on this cash for pot deal. I, in turn, sold my uncle on the idea that I would invest his cash in pot. Screw this up and those backwoods balordi will be the last goddamn thing any of us will worry about."

Across the field Sam saw her brother stand. His legs wobbled, but he stood.

Valentina flicked the sight from Breeze to the man holding the revolver aimed at Jacob. If she fired, she wasn't sure she could turn off the man's motor functions before he shot Jacob. Hell, at three hundred feet using iron sites she wasn't sure she could make the shot at all.

"Let's get this done," Sam said. "Terry, you're up."

Terry checked the load on his snubnose for the umpteenth time.

Sam hung the M16's sling over her shoulder. She nodded at Maurizio and Jo Jo. The four of them crossed the field. Breeze moved out and met them midway. He was walking with a cane and had developed a pronounced limp.

Jo Jo stepped up to search Breeze.

"I don't carry a piece."

"Mr. Binasco wants to be sure you aren't wearing a wire."

"He wants to know what? Fine, here." Breeze lifted his polyester shirt, rumpling the tiger print. He turned in a circle, showing them his pale chest. Next he dropped his pants. A bandage around his thigh where Sam had shot him oozed a little blood. He wasn't wearing any underwear, but he didn't seem to care as he did another circle.

Maurizio looked Breeze up and down taking his full measure. "You the babbo took my cash?"

Breeze pulled up his pants. "To be fully accurate, Sam here took your cash. I stole Sam's cash."

"To be fully accurate, I don't give rat's ass. You had it, and she tells me you spent it or lost it. Point is, you don't have it. You should get down on your knees and thank her. Wasn't for this one, you would be dead. She convinced me to accept your product as payment in kind. Quality is the final question." Maurizio nodded at Terry. "That is where he comes in."

Breeze smiled. "Your royal taster?"

"Something like that." Maurizio let his face go stone still. Together they walked back to the Power Wagon. Big Bob and two other hillbillies stepped back, but kept their hands on their guns, ready. Clem kept the Ruger pointed at the back of Jacob's head.

"Breeze, friend to friend," Sam said, "a sniper has you dialed in. Anything happens to Jake or any of my crew . . . You see my point. You might want to have your boys relax. Anyone's gun goes off, you will be dropped."

Breeze glanced around the woods ringing the meadow. "I used to like you."

"Had a damn funny way of showing it."

"That was business, baby, just business," Breeze said, reaching into his jacket. Everyone froze. Breeze laughed, showing a tortoise shell cigarette case. Opening it, he pulled out a joint. Maurizio shook his head and pointed at the Dodge.

"You aren't a real trusting mother-trucker are you?" Breeze asked.

Maurizio shook his head again.

"Keeping your mouth shut, just in case one of my boys is wired?"

Maurizio nodded. Then flicked his eyes from Terry to the Dodge. On the middle seat sat a large pile of kilo bricks, each wrapped in a black plastic garbage bag and taped tight. Terry took one from the middle of the pile. Jo Jo snapped his stiletto open and passed it to Terry, who made a small slit in the plastic. Taking out a bud he did his connoisseur routine—rolled it between a finger and thumb, sniffed it, then took out his Zig-Zags, broke the bud up and expertly rolled a joint.

The revolver pressed against Jacob's skull, cold and menacing. His eyes met Terry's. This was the deepest down the rabbit hole either of the friends had ever been. Movies made it look cool and fun. This was real. Fuck up and it's permanent.

Terry looked away before Jacob's panic-stricken eyes infected him. He concentrated on his lighter and the joint. Firing the Bic, he let the paper at the tip burn down before taking a deep hit. He held it, offering the joint to Maurizio, who shook his head. Terry looked at the others, holding out the joint.

Big Bob started to reach for it.

Breeze slapped Big Bob's outstretched hand. "This ain't a hootenanny, you fucking hayseed."

Big Bob looked pissed, clutched the Winchester.

Terry jetted a stream of smoke and grinned. "Solid. Nice mellow coming on hard. Yeah, it is the goods. Should go forty, fifty a lid if you brand it right, catchy name. Humboldt Haymaker or some such."

Sam nodded broadly, her eyes flicking to the forest, searching for Callum and his people, hoping they got her signal.

Clem's Ruger was still on Jacob, but he was looking at Breeze.

A bucktoothed, balding towhead aimed a twelve-gauge goose gun at Terry's chest. From three feet he couldn't miss. Terry would have been freaking out, except the pot's buzz was keeping his head calm.

"Hundred and sixty large profit," Breeze said to Maurizio. "All that green and you ain't even smiling a little bit?"

Maurizio shrugged and spun his finger in the air, telling his people to wrap it up.

Jo Jo collected the Lincoln, drove it across the meadow. It wasn't long before the trunk was loaded.

Maurizio leaned into Jo Jo and whispered in his ear, using him as his mouthpiece. "Boss says he is pleased with the deal. He wants to know if you can provide the same product next month."

"Hell, yes. I got enough drying in these hills to make us both rich men."

"Good. He'll be in touch."

"What about Sam and her crew? They traveling under your protection?" Breeze asked.

Maurizio whispered again to Jo Jo, who looked angry but repeated his boss's words. "He says fuck her. Sorry, Sam." He gave her a sad nod.

"Really?" Sam said. "Fuck me? I just made you a bundle."

"You also ripped him off, so you're pretty even." Jo Jo looked from her to Breeze. "Let her crew walk or bury them. They're yours to do what you will." Jo Jo's eyes rested for a moment on Jacob's terrified face. Turning quickly away, Jo Jo walked to the Lincoln and got behind the wheel.

Maurizio took one more look at Breeze, then at Sam's angry eyes. He shrugged and climbed in the back of the big black sedan.

Breeze waited until the Italians disappeared into the forest, then slowly turned on Sam, his face hardening.

CHAPTER 32

"Do not go gentle into that good night."
—*Dylan Thomas*

"Breeze, Breeze, think. Sniper," Sam said. "You want revenge, or you want a walk away?"

"Not really sure at this moment. On the one hand, I'm pissed. But the other hand is full of cash."

"Look at it this way. I brought you a steady buyer. He is going to break you into the lucrative San Francisco market. Fact is, you should kick us a taste. You know, cover my crew and costs." Sam's eyes kept flicking to the trees. *Where the fuck was Callum?*

"You got some balls on you, Sam."

"They're called ovaries—solid steel, clank when I walk." She turned from Breeze to the walleyed man standing over her kneeling brother. "Clem?"

"Yeah, Sam?"

"You really want to take the gun off my brother." She made an exaggerated gesture, pointing at Clem.

"What's that?" Clem's eyes darted from Sam down to Jacob and back. "What are you doing?"

"Telling my snipers that you go first. Can you feel death calling your name?" She whispered his name, slow and spooky.

"Breeze?" Clem was starting to look worried.

"You keep the pistol on that boy. Don't and I'll shoot you myself."

"Sure, sure, Breeze, just—"

"No just. Big Bob, get me Sam's parting gift." Breeze snapped his fingers and Big Bob dropped the tailgate of the Dodge and dragged out a trussed up man with a gunnysack over his head. Big Bob dropped the man at Breeze's feet. With the flourish of a magician Breeze whipped the bag off.

Callum blinked. Even in the dimming late afternoon light, his eyes needed to adjust. He tried to speak but it came out a jumbled mumble through his bloodstained gag.

"I'd offer him a last meal, but 'fraid he couldn't eat it," Breeze said with a cruel smile.

Sam's heart started to pound as it sank in that they were alone and very likely going to die.

"Turns out your ex-boyfriend is a cop," Breeze said. "Had me fooled. Then again, I wasn't balling the dude. You must feel real stupid."

"Son of a bitch is many things, but he isn't a cop. I'd have known." Sam fought for calm.

"You would think so. But nope. Sheriff Winslow intercepted a message from Washington. Word is, this piece of shit was coming after me. DE fucking A. He's one of Nixon's boys."

"Ironic, you used him to set me up for this whole ride, all the time he was setting you up." Sam was riffing. As long as she was talking no one was getting shot. "One question, Breeze. I have to know. Did he give you my mother's number? That how you knew where to find me?"

"That he did, and yes it was," Breeze said. "Thought you might want to pull the trigger. Hell hath no fury and all that."

"Well fuck him, sure, but if he's a cop, Breeze . . . you can't kill a cop."

"No, I can't. That's why I'm gonna have you do it." Breeze put

out his hand, palm up and Big Bob placed an old revolver in it.
"Sam, you are going to shoot this piggly wiggly or I am going to
shoot you and these fine young dudes. You choose."

The towhead aimed at Terry. He had a vacant look that was
maybe more frightening than anger.

Clem pressed the Ruger into the top of Jacob's scalp.

Breeze placed the revolver in Sam's hand. "You are out of options, little girl."

"Don't do it, Sam," Jacob said. "They'll kill us anyway, have to,
to clean up loose ends."

"Little bro has a dark world view," Breeze said.

"Breeze, you promise me, I shoot him, you let us walk."

"Scout's honor." He held up two fingers in a Boy Scout salute.

Sam looked down at Callum.

"Please, no," Jacob said.

Sam aimed the revolver at Callum's head.

Callum's face went from pleading to resignation.

Breeze nodded to Big Bob, who took a Kodak Instamatic from
his jacket pocket and tossed it to him. "Cheese," Breeze said and
snapped the shutter. The flashcube lit Sam pointing the gun at
Callum. "OK, now a fun one, something goofy. No, I'm kidding.
Just pull the trigger and we can get out of this cold and into a warm
bar."

"Don't," Jacob said.

Sam needed to save her brother and Terry.

She needed to pull the trigger.

"I can't."

"Then you choose piggly wiggly over little bro. Clem." Breeze
nodded at the hillbilly. "Time to earn your pay,"

"No. Wait. I'll do it." Sam was resolved. *It is us or them. He is them. Them always loses out to us.* She started to put pressure on the trigger. The hammer rose. The cylinder started to turn.

There was a flash of fire from the grass twenty feet to their left. Three bullets struck the towhead. From the jaw up, his head disintegrated into a bloody puff. He tumbled backward.

Sam swiveled the revolver's barrel to Clem and pulled the trigger. The shot was high and wild. Clem whipped the barrel up from Jacob's head, firing without aiming. He was trying to kill Sam. His shot was low. Blood danced off Callum's head and he fell onto his side.

Big Bob aimed into the meadow, searching for the sniper.

Valentina steadied herself against the redwood's trunk. She took a gentle breath, held it and fired. A three shot burst hit dead center of the giant hillbilly's chest.

Big Bob fell like a tree crashing to the earth.

A bullet singed Valentina's wig as it whizzed past her. Bark jumped from the trunk above her. A second slug dug up the dirt five feet to her left. The shots came from the tree line on the opposite side of the meadow, but their exact location was a mystery. They, on the other hand, sure as hell had her position dialed in. Dropping to her belly she thumbed the M16's selector to full auto. Her people needed her. She let rip with a burst of suppressing fire. Aiming high, the Dodge rocked and its glass shattered from the impacts.

Sardine and Cracker fired a volley toward Valentina's position, kicking up chunks of dirt and grass. She lay motionless.

Breeze took off, heading to the trees from where Sardine was shooting, limping away as fast as possible.

Jacob dropped onto his belly, crawling under the Dodge. He was in full-on freak-out mode.

Clem and Sam stood aiming at each other.

Sam shook her head. "Walk away, Clem."

Clem turned and ran after Breeze.

Sardine and Cracker continued to fire across the meadow.

Valentina rolled to the left. On her back she flipped the magazines and slapped the fresh one home. Bullets sprayed dirt and snapped the branches around her. They didn't have her yet, but they would if she fired or ran.

Terry slipped his hand into his pocket, finger wrapping around the snubnose's grip.

Sam dragged Callum out of the line of fire, putting the Dodge between them and the hillbillies.

Sardine and Cracker poured bullets toward Valentina as fast as they could jack rounds in. She was pinned down. One was aiming to her left, the other to the right. They were walking the shots in. She was running out of time.

Breeze and Clem disappeared into the trees.

Like a stoner Butch Cassidy, Terry pulled the snubnose out. Aiming at where the hillbillies' muzzle flashes had come from, he fired. With five quick, completely wild shots he emptied his revolver into the brush.

His gun clicked empty.

And then it all went silent.

Terry stood in the open, waiting for a bullet that never came. Slowly he turned from where the hillbillies had been to the place he last saw Valentina.

The first wisps of evening fog started to roll into the meadow.

After a long moment, Valentina broke through the brush. Terry moved toward her, slowly at first, then at a run.

Sam looked down at Callum, pushing his blood-soaked bangs out of his eyes. "Don't you die, asshole." She pounded her hand onto his chest. His eyes popped open.

"Stop, I'm OK."

"For now." She struck his chest again.

"Your bedside manner sucks."

Sam snapped her Buck knife open. Callum went silent. Roughly rolling him over, she cut the cord tying his wrists together. Eying the knife still in her hand, Callum sat up and silently rubbed circulation back into his hands. He seemed unaware of the copious amounts of blood running from his scalp onto his face.

Sam folded the knife and dropped it into her pocket. "You're bleeding."

"A bit." He reached up and felt his scalp.

"Is there a hole?"

"Nope, a weird part-line but no hole."

"Too bad. I like your hair."

"Noted. Did Binasco get the weed?"

"No, had some Chinese cat from Oakland take it." Sam spoke looking over him into the forest.

"You saying if I put an APB out on Binasco his car would turn up clean?"

"Yes. But if you want me alive you won't."

"A Chinese cat?"

"That's right."

Callum thought about it. The fog was getting thicker by the moment. "He wasn't my primary target anyway. Breeze? No way I'm going to catch him in this."

"We both know where he's headed."

"Rapunzel's."

"No place else to run," Sam said.

"Thank you for not shooting me."

"Any time." They played it off light, but both knew whatever they had was over. There was no going back from the look in her eyes that had said to protect her brother she would shoot Callum.

At the tree line, Terry and Valentina didn't speak. At first they looked each other over, scanning for bullet wounds or other signs of damage. The fog pressed in on them, keeping visibility down to five or six feet.

"Running out like that, Terry, was fool crazy. Brave, but crazy."

"Didn't think," Terry said and lit a Marlboro. "Kind of spooky out here."

"Funny, I find it cozy." Valentina took the cigarette from Terry. "I'm almost getting used to these." She shivered from the cold. Terry draped his arms over her shoulders and pulled her back into his chest, keeping her warm. "Terr-Terr, I know this must be really strange for you."

"Hush," Terry whispered in her ear. "Some things only make sense if you don't worry about them. That's not right. I'm trying to say . . . When I saw them shooting, you know, at you, and you didn't return fire . . . I thought . . ."

"What did you think, when you was thinking?" she purred.

"Valentina, if you didn't, couldn't, make it out, it would be a tragedy. Made worse if I never said diddly to you about this. I, well, there really aren't words that make sense, but I would miss the hell out of you. I . . ."

"Yes?"

"I never felt this way about any girl, none. But you're not a girl."

"No, Terry, I'm not. I'm a woman."

"Exactly." He hugged her even tighter to him. "Exactly."

"How about that hippy chick waitress?"

"Not my type, as it turns out." He moved her around to face

him. Cupping her face in his hands, he pulled her to him and kissed her, then looked into her amazing eyes. "My mom is going to shit a brick."

"Because I'm black?"

"Something like that."

CHAPTER 33

"Here are we, one magical moment, such is the stuff from where dreams are woven."
—David Bowie

Driving down the mountain, Breeze knew his run was over. It was time to hoist anchor and head south. With the cash from the disco heist and what he had put aside from his pot and pimping empire he had almost two hundred and fifty grand stashed in the safe at Rapunzel's. Plenty for a rich retirement in Baja. He didn't know how long it would take the feds to gather up a tactical force, but he was sure it was better if he left tonight.

There was only one problem.

A big problem.

When he opened the safe in his office and took out the vintage Girl Scouts backpack, the one that usually made him smile, the one that should have been full of money, he found it stuffed with phone books.

Then it hit him. A nagging feeling had been in the back of his mind since the night Sam and her crew had braced him. She left first, leaving behind her brother to do the talking. Why him, why her little brother? The kid and the others must have been a diversion, kept Breeze and his boys busy, giving Sam plenty of time to climb in the window and open his safe. The big boned bitch. He really should have shot her.

"What's wrong, cuz?" Sardine asked. "Look like you been bit by a diamondback."

"I was, name of Sam. How much cash you have?"

"You mean other than what you owe me?"

"I mean that you can get a grasp on this minute."

"I guess a couple hundred between Cracker and me."

"Get it."

"You ain't thinking of blowing town without paying us are you, cuz?" Sardine moved into the doorway, blocking any exit.

"No, I'm just cash-strapped and I need to lay low for a while. I will be back and I will make good on my debts. Does your van have any gas in the tank?"

"Oh, now you want my cash and my van? And you ain't paying us for our labor, provided at no small effort or risk. That sum up the situation, cuz?" Sardine pulled a hunting knife from a scabbard on his belt.

"We're blood."

"That's why you are still breathing and I ain't called Cracker over to help me skin you. You always push us around, well, how's that shoe fit on your foot?" Sardine weighed the knife and looked cold at Breeze.

"Wait." Breeze's eyes darted around the room searching for anything of value. "You don't think I'd leave you holding nothing? No way. Not my mother's sister's kid." He dropped a sheaf of documents onto the desk.

Sardine prodded at the papers with the knife's point. "What're those?"

"Deed to Rapunzel's and the cribs. Yours. All I want is your cash and the van. Can I be any more fair?"

A smile spread across Sardine's face. He called in Cracker and told him they had finally made good. They readily gave up the cash they were holding. As Breeze drove the van away, Sardine slapped Cracker on the shoulder. "What you say we sample some of our new wares?"

"Our what?"

"Hookers, Cracker, a pussy smorgasbord."

Laughing, they crossed the road to explain to the ladies about the management change.

At the Mad River Hospital's ER Callum held off an irate nurse while he dripped blood on the linoleum and called his bosses in D.C. He relayed a version of the events in the high country meadow. He told of the pot deal gone sour, and the informant who tipped him off to it. He rightfully painted Sam and her crew as heroes who saved his life. He gave them Sam's sketchy description of a Chinese man from Oakland; sadly it was all they had to go on. He left Maurizio Binasco out of it. He told them they couldn't trust local law enforcement. By the time a young intern was done putting twenty-five stitches in Callum's scalp, a National Guard chopper set down on the hospital's helipad.

A gauze-turbaned Callum led a mixed team of feds and National Guardsmen in a raid on Rapunzel's. Sardine and Cracker flipped on Breeze faster than hungry baby pigs hit their momma's tit. They gave a description and the license plate number of the rusted van. Callum had no evidence connecting Sardine and Cracker to any of the day's lawlessness. They hadn't participated when Breeze snatched him and he hadn't seen them in the forest. After a vague threat of jail the cousins quickly drew Callum a map of Breeze's hidden pot farms.

The feds taillights hadn't rounded the first bend when Cracker said, "Maybe time we went straight. We can live comfortable off strippers and whiskey."

"Well, strippers and whiskey and pussy. Hate to put the crib girls out of work."

"OK, strippers and whiskey and pussy. Nothin' else, right? I don't want to go to jail."

"I only gave them half of Breeze's stash . . . Can't see any good comes from letting that go to waste."

"But after that were out, right, cousin?"

"Absalootin-tootin, cousin." Grinning like a couple of fools, they left the cold night air and took their seats at Breeze's old booth.

Less than an hour later a Highway Patrol cruiser came upon Breeze by the side of the 101. He'd made it a hundred miles south of Humboldt when the van's engine seized.

Breeze escaped drug charges for lack of evidence, but he was arrested on charges of kidnapping and the attempted murder of a federal officer. Ten minutes into his interrogation he rolled on the sheriff, rushing to be first to make a deal. He was promised a reduced sentence for his cooperation, one he might even survive if he kept his mouth shut about Maurizio Binasco's involvement or any mention of a heist in a gay disco.

Humboldt's very own Sheriff Winslow was arrested that night. He indignantly protested his innocence as they cuffed him and read him his rights. By the time the investigation and subsequent court case was over, he and three of his deputies would be doing hard time.

The local news station took up the story. It went out on the wire, then went national. By the time Sam and the crew hit San Francisco their faces were plastered on the front page of the *Examiner*.

"Local heroes risk their lives to save a federal officer," Sam read.

They were in Valentina's flat, drinking coffee and watching the sun come up. "And Jacob, brother of mine, what goes to the victors?"

"In a Jacksonian sense, that would be the spoils, big sister."

"Exactly." Sam turned over her backpack and dumped all the cash she had taken from Breeze onto Valentina's dining room table. She divided it into six piles. They unanimously decided Jinks got dick.

Terry took his pile of currency and set it on top of Valentina's. "My baby is going to Stockholm."

Valentina glowed. "I love you, my fabulous and dazzling Terr-Terr."

Later, as they were getting ready to drive down to Mountain View, Terry and Jacob stood on the stoop smoking. "What are you going to do with all that filthy lucre?" Terry asked his best friend.

"Give it to Moms, I guess. It's what my pops would have done."

"Sounds about right."

"You ready to roll?" Jacob asked.

"No, think I'll stay here for a couple of days. Me and Val have some things to work out."

"You really are in love." Jacob smiled at the thought.

"Yeah, it ain't perfect, but what relationship is, right?"

"Isn't that the truth. See you at school Monday?"

"Yeah. I think Val would kick my ass if I tried to drop out this near the finish line."

"And she could do it, too."

"I know. Isn't she magnificent, Jake?"

"Yes, she is."

Sam borrowed the Galaxie and she and Jacob drove out of San Francisco. The Transamerica Pyramid stabbed up into the dispersing fog. The double-decker Bay Bridge stretched out toward Treasure Island behind them.

"Candy called it Oz," Jacob said, looking out the back window, watching the city slip away as they headed south on the 101.

"We had some fun there," Sam said. "Don't guess we'll be welcome back."

"No, I'd say the city is off-limits." Jacob continued to look out the back window.

"Jacob?"

"Yeah, Sam?"

"You still hate me?"

"No. Don't get me wrong, all is definitely not alright, but you're my sister. When the shit went down in the meadow, I cratered. Not you. You're more like Pops than I'll ever be."

"You, my brother, are not like any of us. And that is the good news."

Entering the hospital lobby, all of Jacob's attention was on finding Candy. He walked past where Esther sat reading a tattered copy of *Time* with Margaux Hemingway on the cover. When she called his name, he stopped and looked at her, confused.

"Moms?"

"I knew you'd come here. Where is your sister?"

"She's in the car. Candy?"

"Getting better. I spoke to her parents. I told them they could be as angry at our family as they wanted, but not you. You, I told them, are different. Special. A good boy who loves their daughter."

"How'd that go over?"

"About like you'd think." She took out a cigarette and started to light it.

Jacob shook his head. "Moms, can't do that here."

"Since when?"

"I don't know. What room is Candy in?"

"Two-seventeen. Jacob?"

"Yeah?"

"You are . . . never mind. Go see Candy," Esther said, standing. "I need to go thank your sister."

"OK."

"For keeping you both alive, I need to thank her." Esther kissed her son on the cheek and walked away. The fact that Sam was the reason anyone's life was in danger to begin with was left unsaid by Jacob. Stepping into the elevator, he found he was smiling. Screw Sam and his mom and his messed up family.

Candy's parents stood in front of her bed, trying to block Jacob from seeing her.

"I'm sorry," Jacob said.

"Mom, Dad, you can't keep him out."

"Yes, we can," her mother said.

"No, I'm twenty. He's my friend."

"He's just another one of them," her father said.

"He's staying. Please."

Candy's father looked ready to punch Jacob. He also looked like he had never been in a fight in his life.

"Don't make a scene," Candy's mother said to her husband, then spoke to Candy. "Five minutes, and we'll be in the hall." Taking her husband's elbow she led him out. As they passed Jacob they glared at him. He didn't care. He was so happy to see Candy sitting up.

"You look good," Jacob said as the door closed.

"I look like hell. Dirty hair, no makeup."

"You look amazing."

"Do we really want to start with lies?"

"No, my dear, dear Candy, we're not. You look amazing."

Candy laughed, looking into his grinning face.

Jacob sat on the bed, holding her hand. He told her all that had happened, told her Terry was staying with Valentina. She said that was the best news she'd heard yet. He told her about how he'd been terrified when the shooting started, how he'd hidden under the truck.

"Good," she said.

"You're glad I totally wimped out?"

"I'm glad you remained you."

"Who's lying now?"

"Not me." She took his hand and kissed it. "Jacob, this, all this—the robberies, the house creeping, the heist—it is who Sam is. All she'll ever be. You . . . This is, it's just one stop, a blip on your trajectory. See, you are wonderful possibilities."

"I was so afraid, I threw up."

"I'm bored with people too cool to feel anything."

"So you're saying you don't care that I'm a total wimp?"

"It's sexy."

"No, it's not."

"It is to me." Leaning up, she tilted her head back and closed her eyes, her lips puckered ever so slightly.

Jacob leaned down. Moving too eagerly, he clinked teeth with Candy. Pulling back, he started to laugh. "This was supposed to be that magic moment." He was smiling.

"Magic takes practice."

Acknowledgments

A monster thank you to my editors, Elizabeth A. White, whose attention to story is matched by her fine eye for historical anachronisms, and Erika C., who took an axe to my words and never let me deliver less than my best. Together they waded deep into my dyslexic mud and came out bruised and bleeding but not dead.

Erin Mitchell, for midwifing the birth of this beast. The thorough Jaye Manus for the ebook and interior book design. The deeply talented Chungkong for creating the cover art.

My early readers: Tom Pluck, Holly West, and Neliza Drew. Charlie Huston, who reminds me why we do this. Sabrina Ogden and McDroll for being amazing. Book pushers Scott Montgomery and Jen Hitchcock for strong-arming readers into buying my books.

The band Idiot, the dancers of the My-O-My and all the glitter kids we ran with; you remain beautiful and sparkly forever in my memory.

And lastly my amazing wife and sons, they make coming home worth the journey.

Josh Stallings grew up in the shadows of NorCali, down where the lamps have all been shot out with pellet guns and no one asks questions they don't want to hear the answers to. He is the author of the multiple award winning Moses McGuire crime novels; Anthony Award nominated memoir, *All The Wild Children*; and *Young Americans*. His short fiction has appeared in *Beat To A Pulp, Protectors Anthology 1 and 2, Blood and Tacos, Crime Factory, Shotgun Honey* and more. He lives in Los Angeles with his wife Erika, two dogs and a cat named Riddle.

www.joshstallings.net

Made in the USA
Lexington, KY
04 December 2019